So in Love With Him

So in Love With Him

D. Brown-Newton

www.urbanbooks.net

Urban Books, LLC
300 Farmingdale Road, N.Y.-Route 109
Farmingdale, NY 11735

So in Love With Him

ISBN 13: 978-1-64556-744-8
EBOOK ISBN: 978-1-64556-745-5

First Trade Paperback Printing January 2026
Printed in the United States of America

10 9 8 7 6 5 4 3 2 1

Distributed by Kensington Publishing Corp.
Submit Orders to:
Customer Service
400 Hahn Road
Westminster, MD 21157-4627
Phone: 1-800-733-3000
Fax: 1-800-659-2436

The authorized representative in the EU for product safety and compliance
Is eucomply OU, Parnu mnt 139b-14, Apt 123
Tallinn, Berlin 11317, hello@eucompliancepartner.com

So in Love With Him

by

D. Brown-Newton

Dedication

This book is dedicated to D. Brown-Newton. She was born on November 27, 1970, and departed on January 2, 2023. Her memories will live on through her words. She will be remembered as a great author, mother, wife, and friend. May she rest in eternal peace.

Chapter One

Messiah

"Why the fuck are you always bitching?" I asked Tara's annoying ass because this bitch was never fucking satisfied.

"I'm always bitching because you always come here, get your dick wet, and then fucking leave to go back home to that bitch-ass wife of yours," she shouted.

"Watch your fucking mouth, Tara," I warned as I continued putting on my clothes so I could get the fuck up out of her crib before I snapped her fucking neck.

"That's the shit I be talking about. You let that bitch say what the fuck she wants about *me* and *my* son, but *I* have to watch *my* fucking mouth. I'm so over this shit," she shouted, slamming the bathroom door behind her.

No matter how many times I tried to do the right thing, she was never fucking happy, like she didn't know that I had a wife before laying up with me and having my son, Messiah Junior. I had been married for four years and had been fucking with Tara for about two years. My wife, Tami, found out about her when Tara made it known that she was pregnant with me. Tami left me for a good two weeks before realizing that she wasn't about to leave me just so some hood rat chick could have me—her words. I told her that I was done fucking with Tara, and it was just about my son, but I never stopped fucking with her. Tara was on that dumb childish bullshit, and any time I told her that I wasn't fucking with her anymore, she would make it hard for a nigga to see his fucking son. All I was trying to do was keep the peace, so that I didn't have to deal with the bullshit.

"Yo, come out of the fucking bathroom so that I can be out. I've got some shit I need to handle. I'll be back to check on you and shorty later on tonight," I yelled at the closed door.

She came out of the bathroom, wearing nothing but a towel, causing my dick to swell, and as much as I wanted to run up in her ass again, I knew I better head out before Tami's ass came looking for me.

"Dada's been blowing me up, so I need to go and see what that shit is about," I told her, but she gave me a look that let me know she didn't believe me.

She stood there with an attitude, so to avoid an argument, I left a stack on the nightstand and bounced. I bet her ass wasn't that fucking mad because, if she were, she wouldn't have taken my ends. I jumped into my ride to head home, mentally trying to prepare myself for another argument that I knew was waiting on my ass. I knew that I had told Tara that I had business to handle, but I didn't have any business to handle. It was Tami's ass blowing me up because I didn't take my ass home last night.

My jaw tightened as soon as I pulled up to my crib, seeing that Tami had all of my fucking clothes and sneakers thrown out all over the place. She was always on this bullshit that was starting to blow my mind with her stupid ass. I told her ass time and time again that if she was upset with me, it was cool, but don't fuck with my shit.

The front door opened with her best friend, Rema, standing in the doorway, like she was her fucking bodyguard or some shit. Rema was cool because she rocked with my wife hard, but sometimes, she took the shit too far with her fucking mouth when it came to being in *my* fucking business.

"Messiah, she doesn't want to see you, so you need to leave," she said with a roll of her eyes like she was really going to stop me from entering my crib.

I pushed past her ass like she didn't say shit because, if she knew what was good for her, she would take her ass home before she got fucked up.

"Don't come in here with your bullshit excuses because I'm done with you and your bullshit," Tami yelled, coming down the stairs.

"What the fuck are you talking about, Tami? You know I was out there handling fucking business. I'm sick of you with these bullshit tantrums every time I'm not able to answer your fucking calls," I barked at her ass.

"So, you're going to stand here and act like you weren't laid up with that bitch, Siah?" she yelled, grabbing her phone and showing me some fucking Facebook post that Tara posted last night.

I couldn't say a fucking thing because the same fucking clothes that I walked in wearing were the same fucking outfit in the picture. I swear I was fucking Tara up on sight because I told her ass to stay in her fucking lane and to stop thinking this shit was a fucking game.

"I told you to leave this trifling motherfucker alone because he loves them fucking hood rat bitches that don't have shit going for them but a wet, fucking pussy. That bitch isn't good for nothing but lying on her fucking back, but he keeps playing you to be with the ho," Rema said to Tami, but was looking at me.

"Rema, you need to mind your own fucking business and worry about who the fuck *your* nigga is laying up with while you're over here in *my* shit," I told the bitch since she wanted to stand here and act like my nigga, Damien, a.k.a. Dada, wasn't out there doing him.

"I bet you one thing: my motherfucking nigga knows where home is, and if he is out there fucking with those hood rats, I bet you his ass has enough respect for me not to bring that shit home. Cheating is one thing, but to cheat and bring home a fucking baby and continue fucking the ho is some straight disrespectful shit. Tami, I'm out because all this nigga is going to do is have a million fucking excuses about why he keeps fucking the bitch. And please don't use the 'She's not going to let you see your son' shit again because we all know that that's an easy fix. Take your fucking ass to the courthouse, nigga, if the bitch isn't allowing you to see your son," she yelled, leaving.

"Fuck you, Rema," I yelled behind her. "Tami, you need to keep that bitch out of *our* fucking business. That's why shit is the way it is because you've always got her ass in your ear," I said.

"Nigga, please. I didn't have to tell her anything. Who the fuck you think let me know your fucking ass was laid up with that bitch again? If you want to be with that bitch, then be with her. If not, you need to take your ass to court and see your fucking son without having to see her. Every time you give me some lame-ass excuse why you didn't go to court for visitation tells me it's *not* about your son; it's about how you love fucking with that bitch," she cried as the tears fell from her eyes.

"Look, ma, why you keep doing this shit to yourself? I'm going to do this shit the right way. I promise," I replied, wiping her tears.

I knew she felt some kind of way that Tara had my first son, as she should, but I needed her to understand that I knew I fucked up. All I was trying to do was keep the peace, but I saw that Tara wasn't going to make this shit easy until Tami fucked around and left my ass. Tami already had enough grief dealing with her family, who kept telling her how stupid she was for staying with me, and now, all of her friends were in her ear, so I felt that she was just about at her breaking point. She was getting fed up with my ass, and I needed to make shit right before I lost my wife for good.

Tami

The Ave had mad fucking beauty salons, so I knew that this bitch, Tara, walking into the one Rema and I frequented meant she was here to start some shit. I never saw her bald-headed ass at this shop before because the bitch knew she couldn't afford these prices without lying on her fucking back. I couldn't believe that Siah even fucked with this average-looking bitch because she couldn't hold a candle to my ass. The bitch's whole outfit looked like it came from the Rainbow shop down the fucking block. You would think that after having a baby by a nigga like Siah, she would have upgraded by now, but the bitch didn't know anything other than being a hood rat.

"I can't believe Messiah fucked with that dirty, fucking ho," Rema said to me, but was loud enough for everyone to hear.

"Ain't a motherfucking thing dirty about me, bitch," Tara boasted.

"Please don't stand there acting like you're *that* bitch because you managed to trap a real nigga who wouldn't even give you the time of day if it wasn't for his fucking son," Rema shouted.

"So, *that's* what he's telling you pathetic bitches these days? Did he tell you every time he comes to my crib, my son is *never* there? Trust when I say it's *not* my son that keeps him coming back; it's this fire pussy I'm working with that keeps this nigga on his knees," she said, hitting a nerve.

I jumped up so fast that no one could have stopped me if they tried. I was whooping her ass, making sure that she was going to have to use every fucking dime he gave her to get her shit fixed. I tried to tear every strand of fucking hair she had from her fucking scalp as she screamed out in pain. I knew that I shouldn't have stooped to her level, but her mouth wrote a check that her ass couldn't cash. She tried fighting back, but all the rage I had built up in me from the time all this back-and-forth started had me on ten. If Rema hadn't pulled me off her ass, I was going to kill her because all I saw was red. Well, I thought Rema was pulling me off her to help the ho, but Rema started whaling on her ass just as Tara's friend walked in the shop, pushing a stroller that I was assuming belonged to Tara. This was my first time seeing the baby up close and personal, so my emotions got the best of me as the angry tears fell because I just whooped a bitch's ass when I should have been whooping Siah's ass. I watched as Paris and another hairstylist pulled Rema and Tara apart, telling Tara that she needed to go.

"Bitch, you did all of that for what? Trust me when I say that the nigga is still going to fuck with me, and you best believe I'm going to see that ass again. Don't be mad at me; be mad at your nigga. *He's* the one who couldn't keep his dick in his pants. I'll be sure to tell him his stupid, fucking wife was out here acting like a hood rat when I was out here with Messiah Junior," she smirked, leaving the shop.

I really couldn't even be mad at what she just said because it was the truth. *If Siah wanted to stop fucking with her, he would have by now,* I thought before hearing Tara scream.

Rema snatched her by her weave just before the door closed, causing the stroller to jerk, and I thanked God that her friend caught the baby because the stupid bitch didn't even have him strapped in. I knew that I should have snatched Rema up quicker, but all I could think at the moment was that Rema was *my* bitch and would *always* be my bitch. Mila J's song "My Main" would always be our theme song because she was my ride or die, and she didn't give a fuck. Right or wrong, she had my back, and that was why I loved her ass.

"Rema, let the bitch go," I pleaded with her, trying to pry her hands from Tara's hair.

Finally, Rema let her hair go, but not before kicking her, and at this point, *we* got kicked out of the salon too. Once in the car, the hurt was evident on my face, and Rema tried to tell me not to sweat it because, although Siah had a baby on me, she knew for a fact that he loved me. I didn't doubt that he loved me; it was just the fact that he had a kid, and everyone knew that this bitch was his baby's mother.

He had me out here in these streets looking like a damn fool as he ran up in that busted bitch raw like he didn't have a fucking wife at home. I swear, no one knew how much it hurt me to see that baby looking just like his ass. Looking at the pictures that I'd seen, I convinced myself that the baby looked nothing like him, but that was far from the truth. Siah thought that my having his baby was a quick fix to how I was feeling about the situation, but he just didn't get it. Why would I get pregnant when he was still fucking with her, not giving a fuck about my feelings, so having his baby was going to change what? Not a thing, and it was time for me to figure out if I wanted to continue being his wife because I damn sure didn't feel like his wife anymore. He had this bitch thinking that she was on some kind of pedestal because, every time she called, he went running, no matter what we had going on at the time.

"Listen, I have watched you take Messiah's shit for the past two years, and now he has a fucking newborn. If you want your marriage, you're going to have to put your fucking foot down and let this nigga know enough is enough. He does this disrespectful shit because you allow him to keep doing it and taking his ass back. You saw the damn post with your own eyes, and you let him feed you some bullshit, and now, all is good like the shit didn't happen. I'm going to keep it real with you. You give Siah no consequences for the bullshit he puts you through, so why would he change the shit he's doing in these fucking streets?"

"Rema, I just be trying to give him the benefit of the doubt because you know, just like I know, that the bitch do be holding that fucking baby over his head," I explained to her.

"Tami, do you think a nigga like Messiah would ever let a bitch play him? That nigga is feeling that dusty, fucking bitch. If he wasn't feeling that bitch, trust me, not even a damn baby would keep him fucking with her ass. You have to step up your game if you want your marriage before you lose his ass to that hood rat. As you can see, she still looks like a damn two-dollar ho, but she keeps him coming back."

I heard everything that she was saying and was taking it all in because she was right, and I needed to do something, and do it sooner rather than later. I wasn't going to sit back and let this bitch take what was rightfully mine because *I* was Mrs. Messiah Owens.

After Rema and I finished getting our hair done at another shop, I dropped her off at her car before heading to the mall, then going home to deal with my cheating husband. I already knew that the bitch probably called him and twisted the story because he was blowing me up, but I refused to answer. If he wanted to talk to me, it would have to be when I walked through the door.

News traveled fast because my mother left me a not-so-nice message, yelling about Siah having me acting a fool in the streets, like I wasn't raised with some dignity. She had some damn nerve talking about how I was raised. Oh, how quickly she forgot. I was so sick and tired of her and the rest of my family always believing shit that they heard in these fucking streets before getting it from me. I loved my family, but sometimes, I just wished that they would let me live *my* fucking life and learn from whatever mistakes they claimed I was making. My dad was the only one who gave me the benefit of the doubt because I was his baby girl, and he would never believe no shit about me that he heard from the streets. If I were in the streets fighting as a hood rat, like my mother claimed, trust me when I say that my dad knew I must have had a damn good reason.

Envy

Damn, shorty's bad, I thought as I watched how the skirt she was wearing hugged her hips as she swished her ass, knowing she was *that* bitch. I almost forgot that I was at the mall with Camilla until I heard her slick-ass mouth.

"I know you're not ho watching like I'm not standing right fucking here," she barked loud enough for the female to hear.

"Camilla, stop playing," I demanded, heated, but she didn't care because all she did was laugh.

I hated coming to the mall with my annoying-ass sister because, any time I even *looked* in the direction of a female, she always did this stupid shit. She would always pretend like she was my girl if she caught me looking or talking to another female, which always ran them off.

"I'm sorry. I just couldn't help it this time because your ass was drooling from the mouth, and I told you to stop trying to pick up bitches when you were with me. Not one of these females knows that I'm your sister, so all they see is your thirsty ass with a female and still trying to pick up another one," she explained, still laughing.

"Nah, they see a fine-ass brother like myself, and they're wondering what I'm doing walking with a chickenhead," I joked, mushing her ass and walking away from her.

"Meet me at the food court in like thirty minutes," I yelled over my shoulder.

I came to the mall with her annoying ass to help her find a prom dress because my mother wasn't feeling well today. My mother had been under the weather for a few weeks now, and I had been trying to convince her to let me take her to the doctor. She was stubborn and lived by her home remedies, but I tried to convince her that the shit wasn't working because, had they been working, she wouldn't still be sick. She kept talking about she just needed to give it time to kick in, but I told her that she had until the end of the week to show improvement, or I was dragging her ass, kicking and screaming, to the doctor.

I walked into the store behind shorty to see if she would let me holla at her for a minute after leaving my sister, but I didn't want her to think that I was on some stalker shit. Since she was in Sephora, a store I didn't usually shop at, I pretended to be a regular and picked up a bottle of cologne. I didn't even wear the shit they had in the store, but I took the cologne and quickly went to check out because she was already at the register.

"That will be $208," I heard the cashier tell her.

"Let me take care of that for you," I requested, looking at her but handing the cashier my card.

"Trust me when I say I don't need you to pay for anything of mine." She kindly declined, handing me back my card after taking it out of the cashier's hand.

The cashier looked amused as we went back and forth while holding up her line because I was persistent about paying for her items. A nigga like me was used to getting my way, and today would be no different. Shit, she already had me stepping out of my character, following behind her ass into the store like I wasn't that nigga.

"What would your little girlfriend think about you up in here, trying to pay for my items?" she asked, causing the cashier to look at me for a response.

"I don't have a girlfriend," I told her, handing the cashier my card again, and this time, she let the cashier charge the items.

"What's your name, shorty?" I asked her once we were both outside the store.

"My name is Tami. Thank you for your kind gesture, but I'm spoken for," she said, walking off.

"Hold up. Just give me a few minutes of your time." I grabbed her hand, stopping her.

When I released her hand, she just stood there, waiting for me to speak, but for some reason, my eyes were now fixated on her breasts that looked to be about a 36C. My eyes traveled, taking her in as she cleared her throat, bringing me back from the nasty thoughts that I was having.

"My bad, shorty. What are you about to get into?" I asked her.

"What was the point of asking me my name if you're still going to call me shorty?" she sassed.

"My bad. I'm about to go to the food court to get something to eat. Come with me, and let a nigga treat you to something to eat," I said.

"I don't know you, and like I said before, I'm spoken for," she smirked, walking off.

"Damn, shot down in broad daylight," I heard my sister say, laughing like the shit was funny.

"Nah, she probably saw your ass coming and didn't want any problems," I tried to convince her.

"Whatever. I'm hungry. Let's go eat because this mall is wack. I didn't even find a dress yet," she whined, pulling me toward the food court.

After getting something to eat, I headed back to my mom's crib to drop off Camilla and to check up on my mom. I promised my sister that I would take her out to Jersey next weekend because she kept complaining that the mall didn't have anything. I knew it had to do with her not wanting to show up to prom wearing the same dress as another female, so next weekend, I would be spending it at a mall again with her annoying ass. Once I checked on my mom, making sure she was good, I headed out to meet up with my dude, Mason, because I stayed at the mall with Camilla longer than I intended to.

"Nigga, you're always fucking late when you know I told them dudes we would meet with them at 1:00 p.m. This being late shit isn't cool for business," he snapped like he forgot who the fuck he was talking to.

"Nigga, you need to bring it all the way down. I move how I move, and if those niggas have a problem with it, I'll handle that shit," I spat at his ass.

This nigga needed to start realizing that he was fucking with a boss nigga. He was acting like we needed those dudes when *they* needed *us*. If I kept their asses waiting all day, you best believe they would wait because I had the product that they needed to make their fucking money.

"Let's go get this money with yo' weak ass," I told him, laughing.

"Whatever, nigga," he said, jumping into his ride and pulling off after I got in the passenger seat.

I understood where he was coming from about keeping niggas waiting and shit, but he had to understand that *we* were the boss niggas, so if something came up and the time changed, he needed to let those niggas know that they had the option to wait or keep it pushing. It was just that simple. Stressing me about niggas complaining wasn't going to take food out of my mouth when I had mad motherfuckers waiting in line to keep me eating.

I was tired as hell by the time I got back to the crib, and all I could think about was shorty, whom I met today, wondering what she was doing right now. I wished that Camilla hadn't cock blocked. I probably would have gotten her number, even if she didn't want to let me treat her to something to eat. I showered and took my ass to bed because I had shit to do tomorrow, hoping that maybe I'd run into her ass again. I woke up to my phone ringing. I tried to ignore it because I was tired as hell, but it just wouldn't stop. Finally, I grabbed the phone, seeing that it was my sister calling.

"Hey, Camilla. What's up?" I asked her.

"E, I'm at the hospital with Mom; she wasn't feeling well. I'm scared, E," my sister cried.

"Camilla, what hospital is she in?" I asked her, already getting dressed.

I knew that I should have stayed earlier when my mother was telling me she was okay, even though she didn't look all right. I let my business cloud my judgment, not taking heed of her not looking good. Once I arrived at the hospital, I spoke with the security guard, who let me go to the back to see what was going on with my mom. I didn't have to go to the desk because I saw Camilla, so I walked over, putting on my game face because I knew that I needed to be strong for her. They had an IV in my mom's arm, and she was now sleeping peacefully, but her face still looked a little pale and had me wondering what was going on with her.

"So, did they say anything about what's wrong?" I asked Camilla.

"Well, for one, the doctor said that she was very dehydrated, and she came in with a fever of 102, so they put her on an IV and took some blood. She became so weak at home, scaring the shit out of me, and when I saw that she was burning up, I got her here as quickly as I could," she said, tearing up.

"It's okay. You did the right thing by getting her here. Now, we just have to wait to see what's going on with her," I told her, trying to comfort her.

Chapter Two

Tami

I was tired as hell going to work because Siah and I were arguing for most of the night and well into the morning. He had the nerve to be mad at *me* because his busted fucking baby mother got her ass whooped while she was with her son. If she knew that she had her son with her, she shouldn't have been popping off at the fucking mouth. I told his ass I was tired of defending myself when it came to his fucking slut bucket, and he could kick fucking rocks and do him because I was going to do me. He didn't like that shit, threatening me in one breath and then asking me if I was fucking around on him in the next breath. I was so over his bullshit and refused to sweat the bullshit he was on these days, and if he didn't believe me when I said I was done unless he cut the bitch off, I could definitely show him better than I could tell him.

I loved my job, working as a registration clerk at the county hospital, but sometimes, it could be so depressing. But at the same time, it was a reminder that someone was always worse off than you, which, in turn, helped me to stop complaining so much. I clocked in, putting my phone on vibrate because I knew that Siah was going to be blowing me up all day, and I wasn't trying to answer any of his calls unless he was calling to tell me he told that bitch he wasn't fucking with her anymore.

"What's up, shorty?" I heard from behind me. Turning around, I saw that it was the dude from the mall.

"How are you doing, Tami?" he retracted when he saw the look on my face, remembering what I told him about calling me shorty.

"I'm fine, and you?" I asked, being polite.

"A nigga's stressing right now because my mom is here in the hospital," he said with a sad look in his eyes.

"I'm sorry to hear that. I hope she gets better soon," I told him.

"Thank you. Is everything good with you and your people?" he questioned, assuming I was here for the same reason that he was.

"Yeah, I work here, though, and I already clocked in, so I have to go," I said, looking around, making sure my supervisor wasn't watching me.

"Cool. I didn't get a chance to ask you for your number the other day," he said. "Look, before you tell me again that you're spoken for, I just want to be friends." He smirked, waiting.

I knew that I shouldn't have given him my phone number, but I was tired of putting up with Siah's bullshit . . . So why not have a friend? After giving him my number, I told him that I had to get to work. He promised to give me a call later.

The emergency room was crowded as hell today with sick children who were miserable from whatever sickness had brought them here. I was tired as hell and couldn't wait until that clock hit 7:00 p.m. so I could go home and get some sleep. I just knew that Siah was going to be blowing up my phone, but I didn't have one missed call from him when I took my phone out of my pocketbook on my lunch break.

But I had a text message that I knew was from dude, telling me that I gave him my number without even asking him his name, which made me smile. I forgot to ask about his name because, since I had already clocked in, if my supervisor saw me standing there, her ass, without a doubt, would have written me up. So, I texted him back, asking him his name, and when he texted back "Envy," I wanted to ask so badly what kind of a name Envy was, but I didn't ask. He told me that he would hit me up later because they were moving his mom to a room, so he had to go, which was a good thing because I had to get back to work anyway. Since meeting Siah when I was 16, and marrying him when I was 23, I had never even entertained the thought of being with anyone else. But all that shit was about to change.

After clocking out of work, I saw that my front tire on the passenger's side of my car was flat. All I wanted to do was go home and shower. Was that too much to ask for? I swear it was always something. I didn't want to call Siah because I didn't want him to do shit for me, but I had no other choice. I dialed his number, and when it went straight to voicemail, I was pissed and could feel the tears stinging my eyes, threatening to fall. Next, I dialed Rema's number, praying that she would answer, but she didn't. Just when I was about to have a tantrum, right there in the parking lot, I spotted Envy, who was coming in my direction. I tried to wipe away the few tears that managed to fall because I didn't want him to see that I was crying.

"Hey, you good?" he asked me.

"No, I have a flat tire," I sighed.

"I could take you where you need to go," he offered.

I had to think about it because, if he dropped me home and Siah was there, I didn't want to get him caught up in no bullshit. I mean, he looked like the type who could handle his own, but it wouldn't be fair to him, I thought, as I weighed my options. I was already tired and didn't feel like waiting on a tow or someone to come out to change the tire, so I accepted his offer to take me home, praying that Siah was out doing whatever it was that he was usually doing when I got home from work.

"How's your mom?" I asked him once I was seated in the car, trying to make small talk, but also genuinely concerned.

"Her blood work hasn't come back yet, so medically, we're still not sure why she's dehydrated and has no energy to even sit up on her own. She hasn't been feeling well for quite some time now. She refused to go to the doctor, being stubborn as she insisted on relying on her home remedies that haven't been helping at all," he explained with worry in his voice.

"I don't know your mother, but I'm praying that all goes well, and she has a speedy recovery," I offered.

"Thank you. I really appreciate that," he responded.

"How long have you been working at County?" he asked me.

"I've been at Killer County for about two years," I joked.

"Killer County?" he questioned, looking concerned.

"Oh no, I didn't mean it like that. I just meant it takes a lot out of me by the time my shift is over," I clarified quickly because I didn't want him to think County was killing patients when his mother was laid up in the hospital.

"You had a nigga ready to turn this car around and get my mother the hell up out of that hospital," he replied seriously.

"I'm sorry. It came out all wrong, and once it came out, it was too late to take it back because the look on your face scared the shit out of me," I laughed nervously.

"You're talking about my look scared you. Shit, I was scared because that's my mother, the only mother I have, so, yeah, you had a nigga shook. She's not even supposed to be in County right now, but my sister panicked and brought her to the closest hospital, and I don't want to move her now because she's weak," he explained.

"I understand, and trust me, county hospitals do get a bad rep, but she's in good hands. The doctors here are really great," I told him.

We pulled up to my house, and God must have been on my side because Siah wasn't home, and that was a good thing because I wasn't in the mood to explain anything.

"Thanks for the ride, Envy. I appreciate it," I told him, getting out of the car, but he stopped me.

"Do you need a ride to work in the morning since I have to go back to the hospital to be with my mom?" he asked, and I thought it was sweet of him to offer.

"No, I'm good, but thanks for asking," I responded, looking at him . . . feeling something that I shouldn't have.

"No problem. I know you're tired, so I'm not going to hold you up, but I would like to stop by and see you tomorrow. What time do you go to lunch?"

"My lunch hour varies, depending on whether we're busy, so I'll call or text you and let you know," I told him, thanking him again before getting out of the car and telling him that I would see him tomorrow.

When I got inside, I let go of the smile I was holding in because I was really feeling him. He was showing me something that I had been missing in my marriage for a long time.

I woke up the next morning, pissed that Siah didn't bring his ass home again after all that I said to him. I guess the ultimatum meant nothing to him, but it was all good, and I wasn't about to stress because work was stressful enough. I smiled at the thought of seeing Envy today and couldn't wait until my lunch hour. Just as I was about to leave, Siah walked in, looking high as hell, but I continued doing what I was doing, ignoring his ass.

"I didn't know you were still here. Where's your car?" he asked me.

"Had you answered your phone or listened to at least one of my voicemails, you would have known that I was stranded because some-fucking-body slashed my car tire," I said, pissed off.

"My phone was dead. That's why I didn't answer any of your calls. You know if I got the message, I would have been there."

"Okay, I get that your phone was dead, but why didn't you come home last night?" I asked, knowing I didn't have time to be doing this with him, but I was curious to know how he would respond.

"I crashed at the spot because you were already upset with me, so I just wanted to give you your space for the night," he said, but I didn't believe his ass.

"You sure you didn't spend the night with that bitch-ass baby mother of yours?"

"No, I didn't stay the night over there, Tami, because I'm trying to make things right between us, so either you're going to forgive me or not. I'm sick of going back and forth about Tara and my son because both of them are here and not going anywhere as long as she has my son. I'm not trying to hurt you. That's why I promised you that I will not be sleeping with her anymore, and I will be going to court to have my visitation," he said.

"Well, until I see proof of you going to court and requesting visitation, we will continue to have this argument because I've heard it all before. But now, I don't have time to do this with you because I have to be at work in less than an hour," I said, walking away from him and calling my cab.

"If you're not too busy today, I would appreciate it if you took care of my car so that I'll have a ride home after work today," I told him.

"Do you need me to take you to work?"

"No, I called a cab," I said over my shoulder, leaving to wait outside for my cab.

I was in a bad mood at work today because, even though I said that I was over the whole situation with Siah, I wasn't. I loved him and just wanted him to right his wrongs, but all I kept getting from him was excuse after excuse, and to add insult to injury, his ass came home smelling like that bitch. It took everything in me to play along this morning because something inside of me wanted to pick up the lamp and bash him upside his fucking head for standing in my face, lying to me. As much as I loved his ass, I was going to show him that he had the game twisted because a bitch like me was going to show him how it was *really* played, mark my words. I had just finished sending Envy a text message, so I would meet him in the parking lot in ten minutes.

"Hey, I know you wanted to have lunch, but as you can see, my tire is still in the same condition as yesterday, and I need to get home instead of bumming a ride," I said with a smile.

"No problem. You know I don't have a problem taking you home, but I understand the need of not having to depend on anyone," he said, removing his shirt, leaving on his wife beater that showed his banging body and tats that had a bitch fanning herself.

I watched in awe as he did his thing, changing my tire, and just when he was about done, Siah's ass pulled up. He got out of his car, looking pissed off as I stood there, eye fucking Envy and holding his shirt in my hand.

"Who the fuck is this nigga?" he asked, getting in my personal space.

"He's the nigga that's doing what the fuck you were supposed to be doing hours ago," I sassed.

"Tami, don't play with me. I'm going to ask you one more fucking time who the fuck this nigga is," he warned.

Before I could answer, Envy walked over, and Siah's jaw tightened. All I could think was, *Please don't fight at my job*.

"You good?" he asked me, but he was looking at Siah.

"Trust when I say she's good, my nigga," Siah told him.

"As long as you're good, shorty, I'm good," he smirked, taking his shirt from me.

"Don't fucking try me," Siah said, walking up on him, causing me to stand between the two of them.

"If you know what's good, my nigga, you'll fall back," Envy told him, not backing down.

I turned toward Envy, putting my hand on his chest, begging him to leave it alone and just to go back inside.

"Why the fuck you begging this bitch-ass nigga to go inside like he's about to do some shit to me?" Siah barked at me, and before I could stop it, Envy pushed me out of the way and punched Siah in the mouth, and then they started fighting.

I tried to break it up, but Siah pushed me to the ground, hurting my damn knee. Then I was helped up off the ground by one of my coworkers, who I assumed was coming back from lunch. Hospital security was now on the scene, and Siah and Envy were asked to leave. Both left without saying anything to me as they went their separate ways. I swear I didn't expect the shit to go down the way it did. All I wanted was for Siah to see that what he wouldn't do, the next nigga would, but the shit backfired. I was just happy that no report was made because I knew for sure I would have been written up for this shit, I thought, as I headed back inside the building. I wanted to find Envy so that I could apologize, but it was time for me to get back to work, so I just hoped that he was still here when it was time for me to get off.

When I got off work, I didn't have to go looking for him because he was waiting for me. I offered him a smile, but he was wearing a mean mug, letting me know he was upset.

"Are you okay?" I asked him as I walked up to him.

"Look, I don't know what's going on with you and your dude, but I would appreciate it if you didn't get me involved in the bullshit," he said.

"What are you talking—"

"Look, shorty, I'm far from stupid, and I know you were just trying to make that nigga jealous by having him show up, knowing you asked me to change the tire. If you love that nigga, don't play games, and you'll let him live because the next time that nigga squares up with me, his ass is going to be removed in a body bag," he said, walking away, leaving me standing there looking stupid.

Damn, this shit went all the way left, but at the same time, the shit turned me on at how he put his gangster down earlier and now again. I knew I needed to apologize. I shouldn't have used him the way I did, because someone could have gotten hurt. I sat in my car and pulled out my phone, sending Envy a text message to apologize, but he didn't respond, so I started my car and headed home.

Chapter Three

Tami

"I don't understand why you're bent all out of shape about a nigga not returning your text when you say that you're not feeling his ass," Rema said, giving me the side eye, knowing I was feeling his ass.

"I'm not feeling his ass, but yes, I'm in my feelings because all I was trying to do was apologize to him, but fuck it," I told her.

I swear I needed to get out of this house because I'd been in a bad mood all week, because Siah called himself not speaking to me, accusing me of fucking Envy. He had a lot of fucking nerve when he was actually fucking someone and had a baby on me, but my stupid ass forgave him.

"Don't go zoning out on me, Tami. Your ass needs to get up out of this house," she told me, reading my mind as she passed me the blunt.

I took a few pulls and downed a few drinks before I agreed to go out with her instead of sitting alone in the house, wondering if that asshole of a husband of mine was coming home. We decided to pass on going to the club because I wasn't in the mood to watch all the skanks shaking their asses as they decided on which man they would be leaving the club with. We decided to go to a lounge in the village to get our drink on and enjoy some music without all the extra bullshit.

"Rema, that's him over there," I squealed, shaking her, causing her to spill her drink.

"Damn, girl, for someone who's not feeling his ass, you're sure acting sprung," she laughed.

Our eyes met briefly when he turned in my direction, as if he felt someone's eyes on him. I offered him a smile, but he turned back around, kicking it with his friends. I felt some kind of way, but I tried not to show it as I downed another drink.

"Are you going to sit here and stare at his ass all night, or are you going to go over there and apologize? He probably didn't respond because he's a grown-ass man who didn't respond to your text-message-sending-ass, like you're a teenager," she said.

I wanted to go over there, but I didn't know if he would embarrass me in front of his friends, so I was hesitant until I saw him get up to take a call. I stood by the door until I saw him end the call and head toward his car. I was disappointed, but I put on my game face before walking back to the table where Rema was sitting, not wanting to talk about it as I continued to drink. I didn't want to ruin the night for her, but I was ready to go home and sulk alone because I was definitely in my damn feelings.

As we walked past Envy's friends, I heard them talking about how it was fucked up about his mom, so I was thinking the worst. I figured the call was about his mom, so after Rema and I got in separate cabs, I took mine straight to the hospital. I knew that I shouldn't have been going to the hospital in the tipsy condition that I was in, but I was worried about him and just wanted to see if he was okay.

When I got to the hospital, I was happy to see that Curtis was the night security guard on duty. I knew that I was good, and he would let me go back with no questions asked. As soon as I walked toward the ICU, I saw Envy comforting his sister, and I now felt like I was invading their privacy. I decided to turn back, but it was too late because he saw me.

"Why are you here, Tami?" he asked me.

"I-I heard your friends say something about your mom, so I just came here to see if you were okay," I stuttered.

"Look, I appreciate your concern, but I need to be here for my sister right now," he said.

"I understand, and I'm still praying for your mother," I told him before walking away.

While I was waiting for the Uber to arrive, I saw him and his sister leaving the hospital, so I put my head down, praying that they didn't see me.

"Tami," he called out.

I looked up at him, trying not to let the tears fall, and don't ask me why I was on the verge of tears because I had no idea.

"Come on," he said as I walked over to the car, getting into the backseat.

His sister was silently crying, as he tried to comfort her, telling her that their mother was strong and that she was going to pull through. I noticed that he wasn't going in the direction of my house, and I wanted to ask him where he was going, but I decided to sit back and not say anything.

Envy pulled up to a house that I was assuming was his, and I started to get nervous because I knew that I shouldn't be here. Camilla got out of the car and went inside, and he told me to sit in the front with him.

"Look, I don't know what type of dude you're used to, but I'm not that nigga, and I don't have to say that I'm feeling you because I think you know that already. What I don't know is if you're feeling me, but I think you are because, if you weren't, you wouldn't have gone to the trouble of checking on me. As you can see, I have a lot going on and don't have time for the games, so if this isn't where you're trying to be, tell me now, and I'll take you home," he said.

I thought about what he had just said, and I knew that, if I went home, I would be going home to an empty house. I came all this way to make sure that he was okay, so I may as well stay with him because, like I said, nobody was going to be waiting for me to come home.

"I don't want to go home," was all I said as we got out of the car and went inside.

We sat in the living room, and it was awkward because neither of us was speaking as we both seemed to be in deep thought, but the silence was killing me, so I decided to say something to him.

"Are you okay?" I asked him.

"Nah, I'm not okay, but I know I have to be strong for my sister because this shit was so unexpected. The doctor told us that they didn't know what was wrong with my mother, and all of her bloodwork came back good. But now, she's in a fucking coma, and no one has any answers," he said, pissed off.

"I'm so sorry to hear about your mom being in a coma," I said sincerely.

"Thank you," he responded before getting up.

"I hope you don't mind, but I got you one of my sister's nightshirts for you to sleep in because it was either this or one of my T-shirts," he said, handing it to me.

"This is fine. Thank you," I said.

"I left everything that you will need to shower in the bathroom, but if you need anything else, just let me know."

I got up to go upstairs to take a shower, but as I passed the room where his sister was, I heard her crying, so I walked inside.

"Are you okay?" I asked her, knowing she wasn't, but I didn't know what else to say.

"I don't know what I will do if I lose my mother," she said, just above a whisper.

"All you can do right now is pray that she makes it through this. I know it hurts, but trust me, prayer works," I responded, rubbing her back.

"Thank you, and thanks for staying because my brother really likes you," she said.

"I like him too, but my life is complicated right now," I told her.

I sat with her until she was feeling a little better before going into the bathroom to shower and get comfortable. I didn't know where I was sleeping, so when I finished in the bathroom, I went back downstairs and joined Envy on the couch. It was late, and I was tired, so I asked him where I would be sleeping.

"Do you have another room that I can stay in for the night?" I asked him.

"You're not staying up to keep me company?" he asked, now looking at me, waiting for an answer.

"What did you have in mind because it is kind of late," I said nervously.

"We can just watch a movie because I know I'm not going to be able to sleep, even if I tried," he said sadly.

I was tired, but if he couldn't sleep, I guess I could try to stay up and keep him company because that was the least I could do. Halfway through the movie, my phone started vibrating on the table. I tried to ignore it because I knew Siah was just getting home and was wondering where I was. I picked up the phone, turned it off, then sat back on the couch, trying to keep my eyes open to at least finish the movie before telling Envy I was calling it a night. I had no intention of arguing about why I wasn't home when his ass could never find his way home, even though he expected me to accept it.

I woke up to the smell of bacon being cooked, realizing that I had fallen asleep on the couch, lying in Envy's arms. As much as I wanted to stay right where I must have felt comfortable enough to fall asleep, I knew I needed to get up. Camilla was looking at me with a smirk on her face, causing me to smile at her.

"Good morning," I greeted her.

"Good morning. I'm fixing some breakfast before heading back to the hospital," she replied sadly, looking the same as her brother had last night.

I went to the bathroom to handle my hygiene before going back downstairs to help her in the kitchen. I turned my phone back on and had so many missed calls from Siah and a few from Rema, so I stepped away to call Rema.

"Hey, girl. What's up?" I asked as soon as she answered the phone.

"Yo' damn husband has been blowing me up all night, so he had a bitch worried about you. Where are you?"

"After the cab came last night, I had him take me to the hospital to see if Envy was okay," I told her, adding that I couldn't talk and would call her later before ending the call.

Envy

I had just come back downstairs and saw that Camilla was in the kitchen, cooking breakfast, and Tami was on the phone. She ended the call when she saw me. I knew I was feeling her more than I led on because just the thought of her talking to that nigga had me feeling some type of way. I walked into the kitchen, greeting my sister and asking her how she was feeling, ignoring Tami because, like I said, I was in my feelings and had no words for her ass.

"Well, good morning to you too," Tami greeted me, rolling her eyes.

I took a piece of bacon off the plate on the counter and walked out of the kitchen with her following behind me.

"Do you want to tell me what I did to deserve the silent treatment?" she asked with her hand on her hip.

"Next time you want to talk to that nigga, take that fucking call outside," I spat at her ass, but all she did was laugh in my face, pissing me off.

"So, disrespecting my house is funny to you?" I barked.

"No, you acting like a jealous boyfriend is funny to me, and if you must know, I wasn't talking to no nigga. I was talking to my best friend, Rema," she said, walking back into the kitchen.

I didn't know what the fuck this girl was doing to me, but it wasn't a good look, letting her know that I was jealous. She was wearing a smirk on her face when I walked back into the kitchen, right along with my sister, who was giving me the side eye. Camilla knew that I was feeling her, and she wanted me to stop playing games and just tell her, but I wasn't trying to get caught up with her because, regardless of whether she and that nigga were having problems, she was still with his ass.

"Camilla, be ready in twenty minutes because I'm ready to head to the hospital," I said, walking out of the kitchen, avoiding eye contact with Tami.

"Why are you avoiding me like I've got the plague?" I heard Tami asking me, standing in my doorway.

I didn't answer her. Instead, I just looked at her as I took off the beater that I was wearing, showing off muscles and tats, now wearing a smirk on *my* face at how uncomfortable she was looking.

"What were you saying?" I smiled at her.

"I-I said, why are you avoiding me? The least you could have done was give me an apology," she stuttered nervously.

I walked over to her, getting so close that I could smell the bacon on her breath. I was just going to fuck with her, but I couldn't resist myself as I kissed her lips. I thought she was going to pull back, but she didn't. Instead, she kissed me back, and we both got lost in the kiss before being interrupted by Camilla's blocking ass.

"Wow, that was a serious makeup kiss," she laughed, causing Tami to walk out of the room.

"Why are you always blocking? And what the hell do you want?" I asked her, pretending to be pissed.

"You said twenty minutes, so I was just coming to see what the holdup was," she retorted smartly with a roll of her eyes.

After dropping Tami off at her house, I told her that I would give her a call later before pulling out, heading to the hospital.

"It's crazy how you finally find someone that you really like, and she's taken," Camilla said, blowing my mind.

"You sure don't know what *not* to say," I told her, shaking my head.

"I'm just saying, I like her, and I know you like her too because you let her stay at your house, and it's fucked up that she belongs to someone else," she said like she felt sorry for me or some shit.

"Trust me when I say that nigga is about to get his eviction papers," I replied, more confident than I was feeling about the situation.

"Okay, so you're his landlord now?" she joked.

"Whatever," I said, pulling up to the hospital.

When we tried to go to the ICU to see my mother, it seemed as if they were giving us the runaround, telling us that someone was going to come out to speak with us. I felt myself on the verge of going off, but I didn't want to do that in front of Camilla because she already had tears in her eyes at the thought that something was wrong as they put us in a room to wait for a doctor. I knew from experience that anytime they put you in a room before seeing a loved one, it wasn't good news, so I prepared myself for the worst but still prayed that our mother was alive. We sat in the room for a few minutes before a woman in a navy blue pantsuit came in, looking more like a librarian, so I knew that she wasn't a doctor.

"I'm sorry to have kept you waiting. My name is Emily Rhodes, and I'm the administrator at the hospital. I'm here to inform you that when your mother was brought into the hospital, she was misdiagnosed. At the time, we didn't have her medical records because she's not a patient at our hospital, so all her symptoms led us to believe that they were from her being dehydrated. We now know that your mother slipped into a diabetic coma, which was caused by her blood glucose level being extremely low. After receiving her blood sugar test results, we now know that it was hypoglycemia, so our next step of treatment was aimed at getting her blood level raised. We were successful at getting them raised, and she is now conscious and able to tell us that she had diabetes."

I didn't know how to feel. I mean, I was happy that my mother was okay, but I was a little upset that she didn't tell us she had diabetes. Camilla didn't look like she was shocked at hearing my mother had diabetes, which led me to believe that she knew. The only thing that saved this hospital from my wrath was the fact that they didn't know, just like I didn't know.

"Thank you, Ms. Rhodes. I appreciate all that you've done for my mother, and if you don't mind, could you please give me a few minutes with my sister?" I said to her, and once she was gone, I turned to Camilla.

"Did you know that Mom had diabetes?" I asked her, causing her to shift in her seat, and she avoided eye contact with me.

"Envy, I knew, but she didn't want you to know because we all know how you are, so I promised her that I wouldn't say anything. She promised me that she would take the medication, so I thought that, as long as she did that, she was good," she admitted.

"So, if you knew what was going on with her when you brought her to the hospital, why didn't you tell the fucking doctors once you saw the state that she was in?" I barked at her ass.

"Stop yelling at me, Envy. Like I said, I promised her I wasn't going to say anything," she repeated, sounding fucking stupid.

"Thanks for not saying anything and almost killing our fucking mother," I said, causing her tears to fall.

I got up and slammed the door behind me, not giving a fuck about her tears because I was pissed, so pissed that I didn't even go to see my mom. I went out to my car and lit up, knowing I shouldn't have been smoking a blunt in the hospital parking lot, but at this point, I didn't give a fuck. I needed something to calm my nerves because I was ready to strangle Camilla's ass. After all, she knew how I felt about my mother, and keeping something like this from me wasn't cool. I didn't even realize how long I had been sitting out in my car because I must have dozed off, opening my eyes to Tami knocking on the window. It took me a minute to realize that I wasn't dreaming before realizing that she was really standing outside of my car, but I didn't know why since I just dropped her ass off not too long ago.

"I never met someone who loved to be at their job on their days off as much as your ass," I told her after rolling down the window.

"Camilla called me," she said.

"Called you how because I didn't give her your number?"

"I gave her my number to call me if she needed someone to talk to," she explained.

"So, why are you out here, knocking on *my* window, instead of inside, talking to *her?*" I asked.

"I'm not inside because I came to talk to you, so unlock the door so that I can get in," she said, walking around to the passenger side.

I unlocked the door, wondering what she needed to talk to me about because I wasn't in the mood for any bullshit. When she got in the car, I immediately noticed the left side of her face was bruised.

"What happened to your face?" I asked. My jaw tightened before even knowing what happened, but I knew it had something to do with that nigga of hers.

"I didn't come here to talk about what happened to my face. I came to talk to you about you yelling at your sister and not hearing her out. She needs you right now, and she wasn't trying to hurt you by not telling you."

"So, you're letting that nigga put hands on you like the shit is okay?" I asked her, ignoring all that she just said.

"Would you fucking focus and stop worrying about that nigga because, trust, if my face is bruised, his shit is leaking right now," she said with a smirk.

"So, you left that nigga leaking?"

"Yeah, I left him leaking."

"That's my girl," I praised her, lighting up again, taking a few pulls, causing her to suck her teeth.

"Listen, I need you to go back inside to see your mom and talk to your sister because she needs you right now," Tami said, taking the blunt and putting it out.

"I don't have anything to say to her ass for keeping secrets from me that could have cost my mother her life," I told her.

"Envy, you have to realize that your sister thought she was doing the right thing at the time, and she didn't want you to worry."

"Fuck that. She should have told me," I barked louder than I intended to. "I'm sorry. I didn't mean to yell, but she knows how much I care about my mother, and she shouldn't have put her life in jeopardy the way she did. She saw my mother's health failing, and she said nothing, so *that's* why I'm pissed off with her ass."

"She's sorry, Envy, and she's hurting because she knows that she could have lost her mother. She needs you, and your mother is asking for you," she sighed.

"Go back to my house and wait for me. I'll be there in a little while after I see my mom and talk to Camilla. Oh, just to let you know, I *will* be putting hands on that nigga for putting hands on you," I told her, not waiting for a response.

I walked into the hospital, standing outside of my mother's room, taking a deep breath before going inside.

She still looked weak, but she looked better, which made me feel a little better, but I was still mad at both of them.

"Here comes my baby," she said weakly. "Baby, come here and give me a hug. Don't you be mad at your sister. If you need to be mad at someone, be mad at your mama," she whispered in my ear.

"Mom, you should have told me what was going on with you. I kept asking you, but you kept telling me that it was nothing, taking home remedies, knowing you needed insulin," I told her.

"Envy, I didn't want to bother you with what was going on with me because all you would have done was worry," she responded.

"Mom, I'm *supposed* to worry about you, so I need you to promise that you will never keep anything like this from me again. Also, it's not fair to Camilla for you to put pressure on her either. She doesn't know what to do, especially since she promised you she wouldn't say anything. Do you know that she was scared to tell the doctors because you made her promise not to say anything?"

"I know, baby, and I apologized to her already for putting her in that position and having you mad at her."

"I'm not mad at her anymore. I just want her to understand that we're family, and we should have no secrets among us," I said, pulling my sister in for a hug.

"I'm sorry," Camilla cried in my arms, with me rubbing her back and telling her that it was okay.

Chapter Four

Tami

I didn't want to go back to my house after what happened between Siah and me, but I wanted to get an overnight bag. When I pulled up in front of my house, Siah's car wasn't there, so I felt it was safe to go in. I went up to my room, pulling out a few things because, once I left Envy's place tomorrow, I was going to be staying at Rema's place for a few days.

Loud knocking on the door stopped me from packing as I went downstairs to see who had lost their damn mind. I grabbed the bat out of the closet at the bottom of the stairs before opening the door. I thanked God that I had a screen door because it was the police at my door, and I didn't need them to see that bat in my damn hand. I put the bat in the corner behind the door before asking them how I could help them.

"Are you Tami Owens?" the female officer asked me.

"Yes, I'm Tami Owens," I responded, getting nervous because they asked for me by name.

"Ma'am, I'm going to need you to step outside of the home," she said.

"What is this about?" I asked her.

"Ma'am, you need to step outside of the home," her partner repeated.

I stepped out of the house, closing the door behind me because I didn't want them looking inside the house and seeing Siah's blood on the floor.

"Tami Owens, you are under arrest for the assault on Messiah Owens," she said, placing my arms behind my back, handcuffing me as she read me my rights.

I was pissed, so pissed that tears fell from my eyes because I couldn't believe Messiah would get me arrested after he put hands on me first. I was starting to learn a lot about the man that I thought loved me, but how could he love me by being a bitch-ass nigga, pressing charges against his wife? The nerve of him to put his fucking hands on me, and all I did was defend myself, but I guess that meant nothing to him since he still pressed charges like a fucking snitch. I was so embarrassed, being taken from my home in handcuffs because I knew my nosy-ass neighbor had her curtain pulled back, and she was going to have it reported by tomorrow morning to whoever missed it with their nosy ass.

Once I was fingerprinted and had my mugshot taken, I *really* felt like a criminal, and the shit hurt me so fucking bad. The only thing that made me feel good about the situation was that I wasn't a criminal, and since I had no priors, I was eligible for a desk appearance. I used my phone privilege to call Envy because he left me with his keys, and I wanted to let him know what happened to me because I knew he was probably blowing up my phone. He said that he was going to come pick me up, so I went outside the police station to wait for him, and that was when the stress of it hit me all at once. There was just too much going on, and I didn't know how much more I could take because my marriage was failing, and now this bullshit. I felt like I was on the verge of a breakdown as I let the tears fall. Envy pulled up about twenty minutes later, and he was just as pissed off as I was because it showed all over his face.

"Just tell me where I can find his bitch ass," he said as soon as I got inside the car.

"Envy, please, I just want to go get your keys and not think about him right now," I said.

I could tell he was upset, but he left the conversation alone as we drove in silence the rest of the way to my house. I tried my best to clear my head and not think about what happened, but it was hard as the tears fell from my eyes again, causing me to turn my head toward the window so that he wouldn't see me crying. He must have known that I was crying because he remained quiet, just taking my hand in his as he continued driving. That small gesture meant a lot to me as I wiped away my tears with my other hand.

When we got to my house, I went inside and got what I needed, then got back into the car and gave him Rema's address so that he could drop me off. He, being who he was, did the opposite, and we ended up at his place, which I didn't mind, but I had already put enough on him when he had so much to deal with, like his mother being sick.

"Envy, you could have just taken me to Rema's place. You have your own shit to deal with," I said.

"You're good," was all he said as he got out of the car, grabbing my bag.

"Go take a shower and make yourself at home. I'm going to check on my mom and make sure Camilla made it home," he said, leaving me to handle my business.

After my shower, I felt a little better, and when he came upstairs to shower, I called Rema to let her know what happened. She stopped talking to me and was now in the background, yelling at Dada about how she was going to fuck Siah up for being a snitch nigga.

"Rema," I yelled to get her attention.

"I swear I'm going to fucking lose it on Dada's ass," she said, coming back to the phone.

"Rema, you can't blame him for what Siah did," I told her.

"Yes, the fuck I can because he's defending the nigga, talking about he wouldn't do no punk shit like that, but were you not in fucking lockup?" she said, heated.

"Just calm down before your ass ends up in handcuffs, and let me be the first to tell you that the shit isn't worth it," I said seriously.

"Just have my damn bail money, bitch, because you already know I'm going to Central," she laughed.

"I'm about to get off this phone with your crazy ass. I'll call you tomorrow on my break," I told her.

When I walked out of the bedroom Camilla had been staying in, I went downstairs to see Envy sitting on the couch, indulging again. I went and sat next to him, taking the blunt out of his hand, but this time, I indulged as well. I needed this release to free my mind of Siah and my wanting to take his life for all the bullshit he had put me through.

"So, do you want to talk about it?" he asked me.

"Nah, I'm good with just putting it behind me, even if it's just for tonight," I told him.

"Well, I can think of a few things to take your mind off of it," he replied, staring at me with that sexy-ass smirk on his face.

I knew that I shouldn't have been entertaining the thought of sleeping with another man since I was married. I knew that I shouldn't, but, if only for one night, I wanted to live by the saying "married but living single" because that was precisely how I felt right now. Siah slept with his baby mother with no regard for the wife that he had at home, so tonight was fair game. I now had no respect for the husband I had, who was probably between her legs right now anyway.

"Come here," he demanded, looking me in my eyes as I scooted closer to him, never breaking eye contact as his lips touched mine.

He slipped his tongue into my mouth, deepening the kiss as his hands slipped under my nightshirt, caressing my nipples. He broke the kiss, lifted my nightshirt over my head, and smiled after seeing that I had nothing on underneath. He kissed my breasts, sucking lightly, causing me to moan before he pushed me down on the sofa, admiring my body, causing me to now feel uncomfortable at his intense stare. I closed my eyes as I felt his hands separating my thighs as his lips brushed against my clit. I lifted my hips and grabbed the back of his head, enjoying the feel of his tongue dipping in and out of me. I twisted my hips and jerked my body as an orgasm rocked my entire body, sending me into what felt like convulsions.

"OMG, Envy, what are you doing to me? Fuck," I cried out.

He stood, wearing that smirk of his as he removed his basketball shorts and underwear, causing me to gasp at the size of his dick standing at attention. My pussy was tingling with the anticipation of him entering me. He pulled me up and bent me over, entering me from behind, grabbing my hips as he pumped in and out of me. He was fucking the shit out of me, and I tried to keep up with him by throwing back my ass. I met him stroke for stroke, screaming out in pleasure as we both came together. He didn't even give me a minute to catch my breath as he was brick hard. He entered me again, beating the pussy up this time until I came once more. He pulled out, leaving my body tingling all over as I tried to figure out where the hell this man had been all my damn life. Siah put the dick down, but I never experienced what Envy had my body feeling—ever—and I did mean *ever*. Shit, I was in love.

Messiah

"Would you just hold still and stop acting like a damn baby?" Tara yelled.

Tami and I got into a heated argument with me accusing her of fucking that nigga, and when she didn't deny it, I got pissed off. I let my anger get the best of me when I slapped her in the face. I didn't mean the shit, but it was too late to take it back as we started fighting, going blow for blow. I made the mistake of turning my back for a second, and when I turned back around, she hit me on the side of my face with the trophy off the wall unit. My shit was leaking, and I patched it up as best as I could, but the shit wouldn't stop bleeding. I called Tara to come and get me to take me to the emergency room to get stitches, and that shit hurt like hell. She was sitting here, telling me to stop acting like a damn baby, but this shit hurt because whatever they put in that needle to numb the pain wasn't fucking working.

After getting eighteen stitches to my shit, we left the hospital to pick up my son and then my car before going back to her crib to chill for the night. After showering, I was lying on the sofa, with my son lying on my chest, watching ESPN, when my phone started ringing. I grabbed it, quickly answering it, trying not to wake up MJ.

"What's up?"

"Yo, what the fuck is Rema talking about . . . You had Tami arrested?" Dada asked me, causing me to sit up.

"Man, what the fuck are you talking about? I didn't do no punk bullshit like that," I said, heated.

"Well, Tami called Rema and said that she was arrested for assaulting you," he said.

"How fucking long have you known me? You know I don't talk to no fucking police."

"That's what I tried to tell Rema's ass, but she said that they had Tami's name and picked her up from the house."

"Yo, I'm going to hit you back," I told him, ending the call.

"Tara, get your ass in here now!" I yelled, waking up my son.

"What?" she asked with an attitude.

"Did you run your fucking mouth to the police about what Tami did?" I asked, pissed, knowing that she did because who the fuck else knew what happened but her ass?

"Damn right I told them where to find that bit—"

I slapped the shit out of her ass, and she didn't take the slap lightly. She charged me, swinging wildly. I grabbed her hands and pinned her down because, if she had busted my stitches, I was going to kill her ass in here.

"Tara, you better calm the fuck down," I told her, but she was still trying to kick me.

I didn't want to hurt her, but I grabbed her by her neck to let her know that I wasn't playing with her ass and had no problem snapping her fucking neck if she didn't chill the fuck out.

MJ was screaming at the top of his lungs by now, and that was the only reason I let her ass go so that I could pick him up.

"Don't touch my fucking son, Messiah," she cried. "Give me my son and get the fuck out," she said, reaching for him.

"Don't fucking touch me when I'm holding my son, Tara, before I really have to fuck you up in here. If you want to be mad, be mad at yourself because you had no fucking business talking to the police after I didn't tell them shit," I said, heated.

"I'm sick of that bitch. She jumped on me when I was with your son, and you didn't do shit about it to check her ass. Now, she attacked you, and you still weren't going to do shit about it," she yelled.

"She's my wife, and had you kept your fucking mouth shut, you wouldn't have gotten your ass kicked."

"You know what, Messiah? I'm not doing this shit with you no more. Give me my son and go home to your wife," she repeated, reaching for our son, and this time, I handed him to her because I was done with the dramatics with her ass.

I wasn't about to sit and justify why I didn't want my wife locked up because, after all, she was still my fucking wife. What kind of man would I be to press charges on a female like some fucking punk? She gave as good as she got, so who was I to blame her for that? I grabbed my shit and left because Tara wasn't going to let the shit go, and I wasn't going to argue with her any longer in front of my son.

Once in my car, I called Tami back-to-back, just to be sent to voicemail, and I was starting to get pissed off. I wanted to make sure that she was okay and let her know that I didn't do that sucker shit. Tami, of all people, should know that I had been known to do some fucked-up shit, but I would never do her like that by having her arrested. When I got home and saw her car in the driveway, I was happy as hell because I could let her know face-to-face that I didn't do that bullshit . . . but she wasn't home.

I called my nigga, Dada, to see if he was still at Rema's crib, but he had already left to handle some business. I scrolled through my phone until the name Mo appeared, then clicked to connect the call.

"Why the fuck are you calling my phone after what you did to Tami?" she barked on my ass.

"Yo, why the fuck are you acting like you don't know me better than that?" I asked, disappointed that she would believe I could do that shit too.

"So, if not you, then who?" she asked.

"That's not important right now. I'm going to handle that shit, but I didn't call you to get into that shit. I just got home, and Tami isn't here. Do you know where she's at because I checked the police station, and they said that she was released."

She got quiet on the line, letting me know that she knew, but she didn't want to say shit, and I felt myself getting pissed off with her ass.

"So, we're keeping secrets now? I thought we were better than that."

"Siah, don't put me in this situation. She's my friend, my *best* friend," she said, just above a whisper.

"Where is she, Rema? Matter-of-fact, don't even answer that shit. I'm on my way," I told her, ending the call.

I didn't wait for her to answer because I knew that she was going to try to talk me out of coming to her crib.

"Open the fucking door and stop playing," I barked into the phone when she didn't answer the door.

"Siah, you shouldn't be here," she responded.

"Rema, don't play with me. Open the door—now."

She opened the door, rolling her eyes, walking toward the living room, not saying anything to me.

"You can let that attitude roll off your back and tell me where the fuck Tami's at," I warned.

"Siah, why did you come here? You shouldn't be here," she said, ignoring my question.

"Where's my daughter?" I asked, not trying to hear what I shouldn't be doing.

"She's in her room, hopefully, sleeping," she said.

"Well, take your ass upstairs and get her because I'm not going anywhere until you tell me where Tami is," I told her, removing my hoodie and kicking off my Tims, getting comfortable.

Chapter Five

Tami

"You leaving me already, thickums?" Envy asked, grabbing me around my waist, kissing my neck.

"Yeah, I have to go, but I'll call you later," I said, turning to face him, kissing him on the lips.

"You already called in to work, so you have time for me to put it on that ass again," he smirked.

"I have no idea if you have an eye problem or some shit, but in case you haven't noticed, my walk ain't the same from fucking with you," I laughed.

"Come on, just a quickie. I promise I'll be gentle." He tried again, this time grabbing me in a bear hug.

"I can't. I'm going to Rema's place to get a few hours of sleep before heading home to deal with my husband," I told him, causing him to release me quickly as he turned me back to face him.

"I don't want you in that nigga's presence alone, Tami," he spat.

"Didn't I already prove to you that I can handle myself when it comes to him? Trust me, I'm not going to argue with him because I'm not trying to get into any trouble before my desk appearance," I told him, kissing him on his lips again to calm him.

"If that nigga even breathes on you wrong, you better call me," he said, slapping me on my ass, letting me leave.

***

I scrunched up my face and squinted my eyes because I knew for sure my eyes weren't playing tricks on me. Siah was the only nigga that I knew pushing a 2016 QX80 with the custom plate that read "Ghost Ryder." I was bugging out because Rema didn't call me to warn me that he was at her place, looking for me. I wanted to call her, but if her phone rang, he would probably snatch it, knowing my ass was on the other end of the phone.

I circled the block and parked a few doors down to wait until he left before going to her place, even though I knew that he wouldn't recognize Camilla's car. Yes, I had plans on having a conversation with him, but I didn't know if it was going to be a cordial conversation, and I wouldn't dare disrespect where Rema and my goddaughter lay their heads. I didn't understand what was taking his ass so long to leave after finding out that I wasn't there. I had already been sitting in the car for twenty minutes, and he still hadn't come out of her house. Just as I was getting antsy, her front door opened with him holding her daughter in his arms, kissing her all over her face before handing her back to Rema. He said a few words to Rema before jogging to his car, and my mind tried to go there, but I quickly dismissed the thought because it was Rema.

Phoenix stayed with us plenty of days and nights, so he loved her just as much as I'd grown to love her, as if she were my own. I wasn't giving the devil any of my energy as I got out of the car, not giving it a second thought as I stood on her porch, waiting for her to open the door.

"Hey, girl. Why didn't you—"

"What are you doing here, girl? I thought you weren't coming by until after work," she said, cutting me off.

"I called in this morning because I wanted to crash here for a few hours before going home to deal with Siah because Envy was not going to let me sleep," I told her, trying to figure out why she was acting strange and why she still hadn't mentioned Siah being here.

Mama didn't raise no fool, so I decided not to say anything about seeing Siah here, just to see if she would tell me.

"Oh, okay, no problem," she said, picking up a few things off the table.

I noticed the pillow and the blanket, but she still said nothing as I started making assumptions.

"So, what do you have planned for the day?" I asked her.

"Dada just left, still upset with me about screaming on his ass, so I put that ass on the sofa, and I was just about to get Phoenix ready for school before going into the office for a few hours," she said, avoiding eye contact as she spoke.

I started to feel light-headed because Rema had never lied to me before, and it had me feeling some kind of way as I went and sat down on the sofa, trying to calm myself.

"Are you okay?" she asked with a worried look on her face.

"I'm fine. I just haven't been feeling well today," I lied.

"I hope you didn't catch anything from being in that dirty police station," she joked, causing me to fake laughter.

"I'll be okay. I'm just going to lie down for a little bit, if that's okay with you," I said, needing to get out of her presence.

"Girl, why are you acting brand new? You know you don't have to ask," she said.

I feigned sleep in the guest bedroom until I heard her and Phoenix leave. Rema worked at a real estate firm, where the boss showed her special treatment, so she basically did what she wanted regarding her work hours. I knew that she could come back at any time, so I jumped up and started snooping around. I had a sick feeling in my stomach at the thought of my best friend possibly betraying me because it was going to be a hard pill to swallow. Besides the pillow and blanket I saw, there were no other signs of foul play where Siah was concerned. She might have let him spend the night and thought that I would be upset if I found out, so that could be why she didn't mention him being here. I felt stupid for even thinking that she would do something like sleep with my husband behind my back. *She and I are thick as thieves,* I thought as I went back to the guest bedroom and dozed off.

I woke up to the ringing of my cell phone. I looked at the screen, seeing that it was Envy calling. I answered the call, and he wanted to know if I was all right. I told him that I had overslept and was still at Rema's house. I was about to shower and head to my place. I told him that I would call him after speaking with Siah.

After I got out of the shower, I was walking out of the bathroom when I heard Rema downstairs, talking on the phone, so I stood at the top of the stairs, listening, when I heard her say Siah's name.

"Siah, I'm not going to keep this from her any longer. She's my friend, and she needs to know the truth," she said.

"I understand that, but it hurts me to keep looking her in the face and lying to her."

"No, I'm not trying to hurt her, but she needs to know that Phoenix is *your* daughter," she yelled into the phone.

I backed away from the stairs with tears falling from my eyes as I went into the bedroom, trying not to make any noise. She must have thought that I had left since she didn't see my car out front, not knowing that I wasn't driving it. Just to be safe, I hid in the closet, just in case she came into the room to see if I had really left. Words couldn't express what I was feeling right now, and it took everything in me not to confront her. I was beating myself up, trying to figure out how Siah could be Phoenix's father. I cried at the thought that the two people I loved the most would betray me in this way.

I sat in that closet until I heard her leave, probably going to pick up Phoenix from day care. I waited a few minutes to make sure she wasn't coming right back as I quickly dressed, leaving her house with murder on my mind.

I put on my game face before going inside, giving myself a pep talk, reminding myself that I couldn't get into any trouble. When I walked inside, Siah was sitting on the sofa, wearing nothing but a beater and his boxers, watching television. I looked at his head and didn't feel any type of way about it because he got just what he deserved.

"Where you stay last night?" he asked me.

"I stayed at Rema's house," I said, fucking with him, laughing inside at his facial expression because he knew I was lying, but he couldn't tell me how he knew.

"I called, and Dada said that you weren't there," he lied.

"Well, how could Dada possibly tell you that when he wasn't even there?" I asked him.

"Look, Tami, I don't want to argue or fight with you. I just want to know what happened to us, and how we can get back to being us again," he had the nerve to say with a straight face, like he didn't just spend the night with my best friend.

"How about when you stop treating me like I'm some bitch off the street instead of your wife? How could you get me arrested for defending myself? You had no reason to put your hands on me for what you *thought* you knew. I know you're still sleeping with Tara, but do I put my hands on you? No, I don't, and I would appreciate it if you would stop trying to sell me another dream when you know you're still living foul, so please, miss me with the 'you want us back to being us,'" I yelled.

I needed to calm down because I felt myself letting what I found out today get the best of me, and I wasn't ready to reveal what I knew right now.

"Tami, I would never have you arrested, let alone speak to no fucking pigs, and you should know that. If you know nothing else about me, you should know I'm not even built like that," he tried to convince me.

"So, how the fuck did they know my name and where to find me?" I asked him, not believing him.

"I made the mistake of having Tara take me to the hospital, and I didn't know that she spoke to the police about what happened to me. I swear to you that they never even questioned me about anything, so you should be good because I would never admit to that shit," he said, causing me to see red because all I heard was that he had called Tara.

I was so mad but didn't want to react because, at that moment, I felt the need to put hands on him, so I walked away to avoid being arrested again, and this time for attempted murder. He left me alone for a good thirty minutes, coming in just as I was getting off the phone with Envy, letting him know that I was good. I placed my phone down and looked at him, waiting to hear what bullshit he was about to spit, when someone knocked at the door and interrupted him. He looked at me, giving me the side eye, and I looked right back at his ass because I wasn't expecting anyone. I didn't even bother to follow behind him until I heard a female voice, so I went downstairs to the front door, and it was no other than Tara's ass. That was why I couldn't stand this little fucking hood rat. She had no respect when it came to me being his wife.

Granted, she was his baby mother, but she still should have shown some level of respect by *not* showing up at the house where he lived with his wife.

"He has a fever of 101 degrees," she whined to Siah.

"So, you drove all the way here instead of taking him to the hospital?" I asked her dumb ass.

"Mind your fucking business, Tami. This has nothing to do with you," she shot back.

"It has a lot to do with me when you're standing at *my* doorstep with some bullshit excuse because a *real* mother would have taken her child to the hospital if he was *really* sick," I accused because I knew good and well that baby wasn't sick.

"Siah, you've got five seconds to get this bitch from in front of my house before I wipe the fucking ground with her snitching ass," I told him, meaning every fucking word.

At this point, I couldn't care less about a court date and being arrested again because I was getting tired of this bitch playing with me. I heard him tell her to take their son to the hospital, and he would meet her there, but I didn't say anything until she left, and he closed the door.

"See, this is the type of shit I be talking about. No bitch walking should be able to disrespect your wife. Do you know why she thinks it's okay to show up at *my* fucking doorstep? Well, if you don't, let me tell you why. It's because you *allow* her to do whatever the fuck she wants because she has *your* fucking son. If you stop treating that bitch like she's the wife, she'll stop acting like the wife. I know, just as well as you know, that nothing is wrong with your son. She's just playing her mind games again, but I tell you what. If you even think about going to meet her at the hospital, I promise you I will not be here when you get back," I told him, leaving him standing in the foyer.

If his son were really sick, I would never deny him going to see about him, but I knew she was just using his son to get him back to her. He must have told her he wasn't fucking with her anymore after what she did, and that was her way to try to get him to change his mind. I guess he knew that I wasn't playing with him because he didn't go to the hospital, following behind her lying ass. He was trying to get on my good side by cooking me dinner and kissing my ass for the rest of the night, but that shit wasn't moving me. Just like he knew how to pretend, I knew how to pretend as well, and if he thought he was getting some ass, he had another think coming.

Envy

A few weeks had gone by since I'd seen Tami, but I convinced her to spend the night with me last night, which led me to believe that I was feeling her way more than I led on. In our previous conversation, she told me that she was going to talk to her husband about leaving, but now she just kept saying that it was "complicated." She said that she was no longer sleeping with him, but there were some things that she needed to work out before she could leave. So, just knowing that she was still with him was enough for me to fall back, but I didn't because, like I said, I was really feeling her.

"Yo, my mom wants to meet you," I blurted out.

"Meet me?" she asked with her face scrunched up.

"Yeah, she said she wants to meet the woman who kept me and Camilla sane while she was in the hospital. Camilla has been speaking very highly of you," I told her.

"Do you know I've known you for about three months now, and I don't even know what you do for a living?" she said, changing the subject. "I mean, you're living in this big-ass house and driving around in a nice, expensive-ass car, but I never hear you speak of going to work," she added.

"So, out of the three-plus months that you've known me, why are you just asking?" I questioned, pulling her onto my lap.

"I'm asking now because you just said that your mom wants to meet me, and I know nothing about you. You know where I live and work, but the only thing I know about you is that you have a mother, sister, and your fuck game is on point, but that's about it," she laughed.

"If I tell you what I do for a living, I'll have to kill you," I joked, caressing her thigh.

"I'm serious, Envy. I know nothing about you," she whined.

"The day before you walk down the aisle and say I do, I promise to tell you whatever you want to know about me," I told her, shutting her up as my hand was now inside of her boy shorts, dipping my finger in and out of her wetness.

Her pussy was so wet and dripping like a damn faucet by the time I removed my finger from inside of her. I stood her ass up off of my lap, removing her boy shorts and tank that she was wearing before pulling off my boxers, thinking I was about to get up in that pussy, but she surprised me by being the aggressor this time, taking my dick into her mouth. I grabbed her head, pumping in and out of her mouth, as she reached up and started to caress my balls, causing my dick to pulsate in her mouth, letting me know I was ready to explode. She grabbed both my ass cheeks as she bobbed her head faster, and I let go of my load in her mouth, and she swallowed. *I have a little freak on my hands,* I thought as I slapped her on her ass before laying her on her side on the bed. I put my leg between hers before entering her from behind. I thrust in and out of her, causing her to moan, forcing me to go deeper as I beat up the pussy, living up to her statement that my fuck game was on point.

"Envy, fuck this pussy. Oh shit, I'm about to come," she yelled out.

I felt my dick swell up inside of her as her pussy muscles tightened as we both released together, and then I couldn't move. I pulled her closer to me, still inside of her, placing my face in the crook of her neck and staying in that position until we both dozed off. I didn't know how long we were asleep, but we were both awakened by the ringing of her cell phone, which we tried to ignore, but the caller was persistent. She reached around me, grabbing her phone to answer, but the ringing had stopped. Then it rang again, and she answered the call this time. I watched her as she listened to the caller with a worried expression on her face before telling the caller she was on her way.

"Are you okay? What's going on?" I asked her as I watched her worried expression give way to an angry one.

"Siah was rushed to the hospital. Someone stabbed him multiple times," she said, standing with me, catching her just as her knees buckled, and she sobbed in my arms.

"Tami, you have to get yourself together so that you can get to the hospital," I told her.

I didn't know how I felt about her in my bedroom, crying for another nigga, but I had to remind myself that he was still her husband. I helped her get herself together before driving her to the hospital, and as much as I wanted to go inside with her, I refrained from doing so because, since it was her husband, out of respect, I stayed in the car. I reclined my seat because I didn't know how long I was going to be in the car, waiting for her, so I decided to close my eyes and try to get some rest.

Once again, I didn't know how long I was asleep, but it was starting to seem like a crime to get some rest as I was forced out of my sleep by a loud commotion going on outside the hospital. I began to ignore it, but when I looked toward the emergency entrance, I saw that it was Tami arguing with an older woman. When I saw some dude handling her, I jumped out of my ride. Once I got over to where she was, the dude had released her, and she was still arguing with the woman until all eyes fell on me, and the older woman looked at me with disgust in her eyes. I didn't know what I walked into, but Tami was clearly upset as she ran into my arms, sobbing, while whoever the woman was kept asking her who the hell I was.

Chapter Six

Tami

When I walked into the hospital, the first person I saw was Dada, but I didn't even get a chance to walk over to him because the same female officer who arrested me was now standing in front of me. They must have been waiting for me to show up, but I had no idea why. But what I *did* know was that I wasn't in the mood for bullshit.

"Mrs. Owens, we need to speak with you," she said in a tone that let me know that they weren't asking.

I wanted to ask her so badly if she and her partner were the only two motherfucking officers responding to emergency calls. I decided just to see what the fuck she needed to speak with me about, so I followed her and her partner to the end of the hall and into a room, trying to figure out their dire need they wanted to speak to me about since they didn't even give me a chance to talk to anyone about if my husband was still breathing or not.

"Are you aware of what happened, meaning, do you know the circumstances that led to your husband's injuries?" she asked me.

"No, I don't know the circumstances because I just got here after getting the call that my husband was stabbed multiple times. Had you given me a chance to speak to a doctor, maybe I would have known more than what I know now," I spat at her.

"Well, I apologize, but we have a few questions because we are trying to make sense of all that took place this evening. With that being said, do you know a Ms. Rema Royce?" she asked me.

"Yes, she's my best friend, but what does she have to do with any of this?" I asked her with an attitude evident in my voice.

"Were you aware that she and your husband were involved in a sexual relationship?"

"No, I wasn't aware," I lied.

"Mrs. Owens, there was a 911 call dispatched to the home of Ms. Royce. When the officers arrived, they found your husband and Ms. Royce both injured from stab wounds. We do have a suspect in custody who claims she followed your husband, who she claims is her boyfriend, to Ms. Royce's address. She stated that she didn't confront him right away, but when he was at the location for some time, she got upset and went to knock on the door. According to her, when Ms. Royce came to the door, with just a robe on, they had words at the door before she pulled out the knife and stabbed her multiple times. She then ascended the stairs and found a naked Mr. Owens in the bedroom, where she stabbed him multiple times," she informed me.

"The reason we asked to speak to you is because the suspect that we have in custody is a Ms. Tara Richmond, who states that she received a call just before Mr. Owens was set to leave her house, which prompted her to follow him," her partner chimed in.

"Okay, so what are you insinuating?" I asked him.

"We aren't insinuating anything, but we do have to ask if you made the call to Ms. Richmond."

"No, I didn't make any call to Ms. Richmond, and if you don't mind, I would like to go see about my husband and best friend." I stood, pissed off with both of them at this point.

"Mrs. Owens, we'll be in touch," the other officer said, allowing me to leave.

I knew that the officers were probably thinking that I was guilty of something because I didn't show any emotion or shed a tear. I was trying hard not to show them how what they told me affected me because I was angry right then. I wouldn't be human if I weren't bothered, disgusted, and hurt behind being betrayed by the two people that I adored, loved, and would do anything for.

When I got back to the waiting room area, I asked Dada if he had heard anything yet, and he said that they were both still in surgery. Hurt was written all over his face, and I knew he was feeling some of what I was feeling because he and Siah were friends, and he had been with Rema for two years now.

"Did you know?" he asked me.

"No, I didn't know," I responded as a tear fell.

I wiped at my tears as Siah's mother and father walked in, and I tell you no lie when I say that I could feel another piece of my heart being broken. The pain I was feeling was unbearable, seeing his father holding a sleeping Phoenix in his arms.

"Mama Celeste, please tell me that you didn't know," I cried, looking into her sympathetic eyes.

I paced the floor, trying to calm myself because this shit was unbelievable, and I felt like I was stuck in the Twilight Zone right about now. I just couldn't believe that Mama Celeste knew about this shit. No way, not the woman I loved as much as my own mother. Not the woman who I went to about her son when we were having problems, with her telling me how much her son loved me and to stick by him because I was her daughter, and it would hurt to lose me as her daughter-in-law. She knew that he was living foul all along, but she was protecting her son, and I got that, but why tell me to stay if you really loved me like a daughter? I didn't even listen to my own mother when she told me to cut his ass to give him some act right because she believed violence solved everything, so now, I was thinking that maybe I should have taken her advice. Mama Celeste was so passionate when she convinced me to stay with her son, telling me that when a man stepped out, it didn't mean that he loved you any less. It just meant that temptation caught him slipping, which caused him to get caught with his pants down.

All bullshit, I thought as I felt like I was having a panic attack when my breathing became heavy, and I was in dire need of some air. I walked toward the exit with Dada following behind me, asking me if I was okay, but no, I wasn't okay. I was in pain.

"How could she?" I screamed with tears falling from my eyes.

"How could you tell me you love me like your own daughter? I'll tell you how. It's because she doesn't have a fucking daughter. Because if she did, she would have known the shit she was kicking to me was wrong, knowing I would only get hurt in the end. They all just sat back and said nothing—*nothing,*" I yelled.

"Come on, Tami. I need you to calm down, and as fucked up as the situation is, we still need to be there for them," Dada said, but he had the game fucked up, pulling me in for a hug with me pushing him away and looking him in his face.

"Why, Dada? Why should we even care?" I cried out.

"Tami, I know you're hurting right now, but you need to get it together," I heard Mama Celeste say from behind me.

"Why do I need to get it together? Don't you dare come out here acting like you give a fuck about me. I'm so over all of you backstabbing bitches," I screamed in her face.

"Tami, you will *not* stand here and disrespect me," she said.

"Why the hell not? Trust me when I say I lost *all* respect for you, so get the fuck out of my face," I said as my hand went up, and Dada grabbed me just in time because I was going to slap the shit out of that bitch.

Yes, I let my anger get the best of me, but I wanted to hit someone—*anyone*—because so many emotions were running through me right now, and I wasn't going to feel better until I made someone feel pain, just as I was feeling right now.

"Tami." I heard his voice, and a calm came over me as I ran to him and cried in his arms.

"And who the hell is this?" Mama Celeste asked.

"None of your fucking business," I told her, walking off with Envy.

That bitch had a lot of fucking nerve to fucking question me about anything when she helped her fucking son deceive me. I swear I felt like breaking her fucking jaw for standing in my face, acting as if she cared for me, when she knew all along that my best friend was sleeping with her fucking son. I hated them, and I swear that if I never spoke to any of them again, it wouldn't bother me one bit, I tried to convince myself.

Envy

The club was packed tonight and not really my scene, but I had a business meeting set up with a potential buyer. I usually let my dude, Mason, handle this aspect of the business, but I decided to join him since Tami had my head fucked up. I needed a distraction, even if it was only for the night. I swear, I was losing my mind. My business meeting went well, so I motioned for the waitress to bring another bottle of Ace of Spades after deciding to chill before heading home. Mason's girl, Sami, came and joined us after we ended the meeting, and she had a friend with her.

"Hey, Envy, this is my friend, Olivia," she introduced.

I extended my hand, greeting her, and I couldn't help but notice that she was beautiful, and she was wearing the hell out of a teal, off-the-shoulder dress that stopped just above her knees, showing off her thick and sexy legs that had a nigga staring. Mason caught my attention when I saw him grab Sami's hand, leaving me at the table with Olivia, smirking, before walking off when he knew I already had a situation, so trying to set me up wasn't a good idea.

"So, I'm assuming this was a setup?" she smiled.

"That's what it looks like to me, so we might as well make the best of it. What are you drinking?" I asked her.

"I don't drink," she said, causing me to look at her strangely.

"I know you're thinking, why come to the club and not have a drink?" she said.

"Nah, it's just rare meeting a female in the club who doesn't drink, but I don't see anything wrong with it. Shit, that's a good thing," I told her. "So, my dude, Mason, and Sami have been together for a few years now. Why haven't I had the pleasure of meeting you before now?" I wanted to know.

"Sami and I are childhood friends who were always together, but I went away to school, only returning home during school break. I just moved back here for good about a month ago, and we reconnected like I never left," she explained.

"So, what brings you back to the Big Apple?" I asked her.

"A bad breakup and the fact that 'no' meant nothing to him," she said, shaking her head.

"His loss," I offered with a smile. "So, what have you been doing since you've been back?"

"I'm working for the United Federation of Teachers as a coordinator, and I just moved out of my parents' place into a loft not too far from my job. I appreciate my parents allowing me to stay, but I celebrated the day I moved out because they were a bit much," she laughed.

"So, what about you? Do you have a legit hustle outside of the illegal one?" she asked boldly.

"Illegal hustle? You must have me mistaken for someone else. I'm an entrepreneur, making it do what it do," I told her, watching her smile, looking at me like she didn't believe me.

"So, are you seeing anyone?" she asked.

I didn't know how to answer her question because I hadn't seen Tami since the night someone stabbed her husband and best friend. She'd been at his bedside and hadn't returned any of my calls, so whatever I thought we had was on pause right now. She was so upset with him and her, saying that she didn't care if she never saw them again . . . just to become his private nurse, so I was confused about where we stood at this point. I was trying to be patient, but the shit was starting to take a toll on me, not knowing if she still wanted to be with me.

"My situation is complicated right now," I told her, being honest.

"So, what makes it complicated, if you don't mind me asking?"

"Dude meets girl, dude likes girl, girl is married but having problems, dude gets caught up, and now dude is on the fence regarding whether he will end up with girl," I joked, but basically giving it to her straight, no chaser.

"I'm no expert when it comes to relationships, but I can bet money that this one will end how it started," she stated.

"Meaning?" I asked.

"You said that she's married, and I'm a firm believer that when women get married, they weather the storm, sometimes straying away from the storm just to go back to weather that storm. So, she was married when you started, and she's going to be married when she ends it," she explained.

"That was deep," I said, knowing that someone else may not have gotten it, but I knew exactly what she was trying to say.

I was really hoping that Tami wasn't selling me a dream when she claimed to be done with him, but deep down inside, I had a feeling she wasn't done. I just felt like she didn't owe him anything, and she said that he had no one else, but I begged to differ. Where were all those bitches he was cheating on her with? Better yet, let his lying-ass mama take care of his ass like I told her. She didn't see it the way I saw it because she would always say he was still her husband, which made Olivia's statement make a whole lot of sense.

Mason and Sami came back to the table, loving all over each other, telling us that they were ready to go. I knew what the two of them were going to be doing once they got home, the way that they were all over each other. I wasn't ready to call it a night, but I gave him dap, telling him I would holla at him tomorrow. Olivia stood, handing me a business card with her information, telling me to give her a call if I found my situation no longer complicated. I walked out with them, hugging her before walking to my ride, headed home to my big ole empty house to sleep alone again and think about Tami's ass.

I had been calling Tami for the past few days, but to no avail, and I was starting to get fed up with the situation as far as waiting for her to be with a nigga. She hadn't been back to work since her husband had been in the hospital, and now that he was home, she still hadn't returned. Showing up to her house wasn't an option, so I just had to convince myself to say, "Fuck it for now." I guess she would get at me when she was ready to hit me up.

"I miss her too," Camilla said, reminding me that her ass was in the room. "Don't try to deny that you weren't just thinking about her," she stated.

"Have you tried calling her, Camilla?" I asked her, desperate at this point.

"Yeah, but she hasn't returned any of my calls," she said. "Envy, I really like her, and I miss her. I finally had someone to talk to other than you and Mom," she said sadly.

"I miss her too, but there's nothing I can do about it because she's not returning any of my calls either."

"Well, maybe we just need to give her some time to get her situation where it needs to be," she offered, trying to make me feel better.

"Do you have any plans for the day?" I asked her, changing the subject.

"Kami and Prince are supposed to be coming through so that we can hit up the mall, so with that being said . . ." She looked at me with her hand held out.

"What happened to the money I gave you a few days ago, Camilla?"

"Envy, you can't be serious right now. How long do you think $200 lasts?" she said, looking at me like I was bugging for thinking that amount was supposed to last longer than a few days.

"If you can spend $200 in a few days, it's time for your ass to get a job," I told her, peeling off a few bills before heading out.

I was going to go up to tell my mother I was heading out, but she was resting, and I didn't want to wake her. I decided to give Olivia a call to see if she wanted to hang out because I refused to go back to the crib and do nothing alone. I was shocked as hell when she responded immediately with her address because I just knew that she was going to ask me about my situation. I knew she was feeling a nigga, but to keep it real, I wasn't trying to make another love connection. I just wanted to chill.

I was outside of her place, and I guess she was waiting for me to pull up because, just as I was going to get out and be a gentleman and knock on the door, she was already coming out. I still got out of the car, hugging her before opening the passenger-side door for her.

"I didn't expect you to say yes, so I really didn't have anything in mind. Tell me, is there anything you have in mind that you would like to do?" I asked her.

"Well, I have been dying to see *Neighbors 2,* but after dragging my friends to the theatre when the first one came out, they refused to go see the new one. I'm bugging on how they didn't find the first one funny," Olivia laughed.

I didn't want to tell her that I felt the same way as her friends because part one wasn't all that funny to me at all. However, since I asked her to go out, it was her world, and if she wanted to see part two, then part two it was.

"Do you know what time the movie starts?" I asked her.

"Hold up. Give me a minute," she said, typing on her phone.

"Damn, the next one isn't playing until an hour from now," she pouted.

"We can go get something to eat unless you have something else in mind until the movie starts," I told her.

"Well, I don't know how good you are around people you don't know, but my aunt is having a barbecue that I ditched to hang out with you. If you like, we could hang out there and get some good food instead of spending money when we can eat for free," she laughed.

"Shit, I like free. Hit me with the address," I told her, so that I could put it in my GPS.

I didn't need the GPS, but for an address I wasn't familiar with, I always put it in my system because you never knew when you might need that shit again. After giving me the address, Olivia called her aunt, letting her know that she was stopping by with a friend. Her aunt stayed out in Briarwood, a nice little area out in Queens. I was familiar with the area because I used to fuck with a female who lived near there about a year ago.

When we pulled up to the one-family brick home, we saw a lot of cars parked on the one-way street and some people hanging out in front of the house. After opening the passenger-side door for her to exit, she grabbed my hand as we walked into the home.

"Hey, Auntie Elle, this is my friend, Envy," she introduced.

"Hello, Envy, nice to meet you. You two can go on back and get some good food and drinks," she smiled.

"Don't be alarmed, but my mom and dad are here too," she said.

"It's cool," I said, feeling no way about it.

"Wow, let me find out you're a keeper. Usually, just the mention of parents, niggas be running," she laughed.

"I'm not your typical nigga," I told her because it was the truth.

We walked out into the backyard, and whoever dude was on the grill, he had shit smelling good, so good that he had my mouth watering at the thought of fucking up some ribs.

"Hey, Uncle Roy, this is my friend, Envy," she introduced me, hugging him.

After giving me a brotherly hug and telling me it was his pleasure meeting a friend of his niece, he went back to grilling.

"Uncle Roy, we're going to go and get something to eat because our movie starts in an hour," she said to him.

"You're not staying?" he asked, sounding disappointed.

"No, we already have plans to see *Neighbors 2,*" she responded.

"Girl, you don't have to go to the movies to see that. You know I've got the hookup, and if you stay, we can put it up on the big screen, right out here in the yard, as soon as the sun goes down," he said to her, with her looking at me.

"I'm cool with whatever you want to do," I assured her.

"Okay, Unc, we're going to stay."

"That's what I wanted to hear," he smiled, going back to taking ribs off the grill.

We got something to eat and drink, and then sat at one of the tables that they had set up in the backyard. I was going to town on the ribs that Olivia's uncle made with his special sauce because that shit tasted that damn good. I felt someone's eyes on me, and when I looked up, my eyes met with hers, and we just stared at each other until she broke the stare, giving her attention to the little girl who was with her.

Chapter Seven

Tami

Waking up this morning, I wasn't feeling well, but I found the strength to go downstairs to make breakfast for Siah and Phoenix. My life had been turned upside down in a matter of weeks, and to be honest, I didn't even know how I was still standing because, most days, I just wanted to lie down and give up. The hurt and pain that I was feeling daily had to take a backseat. After all, I had no time to dwell on it because I was forced to be there for the two people who hurt me deeply.

Siah was always out in them streets, cheating with this bitch and that bitch, but not one of those bitches was here to care for him. Even his parents were not present because they were too busy playing mommy and daddy to his son, MJ, to take care of him, or so they said.

Siah was able to leave the hospital two weeks after his surgery, but Rema was still hospitalized in a medically induced coma. So, between taking care of Siah and going up to the hospital and taking care of Rema three days out of the week, it was taking a toll on me. Rema had no one but me because her mother passed away last year from complications following her heart surgery, so I had to put whatever I felt about her behind and be there for her. I knew that I was being called all kinds of stupid by my family right now, but what was I supposed to do . . . leave her when she needed me? Yes, I knew that they betrayed me, and I didn't need to worry myself, but if not me, then who, I thought as I put some sausages in a pan.

Siah was almost back to being able to care for himself, which was a good thing. I was exhausted, both mentally and physically, and I didn't know how much more I could take. Sometimes, it was hard to take care of him because looking at him every day without causing him bodily harm was becoming a job of its own.

I hadn't been back to work, but I had to admit that my supervisor, Elle, wasn't as bad as I thought she would be. She had been very supportive of my situation, telling me to return when I was ready and able, which I really appreciated. I was feeling sluggish this morning, and now I was starting to feel light-headed. I thought it had to do with not sleeping as well as I should have.

I backed away from the stove, figuring my light-headedness might have been from the heat, so I walked into the living room, over to the control for the central air, and put on the fan. After placing Phoenix in her highchair and putting her food in front of her, I let Siah know that his food was ready as well before heading out of the kitchen.

I went upstairs to shower and get dressed so that I could go to the hospital to care for Rema because I had officially become her dayshift nurse three days out of the week. I took Phoenix to see her mother every Friday because that was the day that Siah had physical therapy. Siah and I didn't communicate much because I blamed him for having to cut Envy off because of the position he put me in. Envy was calling and texting me, but I just ignored him because I knew he wouldn't understand me caring for the man who hurt me the way that he did. I tried to explain to him that Siah was still my husband, so I felt obligated to be there for him since he had no one else, but he disagreed.

After caring for Rema, I decided not to stay like I usually did because I still wasn't feeling my best, so I walked out. On my way to the elevator, I bumped into Elle, so I stopped to talk to her for a few minutes.

"Hello, Elle. How are you?" I asked her.

"I'm fine. How is Rema doing?" she asked me.

"No change," I responded.

"I'm sorry to hear that, but how are *you* feeling? You look worn out," she said as I subconsciously brushed my hair back with my hand.

I knew I wasn't looking my best because I couldn't even tell you when the last time I had time to get my hair and nails done was. Today, I was wearing a pair of grey sweatpants with a grey T-shirt and sneakers, something Elle wasn't used to seeing me in, so I completely understood her statement.

"I'm feeling okay, just a little overwhelmed these days," I stressed.

"I'm having a barbecue this weekend at my house. Why don't you come by and unwind? Shellie and Rose will be there, so I think it would be good for you to be around your work buddies," she offered, but I hesitated.

"Look, take my address and think about it. No pressure. I just think it would be good for you to get out and have you some me time," she said, handing me the paper with her address on it.

"Okay, and thanks for everything," I told her, leaving.

By the weekend, I was feeling a little better, so I went to get my hair and nails done before finding something to wear to Elle's barbecue later on. It felt good to do something for myself finally, and I was excited about spending some time alone and not having to change dressings and give sponge baths. Having a day to relax finally had me hyped. When I got back to the house, it was already after two o'clock, and the barbecue started at three, so I needed to shower and get ready to head out. Just as I rounded the corner to go up the stairs, Siah came down the stairs.

"I just put Phoenix down for a nap. I'll be back this evening," he said, walking toward the front door.

"Hold up, Siah. Where the hell are you going because I have plans today, and those plans don't include staying in this damn house, babysitting *your* daughter," I told him.

"Look, I have some shit to handle. Just keep her for a few hours, and I promise, I'll be back in time for you to do whatever it is that you need to do," he said with an attitude, slamming the door behind him.

I was so sick of his ungrateful ass to the point that I wanted to pack my shit and move out and never look back. I was so tired of being his doormat that I felt like screaming. I swear that if I could go back to the night at the hospital, I would never return. I felt tears stinging my eyes, and I just let them flow out of frustration with the situation I put myself in. I couldn't even be mad at him because I had no one to blame but myself. I called Elle to let her know that I wasn't going to be able to make it because I didn't have a babysitter to keep my goddaughter, and she told me that I could bring her with me because it was a family barbecue, so I decided to go since I had gotten my hair and nails done.

When I got to Elle's house, I looked around to see if I saw her because many people were there, and I started to feel a little uncomfortable. Phoenix and I walked toward the backyard, where I heard the music. A few kids were playing, and several grown-ups were dancing and eating. Everyone seemed to be having a good time.

"Tami, I'm so glad you decided to come, and who's this little lady here?" I heard Elle say to me, but I wasn't paying her any attention because I had locked my eyes on

Envy, who was sitting at the table with a female smiling in his face.

I broke my stare at the sound of Elle calling my name. Suddenly, I started to feel flushed and needed some water.

"Are you okay?" she asked, concerned.

"Yes, I'm fine. I just need some water. This heat is a killer today," I said, not knowing what else to say.

"Come on inside. I have a few bottles of water in the freezer," she suggested. Phoenix and I followed her inside.

I heard footsteps behind me, but I didn't turn around because I already knew who it was, and I wasn't ready. I had nothing to say to him while he was here entertaining another female. Although I had no one to blame but myself, it didn't stop my feelings.

"Tami, can I talk to you for a second?" Envy asked me, causing Elle to look at him and then back at me.

"Go ahead. I'll take her outside to play with the other children," she said, taking Phoenix's hand, leading her back outside.

We left the house through the front door and were now standing by my car. Just seeing Envy made me realize how much I missed him, but I wasn't going to tell him that.

"So, you really just cut a nigga off, like I did something to you? All I tried to do was be there for you, even if that meant us not being together," he said.

"Envy, there was just so much going on, and I didn't want to put you in the middle of it. I shouldn't have started something with you, knowing that I was married, so for that, I do apologize," I told him.

"Tami, I don't want your fucking apology because I did nothing but keep it real with you, so there's no reason you couldn't have done the same by picking up your phone, letting me know something," he spat.

"I'm sorry. I didn't want to hurt you, so I thought it would be easier just to let you go," I said honestly.

"Why couldn't you let me be there for you? When you told me that you needed to be there for your husband, did I trip or speak about the situation? You shut me out for no reason, and that's some fucked-up shit because I wouldn't have done that to you."

"I don't know what else you want me to say, Envy," I cried, letting the tears fall.

I didn't know if I was crying because of how I did him or if it was all of the stress I had been dealing with, but I just felt like I was about to lose it. I shut him out to take care of a cheating man, only for that man to treat me like his servant and babysitter. I was just so tired, and I didn't know how much more I could take as my emotions got the best of me, and my tears cascaded harder. My body started to heave up and down. Envy pulled me into his arms, trying to calm me down, and I believe that was all I needed because it started to work as a calm came over me.

"Yo, go get in your car. I'll be right back," he said, letting me go, walking toward the backyard.

When he returned, he had Phoenix and the woman sitting with him at the table accompanying him. I had no idea why he would bring her out here when he knew that I was a mess right now, but I breathed a sigh of relief when I saw her go inside the house.

After leaving Elle's barbecue, I let Envy talk me into dropping Phoenix off and coming back to his house so that we could talk. Pulling up in front of my house, I got her out of the car and headed inside, hoping Siah didn't get all up in my face about immediately leaving again. I heard MJ from the foyer, doing his baby talk, which made me smile. Over the last few weeks, whenever he visited, I developed a little bond with him. No matter how I felt about the parents, I would never take it out on an innocent child because it wasn't their fault who they belonged to. Walking into the living room, I could tell that Siah had an attitude just from the look on his face, but I wasn't in the mood to entertain it. All I came to do was drop his daughter off and head right back out without all the extra shit.

"Siah, I'm about to leave for a little while. All you have to do with Phoenix is put her to bed because I'm going to wash her and put her in her pajamas before I leave," I told him.

"Is there something that you want to tell me?" he asked me, and all I could think was, here we go with the bullshit.

"If you've got something you need to say, can you please say it because I need to do what I have to do with Phoenix so that I can go," I told him, sucking my teeth, showing him that he was getting on my damn nerves.

"Don't worry about *my* daughter. Whatever she needs done, *I've* got her," he said with an attitude, but his saying he had her was news to me because I had been taking care of her.

"Okay, Siah. That's good to hear, so I'm going to head out now," I said, walking away.

"Hold up. That didn't mean you were off the hook about what the fuck I just asked you," he said, standing like he was going to do something to me, so I got in my fighting stance because if he put his hands on me, he was going to end up right back in the fucking hospital.

"No, I don't have anything to tell you, but if you have something that you want to ask me and I can answer it, I will."

"Are you pregnant?" he blurted out with his jaw tightening.

"Pregnant? Hell no, I'm not pregnant," I told him, looking at him like he was crazy.

"So, you're going to stand here and fucking lie to my face, Tami? You told me that you weren't fucking that nigga, so who the fuck are you pregnant by because I know it's *not* me," he shouted.

I felt a fucking headache coming on because I didn't know what his crazy fucking ass was talking about, because, if I were pregnant, wouldn't *I* be the first to know? I stood there watching his crazy ass walk over to the table on the side of the sofa and pick up something, trying to hand it to me.

"So you're saying this shit is not yours?" he asked me.

"Nigga, no, that shit is *not* mine, so get that nasty shit out of my face." I backed up because if he thought I was touching someone's piss-filled pregnancy stick, he was bugging.

Suddenly, someone was knocking at the door, and I was saved by the fucking bell from his crazy, fucking ass. I was hoping it was his mother coming to pick up MJ because she never let him stay the night, like *I* was going to do something to him. I turned toward the door, seeing this bitch, Tara, walk in the door like she lived here, pushing by me, bumping me in the process like I wouldn't drag her ass. I didn't even know how the fuck this bitch was home right now, and why the fuck did Siah allow her to walk up in here like she was queen bitch or some shit.

"Siah, what the fuck is *she* doing here?" I asked his dumb ass.

"I'm here to pick up my fucking son; *that's* why the fuck I'm here," she answered.

"Shut your busted ass up because I'm not talking to you. I'm talking to *my* husband."

"She just told you she's here to pick up her son," he said, causing me to lose all respect for his ass because I swear he was a dumb nigga.

"I'm confused because, first off, even if this bitch made bail, wouldn't she be on some restraining order where she shouldn't be anywhere *near* you? And not only that, but also why would you want her ass close to you after what she did to you and Rema?" I asked him. I needed to know what was good because he was acting like he was on drugs since he had never been this damn gullible before.

"Oh, so baby daddy didn't tell you he bailed me out of jail a week ago?" she smirked at me.

"Siah, please tell me this bitch is fucking lying," I yelled at his ass.

"Tami, I couldn't just leave the mother of my child sitting in jail when my son needs his mother," he said stupidly.

"You can't be fucking serious right now. Isn't this the same bitch who almost cost you your life, and if you bailed this bitch out of jail, why the fuck didn't you have her ass taking care of you?" I screamed, pissed off at this point.

"I *have* been taking care of his ass every fucking Tuesday, Wednesday, and Friday when you're at the hospital, taking care of your friend," she smirked, and I swear I didn't give a fuck about a court date, being arrested, or none of that other shit when I popped that bitch in her mouth.

"Yo, chill. Don't you see my motherfucking kids right here?" Siah yelled, grabbing me and pushing me toward the door, telling me to leave. I looked at him as if he had lost his damn mind after all that I'd done for his ass.

"Oh, so *this* is the reason you guys were arguing when I got here? Damn, Siah, I didn't want you to find out like this. I'm sorry your bitch-ass wife went snooping in the fucking garbage, but I'm a hood rat. Ha," she said, holding up that stank-ass pregnancy stick.

I was too done as I grabbed my keys and bag out of the foyer to leave because, if I didn't, I was going to end up on NY1 late-night news for killing both of their asses. I had never felt so stupid in my life, but again, I had no one to blame but myself for trying to do the right thing by him when I thought he had no one, knowing he didn't give a shit about me. I couldn't even get to the car because I had to sit on the porch since I felt light-headed again. I just couldn't wrap my head around why the fuck this shit was happening to me when all I did was be there for people who didn't even deserve my help. I didn't understand why Siah was trying to hurt me when he caused everything that happened to him. So, he was mad at me for what?

I promise you one thing, if I wasn't done before, you best believe I was done now. I couldn't do this shit anymore, and I refused to put anyone's feelings before mine from this day on, I promised myself, meaning every fucking word. Then I grabbed the rail, pulling myself up off the porch and heading toward my car so that I could get the hell away from here.

Envy

After returning to the backyard to get the little girl who came with Tami to the barbecue, I was stopped by Olivia, asking me what was going on. I explained to her that Tami was the "situation" I was referring to, and I needed to handle it. She wasn't pissed or anything. She just said that she understood, telling me that I owed her a rain check because she still wanted to see the movie. She walked me to the front, and I kicked it with her for a minute, telling her that I appreciated her understanding because most chicks would have been flipping out right about now. If I had met her before meeting Tami, she would definitely be a candidate to kick it with to see where it could go as far as a relationship. I knew that I should be kicking it with her since Tami was still married, but I couldn't find it in me because Tami had already made an impression on me, and I was definitely feeling shorty.

I heard Tami's car pull up, so I went to open up the front door for her and was taken aback because her makeup was a mess from crying, and the curls that she was rocking earlier fell, so her hair was all over the place. Instantly, I wanted to know what the fuck happened. I pulled her inside, questioning her because, if that nigga put his hands on her again, I swear he would be getting no pass this time. She sat on the couch and told me everything that went down at her crib. I was pissed, but I was more pissed at her ass for continuing to feel as if she owed that nigga something.

"I'm going to be honest with you because I don't know what's going on with you and why you keep allowing this nigga to play you. He's a fuck boy. There is no other explanation for what the fuck he's doing to you because that's what fuck boys do. I'm going to need you to stop fucking crying because you've cried enough over this nigga. Don't give him one more tear," I told her, wiping her face.

"I'm sorry," she said, just above a whisper.

"Tami, look at me. You have no reason to apologize to me right now. I can't sit here and say that I understand why you stood by him after he did you dirty because I don't understand, but you have nothing to be sorry for," I told her.

"This is why I walked away from you. I didn't want to put you through any of this because my life is a mess right now, and I just want it to stop. I don't want to do this with him anymore because I'm at my breaking point right now," she cried.

She was so upset that she was shaking, and I honestly understood how she felt because, trust me, when I say, I've been there before. When you do everything in your power to be there for someone who hurt you to your core, and they turn around and give you their ass to kiss, they're saying "fuck you." His ass had the nerve to throw the same female who caused all of the problems in her face, so I knew that shit had to hurt. I could tell that she was mad at herself and probably feeling like she wanted to take both of their lives, but she knew that if she did, she would most likely be spending the rest of her life in prison, so I got her frustration. She wasn't feeling well, so she went upstairs to shower, and after giving her a shirt to sleep in, I pulled back the covers in my bed, telling her to get some rest. After kissing her on her forehead, I headed downstairs to get myself a drink and try to figure out what my next move was going to be concerning this bitch-made nigga.

I slept on the couch last night because I didn't want her to feel like I was pushing her to be in a relationship with me, no matter how much I wanted us to be together. I got up off the couch, folded the comforter and sheet, and placed both back into the hall closet for tonight. Then I headed to the bathroom to shower before fixing breakfast for her. I didn't make her a spread because I wasn't great at cooking, so I just cooked some bacon, eggs with cheese, and toast.

"Hey, sleepyhead. How are you feeling this morning?" I asked, walking into the bedroom.

"Still tired, but I'm feeling okay," she responded.

"I made you some breakfast, so when you're ready, just come on downstairs," I told her before going downstairs to fix us both a plate.

My house phone rang, letting me know that it was my mother because she was the only one who bothered to call me on that line.

"Hey, Mom," I said, answering the call.

"How are you doing, son? Camilla tells me that you were feeling down from missing your lady friend," she said, causing me to shake my head.

"Mom, I'm fine, and yes, I was missing my lady friend, but she's here now," I told her, smiling at the thought of Tami's presence.

"Oh, that's good to hear. Why don't you bring her by so that I can finally get a chance to meet her?"

"Okay, Mom, I will. I'm making breakfast, so I'll see you later."

"Poor girl. Why didn't you bring her here for breakfast?" she laughed.

"Mom, I did good this time. I might even cook dinner for her tonight," I laughed.

"Boy, you bring that girl by here, and I'll make sure that I make something special for both of you," she said thoughtfully, like my cooking was going to kill us both.

After I hung up, I finished fixing our plates and pouring both of us some orange juice. Soon, Tami came downstairs, wearing her clothes from last night that I had washed and dried for her.

"After breakfast, I'm going to take you to the mall so that you can pick up a few things until you decide what your next move is going to be. Also, like I told you before, my mom is dying to meet you, and she wants us over for dinner, but if you don't feel up to it, I'll tell her another time."

"No, I'm ready to meet the woman who raised such a wonderful and caring man," she said.

"She utterly failed in the cooking department, though," she added, laughing while pointing to my semi-burnt bacon on her plate.

"Girl, you better stop playing and eat my Cajun-style bacon and act like you know. I put it down in the kitchen," I joked.

After leaving the mall, Tami headed to the hospital to see Rema, and I went to handle some business that needed handling. Camille was hyped about seeing Tami tonight because, after I got off the phone with my mother earlier, she sent me a text message. I didn't want her to get her hopes up about Tami and me being together because she was still married, and until she said that it was over with her husband, I wasn't going to pursue a deeper relationship with her. I knew that it wouldn't matter to Camille whether we were in a relationship. She just wanted to see her. She said that she and Tami could still have a relationship outside of her being with me, which was true, but when Tami got back around that man she called her husband, it was like he played mind games with her that pulled her right back in. So, like I said, I wasn't getting my hopes up this time that we were going to be together.

Chapter Eight

Tami

I was so pissed right now because I had been out of work for all these fucking weeks, and my first day back, and here goes this bitch, Tara, who just walked in the door. I didn't see the baby, so I was wondering why her skanky ass was here in the emergency pediatric department. I looked over at Curtis, the security guard on duty tonight, and gave him that look, letting him know to keep that bitch away from me. I rolled my eyes at the bitch, refocusing on the patient sitting in front of me before Curtis told me that I needed to step out for a second.

"Here you go, bitch. You have been served," she said as soon as I walked out, handing me a big yellow envelope that I let fall to the floor.

"Tara, don't come up here to my job with this bullshit," I said through gritted teeth, trying hard not to lose my cool at my job.

Elle had been more than patient with me, and I wasn't about to let this ugly bitch take me there, and I lose my job. She was doing too much now, but she needed to leave me alone. If she wanted my husband so badly, she could have him because I didn't want his ass anymore. I had no idea why she felt the need to keep fucking with me or even be threatened by me.

"Bitch, I don't care two shits about anything you're spitting right now. All you need to do is take your monkey ass and pick up those papers and handle that, so me and my boo can get married," she said, flashing some bubble-gum-machine-looking ring in my face.

She was a dumb bitch because I wish I would call myself taunting someone who was wearing five carats on their finger with that shit that didn't even look real.

"Curtis, please escort this bum bitch out of the building because she did what she came to do, so she needs to bounce before I drop-kick her ass," I told him, looking at this bitch, praying she put hands on me so that I could lay her the fuck out.

I was pissed off that, once again, Siah had me looking stupid, and at my job this time. I was really starting to realize there was always some shit popping off behind his ass. I was finally happy after spending time at Envy's mother's house because I really had a good time and was finally able to wear a smile on my face since all of the drama I'd been going through. All I wanted was for Siah and his fucking baby mother to leave me the hell alone and let me be. She was still standing there, mouthing off, and I swear it was the devil who told me to kick that bitch in the back, watching her fall to her knees, not caring that she was pregnant.

"Tami, go to your station before your ass gets locked up." Curtis winked at me.

I knew he had my back if that bitch tried to report me, so I picked up the envelope and swished my ass back to my station. After finishing up with registering the patient, I took a bathroom break, and once in the bathroom, the tears fell. I could hear Envy's voice, telling me not to give Siah any more of my tears, but this shit hurt regardless of whether I wanted to admit it to myself. I was bothered by him having her serve me divorce papers, and the fact that he put a ring on the bitch's finger before I even removed mine hurt.

When I clocked out of work, I headed upstairs to visit with Rema, but wasn't allowed into the room. The officer told me that I needed to speak with Detective Amaro first. I didn't understand what was going on with Rema having a police officer outside of her door, like she was in danger, so I went and tried to see if I could get any information from Elle. But I learned that Elle had already left for the day, so I decided to go back to Envy's place and talk to the detective tomorrow to see if I could find out what the hell was going on. Right now, I just wanted to get into a hot bath and soak all of my stress away before my ass really fucked around and had an emotional breakdown.

I looked down at my phone and saw that I had a few missed calls from my mother, but I had no desire to call her back because I didn't feel like hearing her mouth again about me staying with Envy and not her. She went on, saying that was why I was having so many issues now. I never leaned on family; instead, I continually ran into the arms of a man. Well, that was far from the truth. Regardless of whether she wanted to admit it, she was always in the home but wasn't in the home, if that made any sense. She did everything a parent was supposed to do for their child, but the nurturing aspect of being a parent was always missing with her. Whenever it was time to give motherly advice, I always got criticism instead of support. I knew it had a lot to do with her alcohol problem, but that was still no excuse for why she could never be supportive.

I would return her call, but it wasn't going to be tonight. I had to get my mind cleared before dealing with her in fear of snapping on her ass. I swear I needed a mental health day, just one day to forget all that was going on in my life, even if it was just a temporary release from all that sat on my mind daily.

I had just gotten home, and I had to ask myself, where did this man come from, and why couldn't I have met him four years ago? Envy took heed to what I said about needing to soak in a tub after I told him over the phone all that happened at the hospital today. I kissed him on his lips before stripping out of my clothes, walking into the bathroom, and welcoming the smell of the strawberry and cream bath salt that he put into my bathwater. Then I climbed into the tub, lay my head back, and let the water take me to a serene place where all was good in my world.

I closed my eyes as a few tears fell, thinking of all the good times Rema and I shared, realizing how much I missed my best friend. Whenever I felt like giving up, she was always there to talk me off the ledge, and I needed her more than anything right now. Envy was here, always offering me his ear and shoulder, but it just wasn't the same because I felt like I couldn't share some things with him like I was always able to share with Rema. Like today, after being told that I couldn't see Rema, I was disappointed, and I just felt like I had said that to him, he would have been looking at me sideways, so I kept it to myself. Soon, I heard a light knock on the bathroom door before Envy walked in, taking a seat on the toilet after closing the lid.

"You've been in here for a while now. I know that water is cold as hell." He chuckled, putting his hand in the water to prove his point.

The water had since gone cold, but I hadn't noticed it. I knew I needed to get out of the tub before my skin started to get that clammy and wrinkled look.

"Are you okay?" he asked, but I didn't know where it was coming from.

"I'm good," I lied.

"I'm going to need you to keep it real with me, shorty. I know something is bothering you, but you keep giving me little bits and pieces, which is bullshit," he said as if he were annoyed, causing me to shut down.

"Yo, I didn't mean for it to come out that way, but I want you to know that you can talk to me about anything. So again, what's bothering you, and don't give me no bullshit 'nothing' for an answer." He smiled this time.

"It's just that, when I was told today that I couldn't see Rema, I was disappointed, and I know that I shouldn't have been, but I miss her," I said, putting my head down, avoiding eye contact with him.

"Tami, look at me," he said in a stern voice, causing me to focus on him.

"Don't you ever feel that you shouldn't be missing your best friend because she's been your friend since the sandbox, so that shit is normal once being angry wears off. I know you're worried about what motherfuckers will think, and some might even say that you're stupid for feeling that way, me included, but that is until I had to put myself into your shoes," he said, making me feel better and kissing my lips before exiting the bathroom.

Messiah

"Tara, where are those fucking papers that were on the desk in the den?" I asked, walking into the living room, pissed as hell after looking all over and not finding them.

"If you're talking about the divorce papers, I served them to Tami," she responded, going back to rocking MJ to sleep.

"What the fuck do you mean you served her?" I barked, now standing in front of her.

"You had them just sitting there, so I figured you didn't have anyone to serve the bitch, so I did it for you. You're welcome," she sassed, knowing that if she weren't holding my son, I would have slapped the shit out of her ass.

"Tara, don't get shit twisted. Those fucking papers had *nothing* to do with you, so you had no business touching them. I only filed so that she wouldn't be able to," I told her simple ass.

"What the fuck do you mean you 'just filed so that she wouldn't be able to file'?" she said, jumping up in my face with MJ still in her arms.

"You better calm your fucking ass down while you're holding my fucking son, and I meant just what the fuck I said," I told her through gritted teeth, letting her know that I wasn't playing with her ass.

"Well, the joke is on your ass because, if she goes to file, all she's going to learn is that you filed already and counterclaim, so either way, the shit is going to happen if that's what she wants. I'm confused about why you bailed me out of jail and have MJ and me staying here if you never had any intentions of divorcing your wife."

"I never told you that I was leaving my wife, and I bailed your ass out because you're my son's mother, and I know that you didn't do that shit."

"I was there, so how the fuck do you know I didn't do the shit because I swear I feel like slitting your damn throat right about now," she said, letting a few bullshit tears fall.

"I know you didn't do it because you said you didn't do it, and on top of that, your ass is all talk. You're not about that life," I told her ass.

"So, if you believe that I didn't do it, how come, when I said I didn't do it, you never said that you believed me? Instead, you had me walking around here, kissing your fucking ass," she spat.

"Bitch, all that should matter is that I bailed you the fuck out, so you should be kissing *my* fucking ass instead of giving me *your* ass to kiss," I told her ungrateful ass.

"I swear I should have stabbed you," she mumbled, but I heard her.

"Bitch, you're not about that life, like I said, so shut the fuck up," I barked.

"Yeah, I'm going to shut the fuck up, Messiah," she said, getting back up off the couch, putting MJ in his bouncy chair.

"Where the fuck are you going?" I asked her once I saw that she was packing the baby bag.

"I'm leaving because I see that you've got the game fucked up, like *I'm* some stupid bitch staying here when you still want to be with your fucking wife," she yelled, throwing the baby's shit into the bag.

"Tara, don't act like you didn't know that I still wanted to be with my wife because you knew before any of this shit went down, and not a damn thing changed. You can leave, but my fucking son *isn't* leaving with you," I told her.

"Fine," she said, stopping what she was doing as she left the house, slamming the door behind her.

After a few hours passed, I realized Tara wasn't bringing her ass back, pissing me off because I needed to talk to Tami and let her know the reason I filed for divorce. I knew she was probably hurt behind Tara's dumb ass serving her papers, especially thinking that I sent her to do it. So, not only did I have to explain why I didn't send Tara to serve her, but I also needed to tell her my reason for filing for divorce. And if that wasn't enough, I also needed to explain to her why I bailed Tara's ass out of jail.

I wasn't going to tell her that I knew who was responsible for stabbing me and Rema because that bitch was going to get dealt with. I just had to be careful about how I was going to go about it, though. I didn't know why bailing Tara out had her thinking we were going to be together, but I could guarantee her that it was *not* going to happen. The same shit that I had been telling her from the first time she found out about me having a wife remained the same. I told her that I would never leave my wife for her or anyone, and I meant that shit. If she thought that having my seed was going to change that, then she thought wrong.

I had been trying to get up with Dada to explain some shit to him, but he still wasn't trying to hear me. I understood, but I wasn't asking him to be my friend again. I just needed him to hear me out. I even tried to explain the shit to Tami when she was here, caring for me, but she kept shutting me down, telling me to spare her the details. I waited another hour for Tara to return, but she didn't, so I picked up MJ, carrying him to the portable crib that I had in my bedroom before going into the bathroom to shower. After showering, I checked my phone to see if I had any missed calls from Tami, hoping she had at least returned one of my calls or my text messages, but she hadn't. Before going to bed, I called my mother to let her know that I would be dropping the kids off with her tomorrow because I had some business to take care of.

I went down the hall to check on Phoenix, who was sleeping peacefully, so I put the cover back on her that had fallen off before taking my ass to bed. It didn't feel like I had been asleep for any more than twenty minutes before MJ's cries woke me. I got out of bed to pick him up. His diaper was damp, so I changed him, but he was still fussing, so I went downstairs to warm a bottle for him. Coming out of the kitchen, I heard light knocking on the window, knowing it was nobody but Tara's ass, and I should have left her ass out there, but I needed her to get her son so that I could go back to sleep.

After letting her inside, she didn't say anything to me. She just took MJ out of my arms and sat on the couch to finish feeding him, and I took my ass back upstairs to sleep.

Chapter Nine

Tara

When I left Messiah's house, I sat in my car and let the tears fall because I was at my breaking point. I was usually good at handling him, telling me that he wasn't leaving his wife, but it was different this time because when he came and bailed me out of jail and waited for me, it showed me that he genuinely cared about me . . . or so I thought. Then his telling me that he only bailed me out because he knew that I didn't do it was music to my ears, but his believing me wasn't going to help me fight an attempted murder charge without his cooperating with the authorities.

The only thing that I remembered about that night was receiving the call about Messiah being unfaithful, which caused me to follow him since MJ wasn't at home. I knocked on the door and had words with Tami's best friend, Rema, because I wanted to know what the hell was going on between the two of them. When she turned her back to get Messiah, someone hit me in the back of my head. When I came to, I was sitting in the back of a police car with blood all over my clothes, being told by the same officer from the night Messiah was in the hospital that I was being arrested for attempted murder.

Tears were streaming down my face at how stupid I was to go and serve papers to Tami when Messiah never had any intention of serving her. I even lied to her, telling her that Messiah and I were getting married, only to play myself once again because not only was he *not* marrying me, but he also still wasn't willing to be *with* me. I honestly didn't know what kind of hold this man had on me that I couldn't walk away from, I thought, as I found myself knocking on the window after seeing him and MJ in the living room. When he let me in, I just took MJ from him, not saying anything to him as I walked over to the sofa to finish feeding MJ until he fell asleep. A lot of shit didn't bother me because I knew that everything I got I deserved for messing with him, but this shit was taking a toll on me because of his disregard for my feelings.

After MJ fell asleep, I took him upstairs to put him in the portable crib in Messiah's room, and seeing him in his bed, sleeping, caused the tears to fall again. Messiah only gave a fuck about me when it was beneficial to him, and I was starting to believe that if MJ weren't here, he would have left me alone a long time ago.

I needed to find the strength to walk away from this situation because, between fighting his wife, getting my ass kicked, and now facing attempted murder charges, it was time to ask myself if loving him was worth all the pain that I was putting myself through.

When I woke up the next morning, Messiah and Phoenix were gone, and once again, I found myself pissed off. I cleaned MJ, put him in a sleeper, wrapped him in a blanket, and then put him in the car seat until I got myself together so that we could go home. I wasn't about to sit here and wait for Messiah to come back home after he didn't even have the decency to tell me that he was leaving. He was probably going to his fucking wife to say to her that he didn't ask me to serve her the papers and the reason he filed, so the hell with his ass.

I had only been home for about fifteen minutes when I heard someone knocking on my door. I put down MJ, hoping that it wasn't Messiah because I had no words for his ass. When I opened the door, it was Dada standing there, looking sexy as hell with his fine ass, but I wasn't in the mood for his ass because I was already pissed off at Messiah. Dada's parents stayed down the block from me, and whenever he used to visit them, he would always try to get at me, but I always ignored his ass until one night, I was drunk and horny and gave in to his ass.

I was fucking around with him for about two months after meeting him, but it was just a sexual relationship until one night, me and my girl went to the club, and Dada was posted up in VIP with a few dudes. That was the night that I met Messiah because I remember telling my girl that it was sad that all the fine niggas traveled in packs. She followed my eyes when I made the statement, telling me that I better not fuck with his friend, but I didn't give a fuck because I was single and Dada wasn't my man. So, to make a long story short, I left the club with Messiah that night, never looking back, thinking to myself that I had just bagged a boss nigga . . . until I found out that he was married, and I would be sharing his ass.

"Tara, I know you hear me fucking talking to you," I heard Dada say.

"Stop yelling before you wake up my fucking son," I told him.

"I asked you a fucking question," he barked.

"Well, I didn't hear you, so ask me again," I said, annoyed.

"I said, where the fuck have you been?" he shouted, acting as if I didn't just tell his ass not to wake up my son.

"Why is where *I* have been any of *your* business?" I asked him with a roll of my eyes.

"I'm going to ask you one more time where the fuck you've been, so think I'm playing with your ass if you want," he barked.

"No, you're the one playing fucking games, acting like I wasn't locked the fuck up, so let me ask you a question. Why the fuck didn't you come and bail me the fuck out?" I asked him.

"I did come to bail you the fuck out, but you were already bailed the fuck out, and I've been coming here every fucking day, looking for your ass, and you haven't been here. So, again, where the fuck have you and my son been?"

"Dada, don't start this shit again when you know that MJ is *not* your fucking son," I spat.

"Until you prove otherwise, he *is* my fucking son, and if you didn't think he was my son, why the fuck would you allow me to have him every fucking weekend, Tara?"

"You know the only reason I agreed to that bullshit is because you threatened to tell Messiah that we were fucking around and that my son was yours. But you know what? I don't give a fuck anymore. You can tell him whatever the fuck you want to tell him because I'm not fucking with him anymore."

"Yeah, okay. That's what your mouth says, but you know you're not trying to leave that nigga alone. That's why I came to bail out your ass because I knew you didn't try to fucking take his life, and Rema would have whooped that ass on sight. Something isn't adding up, and when I find out who's responsible for hurting Rema, it's a wrap for their ass," he said, getting pissed off.

I just found it comical how he and Tami both found out that Rema was fucking around on him with her husband, but both of them were still going hard for her. But then, when she found out *I* was fucking with her husband, *I* was the hood rat and a million other names. The same shit with Dada when he found out I was fucking with Messiah. I was a ho, but it didn't stop him from sliding up in me every fucking chance he got. All I wanted to do was beat this case, and all of them could leave me the fuck alone because I was done. As far as my son and who he belonged to, it was no longer a concern to him or Messiah because I was finished with him. I sat on the couch, letting him go upstairs to see MJ because, if I didn't, he was never going to leave, and honestly, I didn't have any more fight in me to continue arguing with his ass.

After spending like thirty minutes with MJ, he decided to leave, but not before telling me that if I disappeared with his son again, he was going to fuck me up. I paid his ass no mind because, if he actually cared about my son being his, why the fuck didn't he go to Messiah as a man and tell him when I was locked up? Instead, he allowed Messiah's mother to keep him. He didn't know how long I was going to be locked up, and as far as coming to bail me out, he was a fucking liar because I was in there for a few weeks before Messiah bailed me out. I locked my door behind him, letting everything that he just said go in one ear and right out the other because, like I said, he and Messiah both could kiss my ass.

Tami

My mother was still blowing up my phone, but I continued to ignore her because I still wasn't in the mood to deal with her right now. I finally reached Detective Amaro because I was still barred from visiting with Rema, and I needed to know what was going on. I was en route to speak with him because he told me that once I was cleared, I would be on the list again to visit with her.

When I finally made it down to the police station, I asked to speak with the detective and was told to have a seat, so now, I was just waiting. The longer I waited, the more I began to get nervous because I started to think that maybe they thought that *I* was responsible for what happened to Rema and Siah. I knew that couldn't possibly be the reason since they already claimed that it was Tara who committed the crime, but it didn't stop me from worrying because you never knew with the NYPD. I continued sitting and tapping my fingers on my leg as if I were playing a piano or typing on a computer.

My nerves started to get the best of me since I had been waiting for like thirty minutes now. Just as I thought about getting the hell out of there, I saw a nice-looking older man approach me, wearing a blue suit with his badge showing on the waist of his pants, letting me know that he was the detective.

"Mrs. Owens, how are you? I'm sorry for the delay," he said, shaking my hand before having me follow him.

"I know you're wondering what's going on, and I do apologize for stopping all visits, but if you're cleared, I'll be sure to let the hospital know. Before we get started, I need to ask you a few questions," he said as he grabbed a pen and notepad.

"What relation are you to Ms. Royce?" he asked me.

"No relation, but she's my best friend," I responded as he grabbed what looked like a report off his desk. He took a few minutes looking it over before questioning me again.

"So, you're the wife of Messiah Owens, the same Messiah Owens who was also assaulted at the home of Ms. Royce?"

"Yes."

"So, before the incident, were you aware that they were having an affair?"

"I answered all of these questions already with the other officers," I said, becoming defensive because I didn't want to hear again how they betrayed me.

"I understand if you were questioned already, but those officers aren't on the case anymore, so I need you to answer the questions once more. I know this may be difficult for you, due to the circumstances of the case, but any information you give may be of some help in finding the person responsible."

"I didn't know anything about the two of them messing around because he's my husband and she's my best friend," I lied.

"Do you know a Damien Jones?" he asked, getting on my nerves again because, if he had his name, trust me, he knew that I knew who he was.

"Yes, he's my husband's best friend and Ms. Royce's boyfriend," I told him, rolling my eyes.

I was tired of answering questions like I was being interrogated because most of the questions he was asking, he already knew the answers to. I could hear my phone vibrating in my bag, but I ignored it so that he could finish with his line of questioning, and I could leave.

"One last question, Mrs. Owens," he said, flipping the page of the report that he held in his hand.

"Do you think that Damien Jones may have been responsible for what happened to your husband and friend?" he asked, puzzling me.

"Why are you asking about Damien being responsible when I was told that Tara confessed to stabbing them both?" I asked with a confused look on my face.

"I'm going to be honest with you, Mrs. Owens. I don't believe that Ms. Richmond is responsible for what happened that night. I also believe that the person is someone who knows either your husband or Ms. Royce. I will be keeping an officer on her door until we find out who is responsible or until she wakes up and can tell us herself," he said, also adding that I needed to be careful as well.

I was lost in my thoughts as I thought about what reason he had to believe that Tara wasn't responsible when she confessed. I didn't know if he was insinuating that Dada had something to do with this, but I didn't think so because I knew he cared for Rema too much to stab her numerous times. I would agree that this was a crime of passion, but I honestly didn't believe that Dada was capable of doing such a thing. I heard the detective call me, but shit, I was lost in my own thoughts for a minute.

"I'm sorry. I just don't understand because if Ms. Richmond didn't do this, then who did?"

"That's what I'm going to find out, Mrs. Owens. Thank you for coming down, and I will have your name placed on her visitation list within the hour," he told me, getting up to walk me out.

When I got into my car, I grabbed my water from my cup holder, popping two Tylenols because my head was killing me by now. My phone started buzzing again, and I just felt like screaming when I saw that it was my mother calling once more. It seemed as if she wasn't going to stop calling until I answered.

"Yes, Mother," I said.

"Tami, I have been calling you for days. It could have been an emergency, but I guess you didn't care," she spat.

"Mom, I've been busy. That's why I haven't been able to answer your calls," I told her with a hint of sarcasm in my voice.

"Too busy for your mother? Don't you forget you only get one," she stressed.

"I'm sorry, Mom. I'm just going through so much right now. I promise it won't happen again," I gave in.

"Well, I hope so. Anyway, I was calling to tell you that some woman came by here asking a lot of questions about you and Siah."

"What woman?" I asked her, now interested in what she had to say.

"She said that she was from the D.A.'s office and needed some information about a case that she was assigned to."

"Mom, please tell me that you didn't tell her anything about me or Siah?"

"Girl, don't you insult my intelligence. I told that bitch that I knew she wasn't from no D.A.'s office, and she needed to leave my damn home. I've been calling you to warn you because she looks like she's going to be trouble."

After getting off the phone with my mother, I needed to pop two more pills because I knew trying to figure out who went to my mom's home, asking questions, was going to bring on a stress headache. As much as I didn't want to see Siah's ass, I knew that we needed to have a conversation because something was going on, and I bet money it had to do with his ass.

Envy told me this morning that he was going to be hanging out tonight with his friend, Mason, for his birthday. He invited me, but since I was in a funk about not being able to see Rema, I told him that I didn't want to hang out. Now that I found out that I could see her, I was on my way to the hospital, but I still wasn't in the mood to go out.

After I left the hospital, I was going to stop by and talk to Siah to see if we could have a conversation without all the extra bullshit, and I prayed that Tara's ass wasn't there because she would be that extra bullshit that I was talking about.

I parked my car in the hospital parking lot and went inside, then up to her room. . . . However, the officer at her door stopped me. I had to give him my name before being allowed inside, hoping that my name was indeed on the list. I probably could have gotten in with my hospital badge, but I didn't want to risk my job. That was why I did it the correct way by speaking with the detective.

When I walked into the room, the nurse informed me that she had just finished changing the sheets and cleaning her up. She also told me that the braid I put in a few days ago came out. I thanked her as I grabbed the brush from the top drawer on the nightstand so that I could brush her hair and do her braid again.

After finishing up with her hair, I sat in the same chair as before and grabbed my Kindle out of my bag so that I could read while I waited for the doctor to make his evening rounds. The doctor came at about 6:00 p.m., and he gave me some good news when he said that he would be weaning her off the medication that kept her in an induced coma in a few hours. He stated that it still may take some time for her to wake up, but I didn't care as long as I was about to get back my friend.

After getting the good news, I decided not to visit Siah tonight because I wanted to be here early tomorrow morning. I was going to pray that Rema didn't wake up tonight because no one would be here, so my fingers were going to stay crossed that I was the first face that she saw when she did decide to open her eyes.

When I got home, it was a little after eight, and Envy was already gone, so I sent him a text, letting him know that I had just gotten home and what the doctor said. He told me he would be home no later than midnight, which I knew wasn't the case because anytime he hung out with his friends, his ass *never* got home at a decent hour, and midnight was a decent hour for his ass. I told him to have a good time and to be safe before putting my phone on the charger so that I could shower and call it a night. I made sure to leave my number for the night nurse because, if Rema woke up during the night, I didn't care what time it was. I wanted to know. I forgot that I didn't have anything to eat today when my stomach growled, reminding me. So, I went downstairs to make a grilled cheese sandwich with a glass of warm milk before getting in bed, calling it a night.

Envy

I came out to have a good time because a nigga had been stressed out about Tami sitting on these fucking divorce papers. Tami was served those papers, and she still hadn't signed them, and I was pissed. When she first told me she got the papers, she was all for signing them, stating that she was ready for it to be said and done. So, imagine how I felt, seeing the papers tucked away in her dresser drawer this morning, still unsigned. Trust when I say that I was no jealous nigga, but I just felt like she still had feelings for him, and she was not as ready as she said she was when it came to letting him go. She was honest with me when she said that she wanted to have a conversation with him about sending his baby mother to serve her because she felt it was disrespectful. I disagreed because she shouldn't care who served the papers if she was done with him, as she claimed, but I told her to do what she felt she needed to do. I extended an invitation for her to join me tonight because I knew she was stressed, but she declined, leaving me feeling some kind of way about it because it was like she was here, but she was *not* here. I was so ready to see how far things could go with us, but I honestly didn't think she was ready.

"Looks like somebody's done," Olivia said after walking over with Sami.

"Nah, a nigga's just getting started," I told her.

"Nah, a nigga needs a bottle of water," she replied as she got the waitress's attention to get me some water.

"I know you didn't hire a chauffeur tonight, so you need to take it easy on the liquid devil," she told me, handing me the water.

"Thanks," I said, taking the water to the head.

"I'll be back to check on you," she smirked, grabbing Sami by the hand as they headed toward the dance floor.

I sat back and watched Olivia and Sami turn up on the dance floor as the DJ played "Don't Mind" by Kent Jones. Olivia, moving her hips to the beat of the song, had my dick hard as shit as I thought about sliding up in her ass. After dancing to a few songs, she came back over to the table, fanning herself, grabbing her bottle of water, guzzling it down as I just stared at her ass. Yes, I was looking at her in a whole different light because I wanted to know what it would feel like being between those thighs.

"What?" she smiled.

"Come here," I said, grabbing her hand, pulling her onto my lap.

"Nigga, don't let that liquor get your ass in trouble because we both know you're not ready for this," she said, moving my hand from off her ass.

"Trust when I say he's locked, loaded, and ready to engage," I whispered in her ear.

"And trust, you're not ready for this, like I said, so please don't shoot prematurely," she laughed.

"Stop playing. Let's get out of here and get a room," I told her, rubbing my hand up and down her thigh.

"No need to get a room. You can follow me back to my place," she said, grabbing my hand, pulling me behind her.

I knew my ass was tipsy as a motherfucker, but it had nothing to do with liquor because I wanted to fuck her from the first time I saw her. I dapped up my boys before heading toward the exit, right behind Olivia's fine ass, leading the way.

As soon as we got to her crib, I wasted no time pushing her up against the door as soon as she locked it. I stuck my tongue into her mouth as I pulled up her skirt, putting my hand in her panties until my fingers found her opening.

"Oh shit, Envy," she moaned.

I rubbed her clit in a circular motion before pushing two fingers in and out of her until she came on my fingers. I stood, removing her dress and panties, before kneeling in front of her, lifting her left leg over my shoulder, diving into her wetness. I sucked on her clit, causing her to grab the back of my head as she fucked my face, holding my head in place.

"Oh shit, Envy. I'm about to come," she gasped as I held on to her clit, biting down until she released.

We climbed the steps to her bedroom, and I almost busted my ass because the steps in her loft were built just like a damn ladder, so with my ass still being a little tipsy, it didn't help much, causing her to laugh. Once in her bedroom, I told her she was going to pay for laughing at my ass as I stripped out of my clothes.

"Come sit on this dick," I told her, lying back on the bed, stroking my dick while she stood there, looking scared as shit once she saw what I was working with.

"Come on, shorty. He's not going to hurt you. He aims to please, I promise," I smirked at her.

She slowly eased down on my dick, inch by inch, causing me to moan out at how good she felt, and I wasn't even in yet. Her pussy was tight as hell, and I lost control, grabbing her waist as she bounced up and down, moaning lightly. Once she started really getting into it, she started bucking wildly as she put both hands on my chest, lifting her ass and coming down hard, rotating her hips before repeating the same move. I felt my toes curl and my dick pulsate as I tried to have self-control because I was on the verge of coming, and I wasn't ready to bust.

"Slow down, shorty," I hissed as I tried not to come as she was smirking now.

I couldn't hold it any longer as I held her hips, pounding her shit until we both came, with her collapsing on her back.

Chapter Ten

Tami

I was pissed to the max this morning because Envy didn't come home last night, and he didn't even bother to call me to let me know. He didn't think enough of me to at least call and tell me that he was still breathing, knowing all the shit I was going through. I called his phone, and it kept going straight to voicemail. I then called his mother and sister to see if either of them had heard from him, but they both hadn't.

I went to the bathroom to take a quick shower because I needed to get to the hospital, praying that Rema would be opening her eyes today. I didn't have time to dwell on Envy not coming home right now. I guess when he was ready to talk to me, he would pick up his phone or bring his ass home sooner or later.

When I got to the hospital, Rema still hadn't opened her eyes, so I pulled out my Kindle to read, but was interrupted by my phone vibrating, alerting me that I had a text message. It was from Envy, apologizing for not making it home last night and not calling. He said he had too much to drink, so he stayed at Mason's house. I told him that we were good, but it didn't mean that I believed his ass. I just had other things going on to worry about if he was fucking someone or not fucking somebody last night.

I put my phone back into my bag and reached for my Kindle again, but suddenly, I saw movement out of the corner of my eye. I turned all the way around, and sure enough, Rema was moving. I rushed out of the room, yelling for the nurse because I didn't know what else to do. I moved aside when they rushed into the room. I stood back and watched as the nurse and then the doctor did what they needed to do, and after a few minutes of questioning her, the doctor said that she was stable. She was able to fully follow his commands, so that was a good thing, he informed me.

She was confused at first, like the doctor had mentioned, but after a while, she was able to respond with just a head nod for yes or no. I didn't know if she remembered anything, so I decided to simply be here for her right now and deal with all the other stuff later because I wasn't in any rush to relive the details. I knew she could talk because she didn't have to be put on a ventilator, but I still didn't want her to engage in conversation just yet since the doctor only asked her to respond by nodding yes or no.

"Hey, I missed you," I said, being honest with her as I wiped at the tears that fell from my eyes.

"I'm sorry," she whispered with tears falling from her eyes too.

"Shush. We don't have to do this now," I told her, wiping at her tears, but mine continued to fall down my face.

I stepped away, wiping my tears as I grabbed my bag, leaving the room for a few minutes because I needed to get my emotions in check. A part of me just wanted to hug Rema and tell her how much I missed her and how much I prayed for her to wake up. Then there was another part of me that wanted to strangle her until she stopped breathing, so, yes, I needed a few seconds. I took out my phone and called Siah's mother, telling her that

Rema was awake and asking her to bring Phoenix up to the hospital. She said that she would bring her within the hour, and I told her to call me so I could get her from out front because no one else was on the list.

Just as I ended the call and walked back toward the room, I saw Detective Amaro walk in, letting me know that the hospital informed him that she was awake. He greeted me before walking over to Rema's bed, asking her questions about what she remembered on the night she was stabbed. I didn't understand how the doctor allowed this when she hadn't even been awake for more than an hour.

I was sitting down in the chair after hearing Rema tell the detective that a female attacked her, but it wasn't Tara. I couldn't for the life of me control the anger I was now feeling because this meant that Siah was messing around with someone else who was probably in her feelings to attack him and Rema the way that she did. She said that she was at the door, arguing with Tara, and when she turned to get Siah to deal with her, that was when she heard Tara yell before hitting the floor. She told him that she tried to run, but her legs wouldn't move because she was in shock, and that was when the woman just started stabbing her repeatedly.

The detective asked for a description, but all she could remember was a dark-complexioned woman wearing a navy blue cap on her head, which meant he had nothing to go on. He informed me and Rema to be careful because this woman was still out there, and she probably wasn't going to stop until she felt she had completed whatever she set out to do.

I felt he needed to possibly have a conversation with Siah to find out who the fuck he had been messing with that could be responsible for doing this, because look how Tara's ass acted when I first found out about her and her being pregnant. When he told her that if it wasn't about the baby, not to contact him anymore, her ass lost her damn mind. I mean, crank calls, broken car windows, and late-night pop-ups at the house, showing her ass. It was just crazy how the dick had her behaving, like he was the last man on earth because she just wouldn't stop until he started fucking with her again.

After the detective left, I went over to the bed to tell Rema that Phoenix was going to visit before visiting hours were over. "How are you feeling?" I asked her.

"I'm feeling okay, just missing my baby," she said sadly.

"Well, guess who's on their way to see you." I smiled, causing her to smile.

"Before she gets here, I think that we should talk," she said.

"Rema, I told you that it could wait. Let's just focus on you getting better."

"No, I want to talk about it now because I need you to know that the night that Tara showed up at the house, Siah and I were just talking. He had just gone upstairs to the bathroom when the knock came at the door. What happened between Siah and me happened three years ago, and we were both drunk, and I promise you, it never happened again. When I found out that I was pregnant, I wasn't going to keep the baby because I didn't want to hurt you, but you were so excited and supportive, telling me that I didn't need the father when I told you that he wouldn't want to be involved. I wanted to tell you so many times during the pregnancy, but I couldn't find the strength to do it because I knew it would hurt you. I'm sorry, and if I could take it back, I would, and I promise you that when he was at the house, we were only discussing my telling him that I was going to tell you," she said as the tears fell.

"But why? I mean, we were all cool back then, but you knew how I felt about him, so drinking or not, it shouldn't have happened," I spat.

That was why I told her I didn't want to have the conversation at the hospital because I knew I was going to be in my feelings. Now that I think back, Rema and Siah had always had a love-hate relationship where he always called her his "little sister," so I would have never guessed that they would have taken it there. I didn't understand why people always blamed it on the alcohol when they fucked around and stepped outside of the relationship or betrayed someone who cared about their ass.

My phone was vibrating, and I knew that it was Siah's mom calling to tell me that she was out front. I had more than enough time to know that I was going to forgive her, but I got upset because "blame it on the alcohol" was the anthem for all the cheaters in the world, and the shit was just so tired and played out, I thought as I left the room.

Olivia

"Spill the fucking beans, bitch," Sami yelled through the phone.

"Girl, please. I don't have any beans to spill. I was only calling to see what you're getting into tonight," I told her.

"We're just chilling at the crib tonight with a couple of friends, enjoying food and drinks. You coming through?" she asked me.

"You know I'm coming through, so I'll see you tonight," I told her, ending the call.

I was hoping that Envy was going to be there because I hadn't seen or spoken to him since the night we spent together, and that was like a week and a half ago. I went upstairs, going through my closet, trying to find something nice to rock tonight, just in case he showed up. After deciding on what I would wear, I went and took a shower as my thoughts drifted to him because I was already feeling his ass. I knew he said that he had a "situation," but it must not have been that serious if he was at my crib, fucking me, and he damn sure couldn't blame it on the alcohol because he was sober the next morning when we fucked like two more times before he left to go home.

I didn't want to show up at Sami's crib too early, so I headed out at like nine o'clock, and when I got there, there weren't that many people there yet, causing me to curse under my breath because I was praying that Envy would already be there so that I could make a grand entrance. I was looking too cute, and I wanted his ass to be drooling when he saw me walking in the door, realizing what he'd been missing since he hadn't hit me up since our last encounter.

"Hey, girl. Why you come up in here, looking all sexy and shit? Oh, I almost forgot. You're checking for that nigga, Envy," Sami said, laughing.

"Girl, I'm not checking for no one, so don't get it twisted because my ass always looks sexy when I walk out my door," I told her.

"Well, come on in the back with me because his ass hasn't got here yet," she said, but I already knew that because a bitch was looking for his ride when I pulled up.

We were all sitting around, having a good time, joking and shit while they were getting their smoke and drink on. I didn't drink or smoke, but I was still enjoying myself until I saw Envy walk through the door with his "situation," causing me to roll my eyes. Sami looked over at me, mouthing that she didn't know, but I wasn't going to let him know that I was in my feelings about it as I excused myself and went to the game room where a few of Mason's friends were hanging out. I didn't even know if he noticed me, but I didn't want to be in his presence when he introduced her ass because I wasn't up for any introductions. I sucked my teeth when I saw that they moved the party to the game room like I wasn't in here, trying to avoid any interaction with his ass.

"Olivia, this is Tami, and you already know Envy," Sami said with a smirk. I rolled my eyes at her ass because I hated it when she drank. She always thought shit was funny when it was not.

"How are you, Tami, and good to see you again, Envy," I said, being polite, but I was pissed on the inside.

"What's up?" Envy said, keeping it short with me.

Tami was acting like it hurt her to speak, which made me even more upset that Sami's ass introduced us like I really gave a fuck to meet her. If I wanted to meet her, I would have introduced myself when he told me at the barbecue that she was there. Yeah, I told him I was cool with him leaving with her because he was honest about having a situation, but after sleeping with him, my whole outlook on the "situation" changed. I watched him as he pulled her over to the pool table, handing her the pool stick while he leaned up against her, whispering something in her ear, causing her to laugh. My blood pressure rose just like my anger each time his body went into hers as he attempted to teach her how to play pool.

"Damn, they look like they need a room," Sami said, taking a seat next to me on the sofa.

"I'm about to go," I told her because I wasn't in the mood to sit and watch him be intimate with her, not caring about my feelings.

"Girl, you better not let that nigga run you out of here. Shit, Envy is not the only fine dude in this room. Get your ass up and go mix and mingle," she said loudly, causing a few eyes to look this way.

"Sami, would you be quiet and stop letting the whole room know what you're talking about? And I'm leaving because I'm tired," I lied, and she knew that I was lying because she gave me the side eye.

I didn't know why Sami would try to get me to stay when she had been my friend since we were kids, so she knew my feelings were easily hurt. I did know that it was my fault for sleeping with him, knowing that he wouldn't be mine, but I didn't think that he would outright rub it in my face the way that he was doing right now. I told Sami that I would be right back as I walked to the front of the house because I was getting emotional. I needed a minute to check myself. I rolled my eyes upon seeing Envy coming my way because I was angry with him right then.

"What's up?" he asked me.

"You tell me because I haven't heard from you since the night at my house," I retorted, not holding back.

"I've just been going through some shit," he said.

"So, you were going through some shit when I met you, you were going through some shit when we slept together, and now you're still going through some shit, so maybe you should let that situation go," I sassed because, like I said, I was in my feelings.

"Damn, shorty. I thought we were good," he said, smiling with his fine ass, causing me to smile.

"I thought we were good . . . until you hit and quit without so much as a phone call or text, so, yes, a bitch is in her feelings. Now you show up with your girl, all over her, not even caring about my feelings," I told him.

"Shorty, you knew that I had a situation, and when I came back to the crib with you, I wasn't trying to complicate my situation, but I was fucked up that night. So, my showing up with the female I'm trying to be with has nothing to do with you. We did what we did as two adults, both knowing we weren't trying to be together, so her being here shouldn't even bother you."

"Wow, are you *really* serious right now? I know we weren't trying to be together, but I really liked you, and I just feel that you could have respected me by a call or text instead of treating me like a fucking hit and run," I told him, getting a little louder than I intended to.

"Yo, you're on some other shit right now," he said.

"So, you don't see nothing wrong with fucking me and acting like it didn't happen?" I questioned . . . just as *she* walked into the room, giving him the look of death, telling me she heard me.

Chapter Eleven

Tami

I let Envy talk me into going to a get-together between a few friends of his at his best friend, Mason's, house, whom I had yet to meet. I honestly wasn't in the mood to hang out, but since Rema was doing well and was scheduled to go home in a day or two, I had no excuse to decline this time. It wasn't that I didn't want to hang out with him. I just really wasn't a fan of going somewhere and being around people that I didn't know.

When we got to Mason's place, I was pleasantly impressed, but the glares I was getting from a few of the females had me a bit uncomfortable. So, walking into the game room, Mason's girlfriend introduced one of the females named Olivia, and I acted as if I didn't remember her, giving off the same vibe I was feeling from her ass. I started to think that maybe something did go down with them, but when Envy didn't act any differently toward me, in fact, still treating me as he always treated me in front of her, I let my guard down. I figured what he told me about her was true . . . until I peeped her leave the room just before he said he needed to use the bathroom. I didn't say anything because I was going to give him the benefit of the doubt, assuming he would return within the few minutes it would take him to use the bathroom.

But after like five minutes had passed, I decided to see just how far he had to go to get to the bathroom since he hadn't brought his ass back yet. So, imagine how I felt, seeing him and her in the living room, having what seemed to be a heated argument, but I couldn't make out what they were saying. However, as soon as I got closer to them, I heard the bitch say something about him fucking her, and I wasn't going to lie. I lost it on his ass because, if he knew he fucked this bitch, why the fuck did he bring me here? All his fucking friends probably knew that he fucked the bitch, and now, I was the one looking stupid. I was not one of those females to lose my cool unless it was necessary, and I felt in that moment that it was absolutely necessary, but what I wasn't going to do was step to her ass because I had no beef with her. I managed to calm myself down enough to tell him, "Let's go," so that I could get my shit from his crib and go so he could feel free to fuck whoever he wanted to fuck. I apologized to Mason before storming off outside to wait for Envy's ass to follow, thinking to myself that I should have stayed home.

I was back at Envy's house, sitting in his living room with my arms folded across my chest, being held hostage by his ass, like I really wanted to be in his presence. Since his ass was forcing me to be here, he needed to answer a few questions because I was confused about a few things.

"So, let me ask you something. Why did you fail to tell me that you would be fucking bitches until I handled my divorce?" I asked him, now shaking my leg and wearing a frown on my face, awaiting his answer.

"I'm not out here 'fucking bitches.' I was at the club the night of Mason's birthday and had a few too many drinks, and the shit just happened," he said.

Here we go with what I said a few weeks ago about the cheating anthem that all men and women used, I thought as I just shook my head at his ass.

"So, you're blaming it on the alcohol?" I questioned to be sure.

"That and the fact that I saw the unsigned divorce papers in your top drawer while you got a nigga waiting on you, giving you the space that you said you needed. The nigga had you served, but you found every reason to keep putting off the shit. Then you finally tell me that you're going to sign—just for me to find the papers days later, still unsigned," he barked, telling me how he really felt.

"So, why the fuck couldn't we have a conversation about the shit instead of you acting bitch-made, fucking that bitch because you were in your feelings?" I barked right back at his ass for blaming me for sticking his dick in that bitch.

"Watch your fucking mouth because bitch-made is that nigga *you* married. Stop acting like you don't know that I'm a real nigga," he said.

"So real that I had to find out about you getting your dick wet from her ass, right?"

"It wasn't like that, shorty, and I swear I was going to tell you. Had I known she was going to be there tonight, we wouldn't have gone."

"It has nothing to do with her being there because I still wouldn't have known. The only reason I found out is because you chose to follow behind her like a lost puppy. Then you stand there and have a conversation as if I wasn't in the other room. You thought that I didn't know she was the girl from the barbecue. I knew who she was, and I wasn't tripping because you told me she was just a 'friend,' and when you left with me and she didn't beef, I figured the shit was true. So, either she's one of those bitches who don't care that a man has a girl, or you didn't tell her."

"I told her that I had a situation," his dumb ass said.

“So, now, I’m a fucking ‘situation’? Well, guess what? Your situation is solved. Fuck you and fuck her too,” I said, standing to leave, but he stopped me, grabbing me by my waist.

“Come on; stop playing. That shit was nothing but sex. I hadn’t spoken to her since that night. That’s why she was upset.”

“Wow, so you’re one of *those* dudes,” I said, shaking my head, trying to loosen his grip on me.

“You know better than that, so don’t come at me like that,” he said, kissing my neck.

“Get off me. I’m calling your mother and sister tomorrow to let them know exactly what you did to me,” I told him, wiggling away from him, laughing but not playing with his ass.

“So you’re really going to do a nigga dirty like that?” he asked, still thinking I was playing with his ass.

I had to consider that I had asked him to give me my space, but I also wanted him to know that if we were going to be together, he would have to be honest with me. If he was going to turn out to be like Siah with the lies, he could keep it pushing without me.

I finally decided to do what I told Envy I was going to do. I called Siah to let him know that I signed the papers and would be dropping them off after work. When I left the hospital, I headed to his house, hoping he wasn’t going to be on any bullshit because all I wanted to do was give him the papers and pick up the things that he agreed to have packed for me to take. I got out of the car and knocked on his door before feeling someone’s presence behind me, so I turned around and was greeted by Officer Milford. She wasn’t in her uniform, but I just chalked it up to her stopping by to do a follow-up, but that thought quickly changed as I saw that she was wearing jeans and sneakers.

"How are you?" I asked, not knowing what else to say, just as Siah opened the door.

"Milani, why are you here? Don't you think you caused enough damage with your scheming ass?" he spat at her, and now I was truly confused about what the hell was going on.

"Siah, what the hell is happening?" I asked, but he didn't get a chance to answer as she pulled out a gun, forcing both of us inside.

All I could think about was why I didn't just mail the papers to him and replace whatever I left at his house. Now, I realized who the pretend D.A. was that showed up at my mother's house *and* the person who stabbed Siah and Rema. It all made sense now that she was the one to frame Tara and lie about the statement that she made. I had been with Siah for four years, so I'd be the first to tell you that he didn't have a dick of gold. It was good, but not good enough for these women to be tripping the way they had been.

"I have no idea what's going on, but you need to put the gun down and think about what you're about to do and the trouble you're going to get into," I said, trying to reason with her.

"Shut the fuck up and sit down," she said, pushing me toward the couch, and I swear if she didn't have that gun, I would have fucked her up.

"Look, Milani, I didn't turn your psycho ass in, so you need to leave before I change my fucking mind," Siah told her, but it didn't seem to faze her.

"I'm going to need you to shut the fuck up because, when I wanted to talk to you, your bitch ass didn't have no words for me, so zip it," she said, giving him a look to let him know that she was dead serious.

I saw Siah's jaw tighten, and for some reason, a scene from the movie *Bad Boys* came to mind, so I decided to give it a try.

"Listen, I don't know what's going on, but it has nothing to do with me. I'm just here to pick up my shit and give him these divorce papers. So whatever beef you have with him, you can let me go, and you two can handle it," I told her.

"So much for being loyal," Siah barked.

"Loyal? Nigga, please. Had you known the definition of the word, we wouldn't be in this situation right now," I spat.

"So, you're blaming me for this bitch getting obsessive after telling her that I couldn't fuck with her anymore?" he shouted.

"Who else should I blame, Siah?" I shouted back, pretending that I was going to slap him, but instead, he rushed her, and they were now fighting over the gun.

I stood frozen because I didn't think that it would actually work, but I immediately snapped out of it really fast. Just as I turned to make my way toward the door, the gun went off, and I screamed as her body fell to the floor.

"Call 911!" Siah shouted.

My hands were shaking so badly that it took me a minute to get my phone out of my bag to make the call. After doing so, I went outside to wait for the police to arrive, trying to stop my tears from falling because I felt like I was having an emotional breakdown. One person can only take so much. I was just so done and tired of all the bullshit that I had endured over the four-year course of my marriage to Siah's ass. He had two kids on me, and who knew how many more psychos were going to come out of the woodwork behind his cheating ways?

I had been in denial for so long, and I knew that hate was a strong word, so I was only going to say that I really disliked him. He almost cost my best friend her life, and I could have very well lost mine tonight if it weren't for my quick thinking. One might think that what I did was corny, but he picked up on it, and it saved our lives, so thank you, Mike Lowrey and Marcus Burnett.

Detective Amaro showed up to the scene, and after speaking to him, I went into my bag and threw the divorce papers at Siah, telling him to have a nice life. Once I made it back to Envy's house, I plopped down on the sofa, taking a deep breath as he came and sat down, putting my legs on his lap. He removed my shoes and began giving me a foot massage, causing me to close my eyes momentarily . . . until he started to go into all that I told him had happened.

"Had you listened to me and not taken your ass over there, you wouldn't have almost lost your life," he stressed.

"I know, so please don't rub it in because I'm beating myself up about it enough," I pouted.

"I'm not rubbing it in. I'm just pissed about the shit, and I should put a hot one in Siah's ass for almost getting you killed. That bullet could have had your name on it," he said.

"Who you telling? I was so scared and had to think quickly because all he was doing was agitating her more," I told him. "I'm just glad that it ended with me not being the one fighting for my life, and I'm so pissed that Siah knew all along who stabbed him and Rema and said nothing. He's talking about how he was going to handle it, and I feel that, if he *were* going to handle it, he should have handled it as soon as he was well enough."

"How many times do I have to tell you that his ass is bitch-made? Trust, if it had been me, that bitch would have been sleeping with the worms," he said, dead serious. "His ass was probably *still* sleeping with her and figured he had the situation under control with his wack ass," he added, getting upset.

"Did the bitch die?" he asked.

"I have no idea, but she was alive when the EMT put her on the stretcher, but even if she does make it, she fucked up her life over some dick. She's going to lose her job and probably go to prison, and most likely her partner will too, for going along with this bullshit," I said, shaking my head.

After deciding not to talk about Siah's ass anymore, we ordered Chinese food and watched a couple of movies before taking a shower and calling it a night.

I had been experiencing this sluggish feeling for the last few weeks, so I decided to make an appointment with my primary doctor. I was at work, feeling light-headed, praying that I made it until the end of the day, but if I didn't feel any better after my lunch break, I was going to leave. After finishing up with the patient who was sitting at my station, my next patient, who had to be registered, was already in the back. So I grabbed all of the papers that I needed the patient to sign, and just as I left my station, Elle stopped me.

I wasn't in the mood for small talk because I just wanted to finish up with this patient so that I could leave for my lunch break. Just as I was going to ask her what I could do for her, I felt very dizzy . . . and the next thing I knew, everything went black.

When I woke up, I was in a hospital bed, hooked up to an IV. My head was killing me right now as I reached for the call button for the nurse.

"Hey, Tami. How are you feeling?"

"Girl, my head is banging. What in the hell happened?" I asked my coworker, Trina, who happened to be the emergency room nurse on duty.

"You fainted and landed your ass here, getting tests done," she said. "You were dehydrated, so that's why you're receiving fluids through the IV," she added.

"I need something for this banging-ass headache I've got going on," I told her.

"Okay, I'll be right back," she said, exiting the room.

When she returned, I took the pills she gave me and asked her how long I had been here because I noticed that it was no longer light outside. She said that I had been here since noon, and it was now going on eight o'clock, saying that I had been in and out of consciousness.

"So, what is the doctor saying?" I asked in a panic because in and out of consciousness scared the shit out of me.

"Calm down. It's normal because you were extremely dehydrated," she told me. "Get some rest. The doctor will return as soon as your tests come back, and he'll determine if you need to be admitted."

"Okay. Thanks, Trina."

"No problem. I'll be back to check on you in a few," she said, leaving.

I reached for the plastic bag that held all of my belongings, taking out my phone to give Envy a call, noticing that I had five missed calls from him. He sounded worried when he answered the call, and I didn't blame him after the events at Siah's house. I told him what happened, and he said that he was on his way. I ended the call and called my mother and Rema to let them know I was in the hospital and would keep them posted.

I didn't even realize that I had dozed off, but my mom's loud-ass mouth outside my room awakened me. I heard her fussing with the security guard because he was telling her that she needed to wait until the staff changed shifts, but she wasn't trying to hear him as she started screaming my name. This was the very reason that I told her ass that I would keep her posted because she was off the hook with acting like she didn't have a good upbringing.

"Tami, where are you? Tami?" she continued yelling my name, ignoring the security guard.

As much as I didn't want to get out of bed, I did because I didn't want them to have her ass arrested. I dragged the IV pole with me out to where she was showing her ass.

"Mom!" I called out to her.

"Tami, baby, they weren't trying to let me see you." She rushed over to me, hugging me as she cried.

Now I understand why she was doing all that damn yelling. She was intoxicated, and it pissed me off because this was still my job. When I spoke to her on the phone, it sounded as if she was a little off, but since she told me that she no longer drank, I thought nothing of it. She started drinking after my father left her for another woman when I was about 8 years old. She went from being this independent woman who loved her daughter and would give her daughter the world . . . until he left. Then she would drink day and night without a care in the world, not even to care for me. I had to fend for myself most nights and get myself ready for school most mornings, but I still loved her. My mom had two sisters who could have been there for me, but all they did was talk shit behind my mother's back, kind of how they do me now about my marriage to Siah.

When I was about 10 years old, the school got involved and told her that if she didn't get it together, they would have to involve social services, and that was when she stopped drinking and started being the mom that I needed her to be. If she was drinking again, that only meant that her no-good-ass boyfriend must have left her because she always acted as if she couldn't live without a damn man, as if it were the end of the world. I turned my attention back to my mom, who was screaming my name because I had zoned out for a second.

"Mom, it doesn't take long for them to change shifts, and as soon as that happens, you can come back," I tried to reason with her.

"Why do I need to come back in fifteen minutes when I'm here now?" she said, then staggered, almost falling.

The security guard saw the look on my face because I was on the verge of tears, feeling like that 8-year-old little girl all over again, since she wouldn't listen to me, so he said that she could stay.

"That's what I thought, you damn rent-a-cop," she yelled after she heard what he had to say, but he kept walking, just shaking his head.

Chapter Twelve

Envy

I had been calling Tami all afternoon since her lunch break, but I still hadn't received a response, return call, or text message. Once she didn't come home by the time she usually did, I started to worry, so I decided to go to her job, but just as I was ready to head out, she called me, telling me that she was in the hospital because she had fainted. I grabbed my keys, ignoring the ringing of my phone because I knew that it was Olivia's ass calling me again because she had been calling me all day like a fucking psycho. She was so laid-back when I first met her until I gave her the dick, and now, she was acting like one of those "Fatal Attraction" chicks.

When I got to the hospital, I told the security guard that I was there to see Tami Owens. He told me to go through the double doors and that she was in room ten. Once I reached the room she was in, I could hear loud talking, and when I pushed open the door, I saw an older woman standing over Tami's bed, speaking loudly. I knew she was drunk, but I just walked over to the bed, kissing Tami on the lips and asking her if she was okay.

"Who the hell is this nigga?" she slurred.

"Mom, please. Can you keep your voice down and stop being rude?" Tami told her, sucking her teeth.

Tami never spoke about her mother, and now, I realized why, but I wasn't sweating that shit because, after all, she was still her mother.

"Tami, don't forget that I'm your mother, so don't talk to me like I'm your child," her mother slurred, still being loud.

"I'm Envy," I introduced myself.

"Who in the hell names their child Envy?" she chuckled.

"Mom!" Tami yelled, getting agitated.

"I'm just saying, your little boyfriend has a jacked-up name, but you better watch that one because she named his ass Envy for a reason. Well, I'm going to go and get out of here because you look fine to me," she said, walking out of the room.

I looked over at Tami. She had tears in her eyes because she was embarrassed by her mother's behavior.

"I'm sorry," she said, just above a whisper.

"Don't sweat it. I'm good. How are you feeling?"

"I'm feeling a little better now that they gave me some pain medication," she said.

"Did they say what's going on with you?" I asked her, trying to get her mind off her mother.

"Just that I'm extremely dehydrated, but the doctor is waiting on my test results before he comes back."

"I was headed up here since you didn't answer any of my calls, and you hadn't made it home yet because you always get home at the same time every night," I told her.

"I'm sorry. Just before it was time for me to go to lunch, my ass fainted, but I blame myself because I haven't been feeling well for some time now."

"Had you told me, I would have made sure you took care of it because I can't have my baby walking around, passing out and shit," I said, taking her hand and holding it, putting a smile on her face.

My phone started to ring again, and I cursed myself because I had forgotten to put it on vibrate before coming inside. I took it out of my pocket and put it on vibrate, and the shit vibrated in my hands as I ignored it and stuck it back in my pocket.

"Popular, are we?" Tami asked, looking at me sideways.

I debated whether I should tell her about Olivia becoming a stalker, but if I didn't and she found out, she would start with the "I lied to her" shit again.

"It's Olivia calling me, and she's been on some stalker shit since the night at Mason's crib," I told her.

"Well, if she calls again, hand me the phone," she stated seriously.

"Nah, you're not feeling well, and I'm not about to add high blood pressure to whatever you've got going on," I told her, joking but serious.

Just as she was about to disagree, the doctor walked into the room, and I thought, *Saved by the bell* because she was about to go in on my ass.

"How are you feeling, Mrs. Owens?" the doctor asked her.

"No need to be formal, Dr. Zurosky," she smiled.

"Tami, is it okay to talk about your test results with your guest here, or would you like him to step out of the room for a moment?" he asked her.

"It's fine," she told him, but she looked at me.

"Your hemoglobin levels are low due to iron deficiency. As you know, hemoglobin is a part of your red blood cells, and it carries oxygen throughout your body. Low levels of hemoglobin may cause anemia, which is an illness that makes you feel weak and tired. I'm not too concerned at this point, and this can be corrected by adding different foods to your diet, which I will provide a list for you. Also, you were extremely dehydrated, so drink plenty of fluids and eat foods high in water, such as fruits and vegetables.

I'm going to discharge you, but I want you to follow up with your primary care doctor in a few days, and if you still experience any problems before then, feel free to come back to the emergency room," he told her.

After he left, I let her know that she needed to take care of herself just as she had everyone else. I gave her the same speech that I gave my mother about her health because I cared for her just like I cared for my mother. The nurse came and checked her vitals and removed the IV from her arm before explaining her discharge instructions and telling us that we could leave.

Tami said that she was hungry, so we stopped to get some takeout before heading home. Once again, I could feel my phone vibrating in my pocket, and I hoped that Tami didn't hear it. It could have been business and not Olivia, but I wasn't taking any calls tonight because I needed to take care of my boo, making sure she was straight, so all that other shit could wait until tomorrow.

Once we got back to the house, Tami went to take a shower after we finished eating. She was tired. I had a bottle of water and some Tylenol waiting for her because she stated that her head was still bothering her. She was out like a light a few minutes later, so I went downstairs to call Olivia because the shitload of calls and text messages from her were getting out of control.

Messiah

As weeks went by, I had been trying to see my son, but Tara had not allowed me to because she was on that bullshit again. I swear, if I knew fucking with her was going to cause me to lose my wife and deal with her ongoing bullshit, I would have never gone there with her ass. I was at the point of wanting to cause her bodily harm, but my mom kept telling me to handle it the right way. However, she didn't know Tara as I did. Rema wasn't fucking with me on any level, but at least she let my mom pick up Phoenix every weekend without a problem.

I had just pulled up to Tara's house, praying that I didn't have to put my hands on her ass because all I wanted was to see my son. When she opened the door, she looked like she had seen a damn ghost, and I knew it had to do with her thinking I was going to trip because Dada was there. I saw his car, and I couldn't care less about whatever the fuck they had going on. I just wanted to see my son.

"Messiah, don't come in here starting no shit," she stuttered.

"I'm just here to see my fucking son, Tara, because your monkey ass has been playing games. You're going to stop playing when it comes to my damn son," I told her, brushing past her, going inside.

I felt my jaw tighten and my fist balled as I saw this nigga on the couch, holding my fucking son with a smirk on his face.

"I don't give a fuck what this trick has got you thinking, but this is *my* fucking son," I said, taking my son from his ass, daring him to square up.

I could tell that he was still salty about the Rema situation because his ass had no words for me as he got up and left like the punk he was acting like. I tried so many times to make the shit right with him, but he wasn't trying to hear me, and if he thought that smashing Tara was some kind of get back, he was wasting his time. If he wanted to hit me where it hurt, he had a better chance of trying to fuck Tami because Tara was an open fucking playing field for whoever blessed her ho ass with some damn money.

"If that nigga ever fixes his face to say that this is his fucking son, I'm going to body your ho ass," I barked at her.

"So, now I'm a ho because I don't want to be your doormat anymore? Fuck you, Messiah."

"No, fuck you, and get some clothes on my son so that I can go," I demanded, daring her to say that I couldn't take him.

She took him from me to get him ready, and I swear that I didn't know what possessed me to fuck with her. She was a bird bitch, and Dada was a dumb nigga if he even thought my seed was his when my li'l man looked just like me. I was waiting for those words to come out of his mouth because, when they did, I was going to knock out every fucking tooth he still had and then hang that bitch, Tara, from a fucking tree.

"When are you bringing him back?" she asked, handing him to me, but I ignored her ass.

I lost everything chasing behind these fucking tricks, I thought as I drove to my crib, pissed off at the predicament I was in. I knew what I was doing and the consequences of dealing with Tara. I knew she was a trick, so I shouldn't be so surprised by getting caught up with her. I never expected Milani to be a crazy chick since I met her when she pulled me over for speeding one day. I flirted my way out of that ticket because I knew she smelled the blunt that I had just finished smoking, which gave her probable cause to search the car.

I was riding dirty that day, so I laid the game on thick, and not only did I leave without a ticket, but I also left with her digits. I had no intention of calling her because I didn't fuck with the police, but I called her up on one of those nights that I was going through it with Tami and Tara's trick ass. We linked up the same night, with me smashing, and the bitch was a freak. She had me gone on her head game, but I noticed that she started to get possessive after that night. I paid the shit no mind and continued fucking with her when I knew that I should have taken heed to the shit she was doing because look where the shit got me.

I swear I was missing Tami's ass like crazy, and the saying you don't miss a good thing until it's gone was true because that was actually what I was going through right now. As soon as I pulled up to my crib, I heard tires screech as a car came to a stop right next to my ride, but it was too late to get down as shots were fired, shattering the window, hitting me, causing me to get down so that I wouldn't get hit again.

When I woke up, I was in the hospital, recovering from a gunshot wound to my shoulder, but a nigga was happy to be alive. Whoever the fuck it was better hope I never found out because it was one thing to come for me, but they came for me when I had my fucking son in the car. The doctor said that he was okay besides a few cuts from the shattering glass that hit him, so I was thanking God for not only sparing my life but also my son's life.

Tara's ghetto ass was up here, showing her ass about me putting her son's life in danger and how she was going to make sure I never saw her son again. My being shot probably had to do with her ho ass because she didn't know how to stay off her fucking back and stayed having these niggas thinking I wanted to beef over her skank ass.

I wasn't going to lie and say that I wasn't hurt that Tami didn't show up at the hospital after my mother called and told her what happened to me. I mean, I couldn't blame her for not coming, since she moved on and all, but the shit still hurt because we were in love at one time. I didn't give a fuck if I was with someone or not. If something happened to her ass, you better believe I would have been right there, making sure that she was good. My mother said that it was my own fault because, when she nursed me back to health the last time, I played her by bringing Tara into the home that we shared, which was true, but you would think that, hearing the word "shot," she would have run her ass up here. But I guess that when she said that she was done, she meant it.

Tami

Siah's mom called to tell me that he was in the hospital, saying that he had been shot outside of his house. She mentioned that he was in recovery at the time, and she was calling me to let me know. I still cared about him and his well-being, but he was no longer my responsibility, so I told her that I was glad to hear that he was okay and thanked her for calling. I was with Envy now, and out of respect for him, I couldn't keep running at Siah's every beck and call whenever something happened with him. I knew that he had his mother call me, figuring I would run up there like I did the last time, but not this time; it wasn't going to work. I wasn't about to entertain his ass, just for him to play me like he always ended up doing, so I just wished that he would get it through his skull that he fucked up, and I had moved on. Envy just nursed my ass back to feeling better, so today after work, I was going to go and visit with Phoenix because it had been a minute, and I wanted to see my goddaughter.

After I got off work, I called Envy to see if he had any plans before heading to Rema's place because I didn't want him to say that he was waiting on me, and I didn't come home. I also wanted him to know what my plans were, just in case he thought I was going to see Siah, which I wouldn't have done behind his back. He said that he didn't have any plans, and when I got to the house, we could just order in, which worked for me. I called Rema to let her know that I was pulling up, and when I got there, she was already standing at the door, waiting for me.

"Hey, how are you feeling?" she asked me.

"Much better, and you?" I returned the gesture.

It was crazy how we used to be able to converse without feeling uncomfortable, but this was weird because, when we talked on the phone, we were fine, but now, it felt like we were strangers who were getting reacquainted with each other.

"Phoenix stayed home today because she wasn't feeling well, and I told her that you were stopping by, but after giving her some medicine, she fell asleep," she said.

"That's fine. I wanted to speak with you about a few things, so maybe she'll wake up before I head out," I told her.

"Okay," she responded timidly.

I think that was why she wanted to hash everything out at the hospital. She probably felt safe there, but I would never put my hands on her. Yes, she hurt and betrayed me, but my first reaction to the situation had since died down, and all I wanted to know was why. I sat on the sofa, taking a deep breath, trying to find the right words without sounding as if I were still bitter about the situation. She explained to me at the hospital that it only happened one time, and Phoenix was the product of that one time, but for some reason, I didn't believe her. She may have been telling me the truth, but I just wanted to ask her again to see if her answer had changed, which would let me know if she was telling the truth.

I knew that when you said that you forgave someone, you should just leave well enough alone, but if we were going to continue being friends, I needed this, regardless of whether she understood it.

"I know you told me at the hospital that what happened with you and Siah only happened one time, but you never told me when that one time was. I don't mean to bring it up again, but for me to have closure, I need to know," I told her, being honest.

"It was the night that we were hanging out at the pool hall with Siah and his friends, and you got the call that your mother was in the hospital after falling down some steps. Siah dropped you off at the hospital and told you that he was going to drop me off and come back since your mother was having X-rays done. I was drunk and being annoying, so you told him that it was cool to take me home," she said.

I remembered the night that she was talking about because it was my mother's boyfriend who called to tell me she had fallen because she was intoxicated. I remembered getting to the hospital, asking for my mother because they had taken her to a hospital other than the one I worked at, and they were really rude.

Being drunk caused Rema to be loud and disorderly. When Siah suggested that he take her home, I told him that I wouldn't be long. However, my mother continued to be loud, requesting to see a doctor. So, I told him that he could take her home. My mother's boyfriend didn't stick around, so I called Siah to tell him that he didn't have to come back to get me because I was going to stay with my mother to make sure that she was good. I had no idea that anything went down that wasn't supposed to because, when I took a cab home that morning, Siah was home where he was supposed to be.

"So, my mother being laid up in the hospital meant nothing to you and Siah because, how could you two be fucking, knowing that I was at the hospital, worrying about my mother?" I said to her.

"Tami, like I told you at the hospital, I was drunk, and I forced myself on him, but soon after, I regretted what I did, and it never happened again. I already explained to you how I felt when I found out that I was pregnant with Phoenix. I promise you that I never set out to hurt you. That's why it never happened again. I know I can't take any of it back, but I swear to you that I have never betrayed you in any way since that night because, when I say that it was a mistake and I love you, it's the truth," she said. "I know you want to know why it happened, and you have a hard time believing that it was because of the alcohol, but it was because of the alcohol because, with a sober mind, I would have never done anything like that to you," she continued.

"You really hurt me, and it wasn't so much the act itself. You hurt me because you deceived me for all these years when you should have told me. I shouldn't have had to find out the way that I did, Rema, that's all I'm saying. If you had told me when it happened, sure, I would have been upset, but I would have respected you more for being honest with your best friend that you claimed to love."

"I'm sorry, Tami," she said, wiping her tears.

I had to admit that finding out the details of how it went down really didn't make me feel any better about the situation, and didn't answer the question about why. I had since told her that I forgave her, so I wasn't going to go back on that, but she would have to earn my trust again. I had no idea if it was going to be an easy task, but I was willing to give her another chance to prove it to me. I stayed at her house for about another hour, spending some time with Phoenix, before heading home to have a movie and dinner night with Envy.

Chapter Thirteen

Tami

When I called the next patient, named Olivia Walters, I had no idea that it was going to be Envy's jump-off Olivia. I started to send her to another booth, but since I had already called her, she would have known that I refused to see her. Also, I didn't want her to think that I was bothered by her, so I just decided to do my job. As soon as she sat down, she immediately placed a smirk on her face, but I paid her ass no mind as I began to ask her the questions that I needed her to answer.

"I wish I had known that you worked here because, trust, I wouldn't have come here," she said, but I didn't believe that she didn't know that I worked here.

She was here to play games, and I didn't have time to play them with her because she knew that I was at that barbecue, invited by her aunt, so trust me when I said that the bitch knew that I worked here. These thirsty-ass tricks always wanted to show their ass toward the girlfriend, but never took that shit up with the damn man. When I asked her the nature of her visit, she said that she was here because she had been having lower abdominal pain, adding that her time of the month was late.

I kept my game face on, finishing her registration and sending her back to wait so that she could be triaged. I called the next patient, trying to focus, but it was hard because I knew she was insinuating that she might be pregnant. I was so over the drama that had become my life, and just when I thought it couldn't get any worse, my supervisor, Elle, said that she needed to see me when I finished with the patient I was seeing. I went to her office as soon as I could, as she had requested, preparing myself for the bullshit that I knew was sure to come, because why else would she ask me to her office?

"Have a seat, Mrs. Owens," she said.

I sat, nervous now that she addressed me by my last name when she had always addressed me as Tami.

"I don't know if you were aware that your last patient was my niece, Olivia, and she tells me that you were very rude to her. I don't know what's going on with you and her, but must I remind you that, when you're at work, your job is to be professional at all times?" she reprimanded.

"I don't know why she would say such a thing when all I did was my job, treating her the same as I treat all of my patients," I told her, trying to keep my cool, but I was pissed the fuck off inside.

"I'm not going to write you up this time, but this is a verbal warning, and if you get another complaint, I will have no choice but to write you up," she said, excusing me.

As I was walking back to my workstation, I saw this bitch standing at the emergency room entrance, smirking at me. It took everything in me not to slap fire out of her ass and give her something to *really* report with her dumb ass. I sent Envy a message to let him know that his stalker bitch just showed up at my job and reported that I was rude to her. I also told him that she was insinuating that she might be pregnant, so he needed to be prepared because, if she was, she might be hitting him up to tell him. I put my phone away because he wasn't responding fast enough, and all I needed was for Elle to walk by and see me on my phone.

During my lunch break, I called Rema, and she was mad hype, asking me if I needed her to come to my job. I told her she needed to sit her ass down somewhere because she wasn't fully recovered yet, but she said she didn't care. It felt good to have my friend back, the one who had always had my back, no matter what. I was sitting on the bench outside the hospital, minding my business, when Olivia came out of the hospital, sitting on the same bench. I should have just gotten up and taken my ass inside because this bitch got on her phone, and whoever she was talking to, she was like, "Yes, bitch, I'm pregnant, and now I have to tell Envy he's going to be a father."

Anybody who knew me knew that I didn't fuck with you unless you fucked with me, and I felt she was being petty and trying to get a rise out of me, so I slapped the fucking phone out of her hand.

"Bitch, are you fucking crazy?" she asked with a shocked look on her face.

See, the bitch must have thought I was a pussy because I didn't say anything when I caught her and Envy talking about him fucking her. I tried to show the bitch that it wasn't about her, and I was just going to take that shit up with the man I was dealing with, but she couldn't respect that and instead, took it as if I were a punk. If this bitch even jumped the wrong way, I was going to drag that ass, and I could give two shits about losing my job today because I was sick and tired of these bitches fucking with me.

"If you broke my phone, you best believe you're going to be paying for my shit," she said, picking up her phone from the ground.

"So, you're pregnant, bitch?" I asked her, getting in her face.

"None of your fucking business," she spat.

"So, it's not my business, bitch, but a few minutes ago, you were making it my business. I want to make something clear to you, and I don't want to have to repeat the shit, so you better listen and listen good. You fucked Envy, you didn't fuck me, so the next time you try to fuck around and have me lose my job, knowing that I did nothing to you but service you, I'm going to do more than knock your fucking phone out of your hand. Play with me if you want to, bitch, and if you are pregnant, it better be Envy's because, if you even tell him some shit like that to play games, and I find out that you lied, trust, your mama is going to need that black dress. So again, fuck with me if you think I'm playing," I told her skank ass before going back inside because my lunch break was over.

When I left work, I took my ass straight home because I needed to take a shower and pop a few painkillers since that bitch left me with a banging headache, but it was worth it.

Envy

I had no idea what Tami said to Olivia, but I hadn't heard from her ass, so maybe that pregnancy shit was just to fuck with Tami. I was waiting for Tami to finish getting ready because we were headed out to pick up her friend, Rema, before heading to the club to hang out and unwind. Business was good, and my relationship with Tami had been great, so a nigga felt like he was on top of the world right now.

Tami came downstairs, wearing some off-the-shoulder black jumpsuit, showing every damn curve, and I was about to tell her that she wasn't leaving the house with that shit on, but she gave me that look to say, "Don't start." She was going to have me kill a nigga tonight with that shit she wore because I was sure every nigga in the club was going to be breaking their necks just to get a look.

Once at the club, we bypassed the line and headed straight to VIP, and I was pissed to see Olivia sitting at one of the tables with Mason and Sami. I said what's up to everyone, ignoring her ass, and Tami did the same as she and Rema walked to one of the empty tables. We were all having a good time, drinking and enjoying the music, except Olivia's ass. She seemed to be in her feelings with the way she kept mean mugging me. If she knew what was good for her, she would have a drink, so she could chill the fuck out before Tami came back from the bathroom and saw how her ass was looking at a nigga.

I saw Rema in a heated argument with the dude whom I recognized as her boyfriend, who was at the hospital with Tami that night. I was going to mind my own business until I saw Tami say something to him, and he barked something in her face, so when I stood, my nigga, Mason, stood as well, and we both headed in their direction.

"What's up? Do we have a problem here?" I asked my girl, but I was looking at his ass.

"No problem. We were just headed back upstairs," Tami answered nervously.

"Rema, you good?" I directed to her to make sure.

No, she wasn't my business, but she was my girl's best friend, so if she wasn't good, that meant my girl wasn't good.

"I'm good. Like Tami said, we were just headed back upstairs," she replied, attempting to walk away, but he grabbed her arm.

"I'm not done talking to you, Rema, and you can tell your bodyguards that their services aren't needed," he boasted, but I saw right through that tough guy shit.

"Rema, do you want to have a conversation with this nigga?" I asked her, but Tami answered for her.

"No, she doesn't want or need to have a conversation with him until he learns to talk with his mouth and not his hands," Tami spat.

"Tami, I already told you to mind your own fucking business. This shit here don't concern you," he said.

"My nigga, you need to fall back because coming at this one right here will get you fucked up," I said, pointing at Tami.

"Man, fuck that bi—" was all he got out because I dropped his ass with one punch to the jaw.

I hit his ass so fucking hard that my knuckles hurt like hell, so his jaw better be broken, I thought as I kicked him in the ribs until the bouncers picked his ass up off the floor and bounced his ass out of the building.

"Damn, Tyson. I didn't know you were going to hit his ass," Mason clowned.

"You already know I can't stand a disrespectful motherfucker," I said as I winced in pain.

Once back in the VIP, Tami came over with some ice in a bucket, telling me to put my hand inside to prevent swelling. Crazy-ass Olivia was watching me with a concerned look on her face before getting up and handing me a few napkins because my shit was bleeding.

"Trust when I say he's good because I've got this," Tami told her, knocking the napkins out of my hand and onto the floor.

"Did you hear me say that you didn't have him? I was just offering napkins because his knuckles are bleeding," she spat with attitude dripping from her voice.

"Like I said, he's good, so thank you, but no, thank you," Tami said, getting pissed.

"Olivia, just let him be," Sami said, pulling her away, but she jerked her arm from her.

"I'm sick of this bitch acting like she scares me because I'm far from scared, and I want to see how much you have his back when his son or daughter arrives," she yelled, getting up in Tami's face this time, and I prayed no shit went down.

"Trust me when I say I'm going to have his front *and* back, so if you're pregnant like you claim, I'm going to need you to fall back. That's your first and only warning, so, if I were you, I'd take heed to it and get the fuck out of my face," Tami told her, causing me to feel good about her response.

"Bitch, you sa—"

Whap! was all I heard as Tami slapped fire out of her ass, and they started fighting, and when Sami stepped in to break it up, I guess that didn't register to Rema. Rema grabbed her by her hair, and *they* started fighting like they weren't in a club full of people. Hair was being pulled, punches were being thrown, and I could barely help Mason break up the shit because my hand was fucked up. *So much for me getting out to unwind,* I thought as I watched them looking like they were on a flick of girls gone wild as tits and ass were hanging out, but that didn't stop them. Once the bouncers came and gave Mason a hand, they were still popping off at the mouth, and I was trying to get Tami to calm down, but she was a little firecracker. She told Olivia that she would fuck her whole world up as she tried to get at her again, and that was when I knew it was time to go before she killed that girl up in here.

Chapter Fourteen

Tami

By the time I got home, I was still pissed. I had no words for Envy, and I just wanted to be left alone. I was pissed that I let that bitch take me there and had me in the club, fighting like a fucking hood rat. Anyone who knew me knew how much I despised a hood rat—just to get caught acting like one. I was upset with Envy because, had he not slept with her, I wouldn't have to defend myself against her, and to top it off, I believed the bitch *was* pregnant by him. She left him alone about it until she felt she had to use it to get under my skin, but her not telling him spoke volumes to me because she was on some "I can show you better than I can tell you," shit. I had to really think hard about if I wanted to be in another relationship with another dude having a baby that didn't belong to me. Just the thought of dealing with another baby mother had me wanting to run for the hills.

Rema called to see if I was good, and I told her that I was good, but that was a lie because I was in my damn feelings. When Envy realized that I wasn't speaking to his ass, he left, saying that he was going to the hospital to get an X-ray, but I couldn't care less as I went up to take a shower so that I could take my ass to bed.

When I woke up the next morning, I found Envy asleep on the couch, and I felt bad when I saw that his hand was wrapped. I went into the kitchen to make breakfast so that he could at least eat, and that would be my peace offering for acting like a child about the situation instead of expressing why I was upset. I made some cheese eggs, turkey links, and biscuits, and when I finished, I went to tell him to come eat breakfast, but he was no longer on the couch. I took his blanket and pillow and put both into the linen closet before going back into the kitchen to fix us both a plate.

"So, I take it you're not mad at me anymore?" he asked before stuffing a link into his mouth.

"I wasn't mad; I was pissed, so get it right," I told his ass.

"Pissed about what?" he asked like he was confused.

"I'm pissed because I don't know how to feel about being with another man who has a child on the way who doesn't belong to me," I said, being honest with him.

"I understand where you're coming from, but I didn't set out for this shit to happen," he insisted.

"Well, I beg to differ because, unless you pulled out a condom on her ass, you set this shit up to happen. You should be thanking God that you didn't catch something that your ass couldn't get rid of," I spat. "Olivia is already a pain in my ass and has me acting out of character now, so can you imagine once she has the baby? I don't know if I can go through this again with another baby mama looking for attention," I stressed.

"I'm going to say this, and I promise you that you will never have to call me on it for not sticking with it. If Olivia gets lucky enough to get pregnant by me, and I prove that it's mine, I will be there for my child. I will not, and I repeat, *I will not* put you through none of that bullshit your husband put you through. If that means court the day after she pushes out the baby, so be it because that's the difference between a fuck boy and a real nigga," he tried to convince me.

I wanted to believe him, but after dealing with Siah and Tara, it was tough because Siah said that same thing in the beginning, and we saw how *that* turned out. I didn't realize how bothered I was about the whole situation until I felt a few tears threatening to fall, but instead of letting him see one fall, I left the kitchen, no longer hungry. I didn't want to be upset with him, but I left one man to run into another one who put me in the same situation that I was running from when I met his ass. Envy left me alone for a few hours, so I was upstairs, watching the Lifetime channel, until he decided to come and interrupt me. I didn't mind, but I wasn't going to let him know that.

"I'm not coming up here to upset you again. I just wanted to come and tell you that I'm sorry," he said, but I wanted to hear what he was sorry for.

"So, if you're so sorry, tell me why," I said, looking him dead in his face, waiting.

"I'm sorry because I finally met someone like you, who I'm really digging, and you were honest with me about your situation, and I just feel that I should have been patient with you. If I knew that I wasn't willing to wait, I should have told you instead of giving another female what I only wanted you to have. My sister and mother adore you, and I'm sorry that I might have messed up giving them the chance to love you like I do," he said, and I sat with my mouth open in total shock because it was not what I expected.

I was going to question him, saying that he loved me, since he hadn't known me that long, but after I thought about it, what was *not* to love about me? I wasn't sure if I should return the gesture because I wasn't sure if I was there yet, but his words touched me, and a few tears fell.

"I'm sorry," he whispered in my ear. "So, we good?" he asked while placing kisses on my neck.

"We're good," I told him.

"Okay. Well, I need you to get dressed. Mom invited us over for dinner, and she said that she wasn't taking no for an answer."

"My body is hurting from fighting in the club last night, but I am going to go and take a shower and get ready. I'm not about to give up on Sunday dinner because, if I do, I know we are going to be eating Chinese, and I *am* tired of Chinese," I told him, fucking with him.

"You know I gets busy in the kitchen, so stop playing," he said, slapping me on my ass when I got up to go to the bathroom.

I was dressed and ready to go to his mother's house in about an hour, and I couldn't wait because I was starving since I had no breakfast or lunch thanks to Envy's ass.

Olivia

I had a banging-ass headache from Tami pulling my damn hair at the club on Saturday, and I was still pissed off. I had no intention of fighting with anyone. All I was trying to do was give him some napkins because she wanted him to stick his hand in ice, which I got, but he was bleeding. She took what I was trying to do the wrong way, and when she started flexing, I had to let her know that I wasn't scared of her fucking ass. The only reason I bowed down to her at the hospital was because my aunt threatened me and told me that if she found out I was lying about Tami being rude, she was done with me, and I believed her, so that was why I let that shit slide. My aunt was the reason that I had a car and was able to pay for that expensive-ass loft that I was living in, so I wasn't willing to fuck that up for anyone. Every fucking dog had their day, and trust me, if Tami kept thinking she was *that* bitch, her day was going to come sooner than later.

I wasn't going to say that I was not in my feelings about how Envy was handling me, especially after I said I was pregnant. I mean, he didn't even call to see if I was bullshitting or not about being pregnant, and it pissed me off. Sami was upset with me because she felt that the whole fight situation could have been avoided if I respected that Envy didn't belong to me. She said that when his girl said she had him, I should have backed off out of respect. I didn't see it that way because his so-called girl didn't have to knock the napkins out of his hands like I just fed him some poison or some shit, so she was being disrespectful first.

When I found out that I was pregnant, the only reason I didn't say anything to Envy was that I slept with someone about a week before we hooked up, so I wasn't sure if he was the father, but he didn't know that, so he could have reached out. I knew his not reaching out had to do with Tami, but what kind of man lets a woman dictate what the fuck he should do or not do? If he was a real man, it should matter to him if he fathered a child, regardless of the situation that his ass was caught up in.

When I got off of work, I so wanted to go home and soak in a tub of water, but I told Sami that I would meet her at Carmela's, this Spanish spot, because she wanted to talk to me. I wasn't really in the mood, but since we were friends, and it was my fault that she had to fight when the shit had nothing to do with her, I could at least go and get my tongue-lashing if it meant that we could go back to her not being mad anymore. When I arrived at the restaurant, I parked and went inside to wait for her because she said she would be about fifteen minutes after me, as she had left work later than I did.

"Hey, girl," I greeted her. "What's up? How you feeling?" I asked.

"I'm good, but let me just get to what I invited you here for," she said, like she was at a business meeting or some shit.

"So, why didn't you tell me that you were pregnant? And are you actually pregnant by Envy?" she asked, but I didn't know if I should tell her that he was a possibility, just in case she was asking for Mason.

"I was going to tell you, and I didn't mean for it to come out that night at the club, but that bitch was really feeling herself. I felt like I needed to knock her ass down a few notches because she was going hard for no reason. I'm pregnant, and it's Envy's baby, but I wasn't going to say anything to him until it was time for us to do a paternity test because I knew he was going to deny my baby without a doubt," I told her.

"Well, what did you expect after you gave up the ass when you knew he was with someone else? So, any man would think that you were out there since you had no regard for the next chick," she said harshly, and I didn't know where *that* shit was coming from.

"Why are you coming at me like that?" I asked her.

"I'm sorry; I didn't mean to. I'm just so fucking pissed that you had me fighting in the club when I told you to fall back. I know you got upset, but there's a place and time for everything, as I tried to explain. Tami is Envy's girl. So, if she said that she had him, you should have fallen all the way back because, if that were my man, I would have felt the same way. You already knew that, since you slept with him, there was beef between the two of you, so again, that shit could have been avoided.

"I know I'm saying the same shit that I said to you on the phone, but I just felt that you weren't hearing me. So, that's why I asked you to meet up with me. Mason and Envy are best friends, like you and I, and they are going to always hang out together. So, that means that Tami is going to always be around for that reason. If you feel like you can't handle that, I just won't invite you if I know that she will be in attendance," she said.

I felt like she was taking sides, but I let her have that because I wasn't about to be up in here arguing with her about Envy and his bitch.

"I get what you're saying, and trust me, I'm over it. No ill feelings, and like I said, when my baby is born, I will offer him the paternity test if he wants one. You don't have to worry about inviting me to any future outings because I'm not going to say anything to either one of them," I assured her.

I felt like she was on some bullshit, but I honestly thought that Mason had her ass come and talk to me because Sami never had a problem with me when it came to fighting bitches. I let it go, and we ordered food and kicked it until it was time for us to head home because we both had to be to work tomorrow. Once I was in my car, I sat for a minute, just thinking about all the shit she said to me, and once I thought about it, I felt slighted. She was acting brand new, like she wanted to be friends with the bitch because she was Envy's girl, and if that was how she felt, she should have said the shit. If she thought I was going to say that I wasn't going to come around, she would have been waiting forever. I was not about to make his bitch feel comfortable because, every time she saw me, I wanted to remind her that her dude slept with me, and I was carrying his baby, so, hell no, I wasn't going to fall back. I stopped at the drugstore on my way in to get some Epsom salt because I was going to soak my sore body.

Chapter Fifteen

Tami

Since the night at the club, everything had been going well between Envy and me because we had been having a drama-free relationship. Mason's girl, Sami, apologized, saying that she wasn't trying to jump in the fight. Instead, she was trying to break it up, and I believed her. We hadn't been out, but tonight, we were going on a double date with them to dinner, so I was upstairs, getting ready because Envy was already dressed and waiting. He knew I always needed at least thirty minutes longer than it took him to get ready because I needed to look like the diva that I was before walking out the door.

"I'm going to start making your ass wear some damn jeans and sneakers," Envy said as soon as I walked down the stairs.

"Why are you always trying to start? I can't help that my body makes this simple outfit look like I'm ready to hit up a club or two. Would you rather a chick with no tits, hips, or ass?" I asked him.

"Hell no. I'm just going to start keeping your ass in the house because it's a crime to look this damn good, which is going to make it a crime when I fuck some nigga up over your ass," he said, pulling me into him.

"If you want to make it out with your friends, you better release me now because, once you wake her up, you're going to have to play with her," I told him, pointing to my kitty.

"Well, bend over the couch and let me take care of that real quick," he said, squeezing my ass.

"As tempting as that sounds, we can't keep your friends waiting, but when we get home, it's on and popping," I said, teasing him as I rubbed up against him before heading toward the door.

I watched him and laughed as he tried to adjust his dick in his underwear because I woke up the beast he was packing. He was always talking about what I was wearing when he knew that wearing those damn grey sweatpants always had his dick on display. He always had thirsty bitches breaking their necks, just to get a peek, but unlike him, I didn't get all crazy about it because all that dick belonged to me.

When we got to the restaurant, Mason and Sami were already waiting, saying that it was like an hour wait because it seemed like everyone and their mamas were on date night tonight. I really wanted some seafood, but I didn't know if I wanted to wait a whole hour just to be seated, and Sami agreed. We ended up at a steakhouse, and although it wasn't what I wanted, the drinks and conversation made up for it because I had a good time and was happy that I decided to give Sami a chance because she was cool. We said our goodbyes, agreeing to do it again soon, before going our separate ways, and I couldn't wait to get home because I had some riding to do.

Just as I was about to talk dirty to my man about what I was going to do to his ass when we got home, my phone rang. It was Rema, and I started to let it go to voicemail, but something told me to answer the call.

"What's up, Rema?" I asked her while massaging Envy's dick through his sweatpants, but I stopped at the sound of her voice.

"Ta-Tami, Dada is here, and he done lost his mind up in here, scaring Phoenix," she said in a shaky voice, letting me know she was scared too.

"Get the fuck off the phone, bitch," I heard him yell before the call ended.

"Envy, I need you to get to Rema's house now!" I said in a panicky voice.

"What's going on?" he asked as he made a U-turn.

"Dada is at Rema's house, bugging out. She said he's scaring my goddaughter. While she was talking to me, I heard him tell her to get off the fucking phone before the call ended," I said, trying not to cry.

I was worried because, when Dada drank, he could get really crazy, and I knew this from witnessing him in action. Rema and I went out one night after he told her that he didn't want her to go out to the club, but she went anyway. He must have hit the bottle the entire time we were out because, after the club, I decided to crash at her crib, and when we got there, his ass was acting real crazy. He hauled off and put his hands on her, and once he yoked her up, trying to choke the life out of her, I had to get involved. I knew that there wasn't too much that I could do, since he was a man and a strong man at that, so I jumped on his back, punching him in the back of his head. I was trying to get him to release her, but he flung my ass off like I was a rag doll, causing me to hit my head. He went right back to choking her and telling her that if she ever disobeyed him again, he would kill her, and if Siah didn't get there when he did, I think he would have succeeded in killing her ass up in there.

Siah had to whoop his ass, and the sad part about it was, when he sobered up, he didn't remember any of the shit that happened, so that let me know he had to be high on some shit. He never had another episode like that after that night. Well, I never witnessed one, but I needed

Envy to hurry up and get there because my leg started shaking since I was worried and nervous at the same time. Rema wasn't answering her phone, so that made it much more worrisome, and although Envy was driving as fast as he could, it just didn't seem fast enough for me.

"How much longer?" I asked him.

"Tami, I'm going to need you to calm down. I'm going as fast as I can," he said, but it was easy for him because he never had to witness Dada lose his damn mind.

I tried my best to calm down because it wasn't going to help the situation, so I sat back and put my head against the headrest, closing my eyes, praying that his ass would leave. When Envy pulled up to Rema's house, he had to park a few doors down because two police cars were parked in front of the house, and another one was parked on the lawn. My heart raced as I jumped out of the car, trying to get inside her home, but an officer standing outside the house stopped me, telling me that I couldn't go inside. I tried to explain to him that my best friend and goddaughter lived here and that I needed to go inside, but he wasn't trying to hear me. I started crying because I didn't know what was going on inside, and when the ambulance pulled up, my heart raced again.

"OMG, is someone hurt inside?" I asked the officer as the tears fell.

"Ma'am, I'm going to need you to step back," he said sternly.

"Why can't you just tell me what's going on when I just told you that my fucking friend and her daughter live here?" I shouted because he was getting on my nerves.

Envy walked over, trying to calm me down because I swear I felt like fucking up that police officer. He was being so inconsiderate. He could have told me something. She was my family, and I was the only family she had, but did he care? Hell no. My nerves started to get the best of me when I saw a *second* ambulance pull up and a few more police cars as I broke loose from the grip that Envy had on me. I ran past the police officer, who was holding back the crowd that had now formed outside of her house, all wondering what was going on like me.

When I made it to the front of the house, I dropped to my knees at the scene before me and let out a gut-wrenching scream as the tears fell from my eyes.

Envy

I watched as the tears streamed down Tami's face and wished that I could take away the pain she was feeling right now. She had just gotten her best friend back, and now, she was gone because of a fuck nigga who couldn't accept the fact that she didn't want to be with him anymore. When we got to the house that day, we were told that it looked to be a murder-suicide with him killing Rema, then taking his own life. I knew that Tami's life as she knew it was not going to be the same, and I was going to have to do whatever I could to convince her that life goes on. I knew that it wasn't going to be an easy task since she blamed herself for us not getting there in time. I tried to convince her that it wasn't her fault, and she didn't need to blame herself. I swear, I have tried everything to bring her back from the depressed state that she was in, but to no avail.

When she saw Phoenix at the funeral, that was the first time I saw a smile on her face, so I figured that's what she needed right now. Messiah, her punk-ass ex-husband, kept giving excuse after excuse about why she couldn't visit with her goddaughter, so as much as I didn't want to deal with him on any level, I was willing to do whatever I needed to do for her, so I hit him up.

The nigga was on some bullshit at first, but after letting that nigga know what it was, he said it was cool. He said that I needed to pick her up from his mom's crib, like he didn't want me to know where his new spot was. I told you he was a fuck nigga because what nigga you know would give up his mom's address if he was worried about a nigga hitting him up?

I told Tami that I was going out to handle some business and would be back in a few. After picking up Phoenix, we were headed back to my house, and I couldn't wait to see Tami come to life once she laid eyes on her goddaughter. Phoenix didn't look too happy until I told her that she was going to visit Tami. By the big smile that she had on her face when I told her where we were going, I could tell she missed Tami just as much as Tami missed her.

I took her hand as I helped her out of the car, and once inside the house, we went upstairs to the bedroom where Tami was. As soon as she saw Phoenix, she jumped out of bed, hugging and kissing her all over her face as her tears fell. She almost made a thug cry, watching the love the two of them showed each other, but I held it together.

"Thank you so much, Envy. How did you get him to let you bring her to see me?" she asked through her tears.

"Let's just say we came to an understanding," I told her, causing her to jump into my arms, kissing me all over my face, and causing Phoenix to laugh.

"Well, whatever you did, thank you so much," she said, wiping at her tears.

It felt good to see her slowly getting back to herself, and I just prayed that when it was time for baby girl to go home, she didn't go back to that dark place. I treated them to dinner . . . Well, it wasn't quite the kind of dinner I had in mind because we were eating pizza at Chuck E. Cheese's. But I'm not going to lie and say that we didn't have a good time because we did. We both played the games, and I was running around like a big kid, trying to get Phoenix as many tickets as I could. Phoenix even had me sitting in the ride that snaps your picture while Tami clowned me, laughing so hard that all I could do was laugh with her.

As soon as we got home, I took a sleeping Phoenix out of the car and put her to bed, removing her shoes and covering her up before joining Tami in the bedroom. I stood near the door and watched her as she undressed, getting aroused at the thought of sliding up in her, but I didn't know if she was ready. We haven't had sex since she's been grieving, so just the sight of her standing there looking sexy as hell had me wanting to fuck the shit out of her.

"Thank you again for all that you do for me," she said, walking over and wrapping her arms around me, pressing her naked body up against mine.

I caressed her ass as I whispered in her ear, telling her that I would do whatever it took to see a smile on her face before tonguing her down. I hungrily sucked on her tongue before traveling down her body until I was sucking on her clit. She placed her leg on my shoulder and grabbed the back of my head, riding my tongue while screaming out my name, telling me she was about to come. I quickly removed my clothes and pushed her down on the bed, as she bent her back and hiked up her ass. Then I went knee-deep into the pussy. All that could be heard was the sound of me beating the pussy up and her moans, causing me to grab her hips and ram my dick in and out of her, hitting her with long, deep strokes. I felt myself about to come, and she knew it because she threw that ass back, meeting me stroke for stroke, until I released all my seeds inside her. We both collapsed, and I pulled her into me, whispering in her ear that I loved her before dozing off, feeling complete.

When I woke up the next morning, Tami was in the kitchen making breakfast, shaking what her mama gave her to Tory Lanez's song, "Luv."

"You good?" I asked, hugging her from behind and kissing her neck.

I asked if she was okay because Phoenix was leaving today, so I just wanted to know what state of mind she was in this morning.

"I'm good, but I'm not going to lie and say that I'm not a little sad that she has to go," she admitted.

"Well, if it makes you feel any better, I feel kind of sad too that she has to leave because I really enjoyed having her here. Maybe we should have one of our own to run around here," I said, joking, but low-key serious.

"Did you forget that you might have a little one on the way already?" she responded, moving out of my arms.

I didn't want to get into an argument about Olivia right now, so I knew that I needed to say something to get her back to dancing and smiling again.

"Tami, like I told you before, I would never turn my back on any child that belongs to me, but just remember that having a child with you would be a child that was conceived by love. I don't love Olivia, and I will never love her, so with that being said, let's not even discuss that child unless those papers come back saying 99.9 percent that he or she belongs to me," I told her.

"You're right, and I'm sorry," she said, kissing me on my lips before going back over to the stove to finish breakfast.

I decided to leave the having-a-child talk alone for right now, and, instead, enjoy breakfast with her and baby girl before going to take her home. When it was time for her to leave, Phoenix was sad too, but I told her that she could come back next week, and that put a smile on her face.

After dropping her off, I headed to Mason's crib to find out if all was good with business because I haven't been handling business as usual. I prayed the whole ride over to his crib that Olivia's bitch ass wasn't over there because I didn't want to see her ass until it was time to take that DNA test.

"Yo, what's good, my nigga?" Mason greeted me.

"I'm just trying to get back to this business," I told him, dapping him up.

My whole facial expression changed seeing this bitch sitting in the living room with Sami, but I ignored her and followed Mason to the game room. I heard her say some slick shit to Sami. I just hoped that she didn't bring her ass in here tripping because I previously told her that I didn't have shit to say to her until she has the fucking baby.

Chapter Sixteen

Tami

My heart still hurts, and I'm trying so hard to go back to living an everyday life, but it hasn't been easy. I'm still having a hard time blocking out Rema and Dada lying dead on the living room floor in a pool of blood. That day, I felt I lost a piece of me because, regardless of her faults, she was the sister I never had but always loved. I'm thankful that he spared my goddaughter's life, but I hate him, and I hope that he's burning in hell right now. I'm also grateful for what Envy did in getting Siah to let me visit with her because he was being a real bitch toward me. He kept giving me excuse after excuse about why Phoenix wasn't allowed to see me, but I knew it had everything to do with him still being bitter about my leaving his ass. I have no idea what Envy said to him to get him to budge, but I appreciate him. I know that he can't stand Siah because he always said Siah was a bitch-made nigga, and he ain't never lied.

I was feeling sad that Phoenix was going home, but I knew that I needed to be strong, so when I heard Envy get up, I put the music on in the kitchen and pretended I was good. When they left the house, I cried like a baby because having Phoenix here gave me back a piece of my friend. She reminded me so much of her mother, and that, alone, made me want to kidnap her and never give her back. But I knew that I needed to get myself together because life goes on, and I had a job with people who had been more than patient with me, but it was time to go back now.

I didn't know how to feel about Envy saying that we needed to have a child of our own because, although he wasn't worried about Olivia, I must admit that I'm very much worried. If her child is his, that means that he has to deal with all the pettiness that she's going to dish out, and if I'm with him, she is going to make my life a living hell. It's going to feel as if I were dealing with Siah and Tara's ass all over again, so having a child with him is not in the cards for me right now.

I feel that our relationship is going to end if that's going to be his baby mother because I will *not* put myself in that situation again with any man. My mental state right now will have me killing her, and all that's going to do is have me spending the rest of my life behind bars.

I've been going through so much and dealing with my mental struggle, soon realizing that my mom hasn't even called to check on me. She must not have cared how I was doing after losing my best friend, and that shit hurt like hell. The only one who reached out to me via text messages was Sami, checking on me every day. Even when I didn't take any of her calls, she still made sure to text to let me know that she was thinking about me, and that small gesture meant a lot to me.

Envy said that he was going to catch up with Mason after dropping off Phoenix, so I was home alone, but not for long. I decided to go out to get my hair and nails done for work tomorrow since it would be my first day back after being out for so long. I wanted to go back looking like my pretty self, instead of how I've been looking, so I decided to call Sami to see if she wanted to go with me. She said that Olivia was over, so she would have to take a rain check. Since I knew that Envy headed that way, I decided that after getting my hair and nails done, I was going to do a petty pop-up. I know that I said all that stuff about her making my life a living hell, but I was going to remind that bitch that *my* man was just that—*my* man.

I pulled up to Mason's house about an hour later and knew that Envy was still there because I hit him up, and he said he was. He told me that the trick was there, but he wasn't sweating her. I wasn't sweating her either, but like I said, I felt like being petty today.

"Hey, girl, what you doing here?" Sami asked with a smirk on her face, knowing damn well that I was doing a pull-up because I'd told her ass. I told her my pull-up game was strong, and I knew that she didn't believe me, but I guess she'll take my word next time.

She let me in, and I walked past Olivia, making sure to roll my eyes as I kept it pushing to the game room where my man was chilling. Envy and Mason were playing the game, so they didn't even see me walk in, but when my familiar scent filled the room, Envy's ass turned around with the quickness.

"What you doing here, bae?" he asked me, pulling me in for a hug.

"I was lonely sitting at home by myself," I pouted with a smile on my face.

"You full of shit," he laughed.

"Let me finish kicking Mason's ass real quick, and then we can leave to get something to eat," he said.

"Nah, I'm going to chill with the ladies." I winked at him, walking back into the living room.

"So, Sami, what's been going on?" I asked her, taking a seat right next to Olivia on the couch.

"Ain't shit. What's been going on with you?" she said, trying to hold in her laugh.

"Sami, I'm going to go because I see that losing her friend done fucked with this bitch's head if she thinks I'm about to sit and chill with her ass," Olivia said.

"What the fuck did you just say?" I jumped up.

"I didn't stutter. You heard exactly what the fuck I—"

She didn't finish what she was saying because I popped the bitch in the mouth, not giving a fuck about her being pregnant. Then again, I did care that she was pregnant. That's why I popped the bitch in the mouth and didn't kick her ass in the stomach, just in case it was Envy's baby she was carrying. Envy came out of the game room because this bitch was screaming his name like she was his bitch, and he was going to come to her rescue. He came into the living room to see that bitch holding her face. He looked confused about what the fuck just happened.

"Bae, let's go. I'm ready to go get something to eat," I said, pulling him toward the door. "Later, Sami. I'll hit you up later, and good seeing you again, Mason," I added, as we exited the front door. "I'm going to drive to the house. We can just order in and watch a movie since I have to be back at work tomorrow," I told him, as I got in my car and pulled out.

Envy

When I pulled up to the house, Tami was already there, but I sat in the car for a few minutes before heading inside to deal with her. I needed to know what the hell just happened because it was so out of character for her, and the shit had me bugging. When I walked in, I had no intention of arguing with her, but I needed her to help me understand what the fuck just happened and why.

"What took you so long?" she asked me.

"I was sitting in the car, trying to figure out what the hell that was that you pulled back at Mason's crib."

"What are you talking about? All I remember is coming here to chill with you. I didn't know she was there, and she didn't want me there, so she got slick outta her mouth, so I popped her in it," she said, flicking channels on the television and pissing me off.

"Tami, you *do* know that that girl is pregnant, right?" I asked in disbelief at how she was acting.

"I know she's pregnant. That's why I popped her in the damn mouth as opposed to her stomach," she said, and I just looked at her like she was crazy. "What? Please don't tell me you got some feeling about what happens to that trick," she spat.

"I don't give a shit about her, but I do give a shit about you, so I'm going to ask you again. Are you all right?"

"I'm all right, Envy. I'm just tired of always doing the right thing. I'm tired of being there for motherfuckers who are never there for me. And I'm tired of being loyal to everyone, and no one is loyal to me. First, it was Siah, then Rema, and now you, so, yes . . . I'm all right. I just felt like being petty to the bitch that's carrying my man's child. Is that all right with you?" she snapped.

She got up off the couch and stormed upstairs, leaving me feeling like shit, so I went upstairs and found her on the bed, crying. I went to her to apologize, but before I could say anything, she started speaking again.

"I'm sorry for going off on you like that, but I held that in for too long until I just exploded. So, for that, I do apologize. I want you to open your eyes and see that I have no one who cares about me or even supports me when I need them. How many family members did you see at Rema's funeral or even show up at the house, for that matter? I always had Rema, whether you or anybody wants to believe it. And to be honest, she was all I had. I miss her, and I don't know how to go on without her. I lashed out tonight because I'm hurting, and I'm not as strong as one might think. All I want from you is what I give. Nothing more, nothing less, because I don't think that's asking for much. I love you, Envy, but I honestly don't know if I can stick around for the long run because my heart isn't strong enough to watch you father a child with another woman. I've been there and done that," she cried.

"Tami, I love you too, and I don't know how to stop your heart from hurting, but what I do know is that I promise to try to mend it. I also promise you that I will never make you feel the way that he made you feel. You will always be my priority and a part of any decisions concerning any demands that she may have regarding the child, if it's, in fact, mine," I told her, looking in her eyes, letting her know that I was being honest with her.

"I hear you, Envy, and please, believe me when I say that I want to believe you, but that's the same shit he said, and he did the opposite of what he said he was going to do," she stressed.

"Listen, the situation as far as having another female pregnant is the same, but don't put me in the same category as that nigga because I'm a *real* nigga, and my word is my bond. I love you, like I said, and I want to be with you, but if you feel the need to keep throwing the shit in my face, I'll understand if you want to part ways now," I said, pissed that she's blaming me for her ex's mistakes.

If she wanted to keep it all the way real, that nigga was her husband. I didn't owe her shit. She was the one who bounced on me and went back to that nigga, leaving our relationship in limbo. I had no idea where the fuck I stood with her, so if she wanted to blame someone, she needed to blame herself. Just thinking about the shit had me pissed to the max, so I left the bedroom to blaze a blunt before I said some shit that I most likely was going to regret later. Tami needed some time to marinate if she was going to be able to ride with a nigga if Olivia's baby was mine.

I was downstairs for about an hour when she finally came down, sitting beside me on the couch. She looked like she had been trying to put her words together before saying whatever it was that she wanted to say. To be honest, I was sick of talking about it. The fucking baby probably wasn't even mine, but here I was, already dealing with bullshit.

"Whatever you're about to say, just don't let it be that you're sorry because I really don't want to hear 'sorry.' I want to hear you say that you're going to ride this out with me because, if not, like I said, it's best we part ways. I'm not going to continue to fight with you about a baby that we don't even know is mine. And yes, I may sound like a broken record right now, saying the same shit, but I want you to get it and understand it. So, what's it going to be?" I said, helping her out because had she started with "I'm sorry," I was going to lose it on her ass.

"I wasn't going to say, 'sorry,' but after thinking about some of the stuff that I said, I did want to tell you that I shouldn't be comparing you to my ex. I don't want to part ways, but you can't tell me how to feel or how to react to a situation when I'm the one in that situation. I'm going to rock with you because I love you, but don't you ever think that you have control of what I feel and what I should say or not say," she said, rolling her eyes, thinking she checked me.

Sami

"So, where the fuck was you last night?" I asked Mason when I got up this morning.

After Envy and Tami left yesterday, Olivia was going off about how I didn't have her back and how she didn't understand why I was friends with Tami when I was supposed to be her best friend. I told her ass that I didn't know that I was limited to having friends just because I was friends with her, so she got pissed about it and left. This nigga here calls himself going after her to see if she was okay, but never brought his bitch ass back into the house. I got tired of waiting on his ass to return and fell asleep, but I woke up to his ass lying next to me in the bed this morning, so I kindly woke up his ass.

"Why you waking me up with this bullshit early in the fucking morning?" he snapped.

"Nigga, if your ass came in last night, you would have gotten hit with the 'bullshit,' as you call it, but since you didn't, you're going to hear it now. You went outside to see if Olivia was all right to drive home, which *wasn't* your place, but I let it ride. But for you *not* to come back inside, you had to have me fucked up. So, again, where the fuck was you last night? And what time did you slide your ass up in this bitch?" I snapped back.

He got up with an attitude, throwing the blanket off him like he was a fucking 2-year-old having a fucking tantrum. Do you think I gave a fuck? Nope, because he wasn't going anywhere until he answered my questions. I wasn't insinuating that something was going on with the two of them, but I have been seeing shit that just wasn't sitting right with me. So, his running behind her yesterday just triggered some things that I noticed before, like when she comes over and he's here. And it doesn't matter what room in the house she's in because he's always there. If I step out of the room, I could clearly hear them talking before reaching the room on my way back, but as soon as I enter, there's nothing but silence. I watched him go into the bathroom and lock the door like the shit fazed me. I was going to be sitting here waiting on his ass, but after a few minutes turned into a few more minutes, I knew he was taking me for a joke. He knew that I had to get ready for work, and I wouldn't be able to wait out his ass, so I went downstairs to shower so that I could get my ass ready for work.

When I came out of the bathroom, I hurried upstairs, wearing just a towel wrapped around me because I didn't take my clothes downstairs with me. I was cold because, no matter how many times I told Mason to stop turning on the central air, he never listened. Somehow, he stayed hot for whatever reason.

As soon as I walked into the room, he jumped out at me, scaring the shit out of me with my towel falling to the floor. He was bent over, laughing, like the shit was funny, but my heart was still beating as fast as hell as I tried to catch my breath from running across the room.

"So, it's funny that you almost gave me a heart attack?" I asked with a roll of my eyes.

"That's what your ass gets for talking shit like I was with your wack-ass, fucking friend," he said, grabbing me.

"It wasn't even about that. It was about you leaving and not fucking coming back without saying shit. Olivia came into the equation because you had no business running behind her ass, especially when she was mad at *me,*" I told his ass, but all he did was rub up against me as I felt his morning wood against my ass.

He pulled off his boxers, bent me over the bed, and entered me from behind, causing me to moan out. I didn't want him to know that I was enjoying him plunging in and out of me when I was supposed to be mad at his ass, but I couldn't help it.

"I knew all you wanted was some dick," he said, sucking on my neck as he deep-stroked me, causing me to close my eyes, enjoying the pleasure that he was giving my kitty.

I got so lost in what he was doing to my body that I wasn't thinking about being mad at him, or the fact that I had to be at work in less than an hour. I tried my best to resist the urge to scream out again because he was being extra cocky with it, but I couldn't as I arched my back, screaming out for him to fuck me harder. *Big mistake,* I thought as soon as the words left my mouth. Now, he went animalistic on my ass, fucking me hungrily as if this would be his last time in the pussy.

I felt myself on the verge of exploding, so I bit down on my bottom lip, trying to fight the urge to let go because I was enjoying it that much. But when I felt him grab my hips, I knew he was about to explode too, so I let go, and we came together. I couldn't even catch my breath because I had to take a quick shower, knowing I would be late for work. I know my job is just about sick of me because I have a history of being late due to Mason with his morning quickies, so if my ass got fired, it would be his fault. He keeps telling me that I don't need to work, but I like my independence and not sitting at home, waiting on a nigga to take care of my ass. I didn't want for nothing with Mason, but I learned a long time ago to always stack my money. So whenever he gave me money, I never go materialistic or crazy because you never know when that shit was going to end.

"Don't even think about it, Mason. I have to wash up and get out so that I can get my ass to work," I told him upon seeing him entering the shower.

"Call out," he said, entering me like I didn't just say anything to him.

My pussy was sore, but that didn't stop me from backing up my ass, taking all nine inches of his loving. After getting off for a second time, I showered and called my supervisor to let him know that I wasn't going to make it in today because I wasn't feeling well. I knew that meant if I wanted to keep my job, I needed to head my ass over to the emergency room for some proof. Mason was getting dressed, so I told his ass to take me to breakfast since he was the reason I wasn't going to work . . . again.

"I'll take you to get some breakfast and then drop your ass over at 'killer county,' where ole girl works. Maybe she could hook you up without seeing the doctor," he said, talking about Tami.

Chapter Seventeen

Tami

My first day back at work wasn't too bad because time went by quickly, and by the time I looked at the clock, it was time for lunch. I went out front and sat on the bench to give Envy a call to see how his day was going. I was trying to feel him out after the heated conversation that we had this morning. I'm not going to front, though. He had me a little shook when he was like we should part ways because that's not what I wanted. I never had any intentions on breaking up with him. I just wanted him to understand where I was coming from and what I was feeling since he was trying to tell me how I should feel.

"Hey, what you doing?" I asked when he answered the phone.

"Chilling with Mason," he answered dryly.

"So, are you home or are you at Mason's spot?" I asked.

"I'm home. He stopped by after dropping Sami off at County," he said.

"Oh, okay. Is she all right?" I asked, concerned.

"Yeah, she called out of work and needed some type of proof of her being sick so they don't fire her ass," he explained.

"All right. I'm going to see if I can find her since I'm on my break," I told him.

"Cool," was all he said, ending the call.

I wasn't feeding into his rude ass today. I walked over to the emergency room department, and after getting the room number where Sami was, I walked in. She was sitting on the bed playing on her phone.

"Hey, girl, what's up?" I laughed, since I already knew why she was here.

"If you're laughing, you already know what's up," she laughed.

"OK, so what's the reason you're here today and on a level of one to ten, what would you say your level of pain is?" I laughed, pretending to be the doctor, causing her to burst out laughing.

"You play too much. I'm ready to get up out of this depressing place, and if you got some pull, I need you to use it and get me up out of here," she said.

"Nah, bitch, you should have taken your ass to work," I told her.

"Girl, Mason was on some bullshit this morning, which ended with us fucking and my being late for work. Then he came into the shower wanting some more when I was trying to get washed and out of there after our first session. Then he told me to call out, so I did. Now, I'm here, pretending to be sick to get a damn note because my job is about sick of my ass right about now," she said, shaking her head.

"So, what was he tripping on?" I asked, confused, because it couldn't be that bad if they were fucking.

"He wasn't tripping; I was because, after you left yesterday, Olivia was in her feelings because she felt that I should have had her back. She felt that I shouldn't even be friends with you, since she's my best friend, but I kept it real with her ass and told her that she deserved that slap. As far as my being friends with you, I told her that I didn't know that I wasn't allowed to pick my friends simply because I was friends with her."

"Are you serious?" I asked in disbelief.

"Wait, that wasn't the fucked-up part. So, Olivia got upset and stormed out of the house, and this nigga ran behind her to make sure that she was 'cool to drive.' How about his ass didn't come back in the house, so when I woke up this morning, Mason's ass was in bed, and I went the hell off on his ass. I wanted to know where the hell he went and stayed all night."

"Hold up. So, Mason went after Olivia, and you didn't stop that nigga? You better than me because he had no business checking on her, especially if you, her best friend, didn't take *your* ass out there. So, do you think they creeping?" I asked her.

"I don't know, but he said all he did was make sure she was good, and she left after she said that she was. He said he left after her to go take care of some 'business,' but like I said, I don't know. But what I *do* know is that the two of them better not be that stupid to cross me," she said.

"I feel you, but next time that nigga come outta his face talking about checking on a bitch that's not his, you better check that ass right then and there. Never give that nigga room to think that that shit is cool," I told her because I was having a hard time coming to grips with how he made it out the front door. "Girl, my break is over, so I have to get back. Call me later," I told her as I walked out.

When I got off work, I didn't get a call from Sami. I walked to the back to see if she had been discharged, and she wasn't, so I returned to her room.

"Why the hell you still here?" I asked her.

"Girl, that's why it doesn't pay to lie because my ass had to sit here all day, waiting for some damn bloodwork to come back. The doctor just came in to tell me everything came back normal, and my feeling light-headed and nauseated could be from fatigue, caused by overworking myself. I wanted to say the only 'overworking' I do is when I'm putting it down in the bedroom," she laughed.

"Do you want me to drop you off, or did you call Mason already?" I asked her.

"Nah, I didn't call him yet, so I would appreciate it if you would drop me off. I'm just waiting on the discharge papers and my note for work."

"OK, I'll be in the car out front," I told her.

I was sitting in the car, playing *Angry Birds Pop!* when something told me to look up, and I wished like hell that I didn't. I saw Tara and Siah leaving from the emergency room exit, and she was still very pregnant. *I guess he's claiming that baby too,* I thought as I just rolled my eyes at the sight of them because he knew his ass was feeling that trick all along. I leaned my seat all the way back because I didn't want him or that bitch seeing me, because then, her ass would have gotten the satisfaction of knowing I saw them together.

"Girl, who the fuck you hiding from?" Sami said, causing me to jump because I didn't even see her ass walk up on my car, let alone open the door.

"I'm hiding from my bitch-ass ex-husband, who said he didn't father that bitch's baby, but from where I'm sitting, it looks like he's claiming it. I didn't want them to see me because I didn't have time for the drama that always follows whenever I'm anywhere around them two," I told her, putting the car in drive and pulling out.

"I bet your ass happy now that you didn't have any kids with him," she said.

"It's still like having kids with him because he's the father of my goddaughter, so he's being a bitter-ass man because I left him. He wouldn't let me see her after the funeral, so it took Envy to hit him up before he even agreed to allow her to visit with me, with his punk ass," I said, getting pissed off just thinking about it.

"So, he just going to be fucking with you for no reason when it comes to getting her because he knows that he can," she said, and she hit that shit dead-on because it's all a game to his ass.

I dropped her off at her house and headed home to shower and cook some dinner because I was making it an early night. Envy's mom invited us to Sunday dinner this week, so I was looking forward to seeing her and Camille. I haven't seen them since the funeral because I didn't want to see anyone.

When I got to the house, Mason was gone and so was Envy, so I went up to take my shower before hitting him up to see where he was at. He didn't mention going anywhere when I told him I was dropping Sami off.

After showering, I saw that I had a message, so, thinking that it was him, I grabbed my phone to see what excuse he had for leaving the house before I got home. I looked and saw that it was a message from Siah's punk ass, so I opened the message to find out why he felt the need to text me.

Siah: Hey, Tami, why didn't you say hello when you saw me today? That was some rude shit, but it's all good.

He was tripping, and I wasn't about to respond to his ass because that would have just been a war of words, and I wasn't in the mood. I went downstairs to the kitchen to take out the chopped meat, so that I could make a pan of baked ziti with a salad. I heard my phone ringing, so I ran upstairs to get it, thinking it was Envy's ass, but I saw that it was my mother calling. I haven't spoken to her, and she didn't reach out to see if I was okay when Rema was murdered, so I was wondering what the hell she wanted now. I started just to let it go to voicemail, but she was still my mother, so I answered.

Envy

I knew that Tami was going to be pissed because she just spoke to me before dropping Sami off at the crib, and I didn't tell her that I had to make a run. Mason and I bullshitted all day playing a game, so I forgot that I promised to drop off some money to Olivia because she hit me up claiming she needed some copay for her doctor's appointment tomorrow. I know what you're thinking, but if the kid is mine, I didn't want to feel like shit for not doing my part, so that's why I agreed to help her out. I know I should have said something to Tami about it after telling her that I was going to include her in all my decisions regarding Olivia. I wanted to tell her, but it would only cause an argument, so I figured if I could prevent us from arguing, it was best to keep it to myself. When I got to the house, she was in the kitchen cooking, so I went and kissed her, but the look on her face told me she was pissed.

"Why didn't you tell me that you were stepping out?" she asked me.

"I was bullshitting with Mason and forgot that I needed to stop over by my mom's crib to take Camille some money," I lied and felt like shit.

"I miss them and can't wait until Sunday to enjoy some of your mother's good cooking," she said.

"You and me both, but you just worry about what you got cooking up in here. I'm going upstairs to shower," I said, slapping her on her ass.

As soon as I got out of the bathroom, I dressed in some shorts and a T-shirt so I could get back downstairs because a nigga was starving. I grabbed my phone and saw that I had a text message from Olivia, thanking me, as if she hadn't already thanked me when I handed her the money. I swear these bitches are always trying to be messy because for her to text what she said to me already, she probably was hoping that Tami saw it. I just deleted the message, shaking my head, regretting my decision already of going behind Tami's back for her ass. I swear, the next time, I'm going to send that shit by someone else because I see she's on some bullshit. Tami had it smelling good downstairs, and when I saw that she made ziti, my ass couldn't wait to dig in because I loved her baked ziti.

"My mom called me today," she said, as she sat down at the table to join me.

"She finally reached out, so that's a good thing. What did she want?" I asked her because I knew she was upset that no one in her family reached out when she needed them.

"She sounded like she was drinking, but she said that she was just calling me to tell me that she missed me and wants to see me," she said sadly. I know how she felt about her mother's drinking problem, so she battled with herself between being in her life or just letting her be.

"Well, I think that you should see her because she's still your mother, and you only get one. She's dealing with her demons right now, and I think she needs you, even if it's just listening to her talk bullshit."

After dinner, I helped her with the dishes. Then we went into the living room to watch a movie before calling it a night. Tami had to work in the morning, and I had business in the streets. Before I could even get into bed, my phone was alerting me that I had a text message, and I got pissed off, but at the same time, I felt thankful that Tami was in the bathroom. It was Olivia asking me if I could go with her to her doctor's appointment, but I ignored the text and turned off my phone. Tami came out of the bathroom and got into the bed and I pulled her into me, kissing her on her neck before taking my ass to bed, praying that my good deed didn't come back and bite me in the ass.

The next morning, when I got up, Tami was already gone, so I powered back on my phone to find numerous messages from Olivia's ass, so I decided to nip the shit before she started her bullshit again.

"Listen, Olivia, when I agreed to help you out, that didn't mean you had the green light to fucking harass a nigga," I said, not giving her a chance to say hello.

"I wasn't trying to harass you; it's just that you said you were giving me the money because, if it turns out to be your baby, you will feel bad. So, I was just thinking that maybe you wanted to come to the doctor's appointment so you don't miss out on hearing the baby's heartbeat or how he or she is progressing," she said.

"I understand all of that, and yes, it will fuck me up if it's my baby, and I missed all of that, but I'm in a relationship that I need to respect, so, please, don't hit my phone again," I said, ending the call.

I pulled into the parking lot just before the Williamsburg Bridge, waiting on my li'l nigga Snoop to drop off his count for the week. I would usually have his ass meet me at the spot out in Queens, but I had some shit to take care of in Brooklyn that I couldn't be late for.

"What's up, Boss Man?" he asked, once in my car.

"Chilling. Is the count right because I don't have time to count that shit right now?"

"Come on, Boss Man, you know my count is always right," he said, like his ass was offended, but I didn't give a shit.

"That's what I want to hear, so get up outta my ride," I told him jokingly, but serious as hell because I needed to go.

"That's some cold shit, man," he said, getting out of my car and hopping into his, pulling out.

I pulled up to the jewelry store, and Camille was already inside waiting on me with a smile so wide she made me smile. "I never thought I would see the day that you would be trying to propose to someone," she said, still smiling.

"I know, but I believe she's the one, so just help me pick out the ring because I'm going to do it at Sunday dinner," I told her.

"All right, big brother. I'm so proud of you," she said, making me feel good about my decision.

I was nervous as hell because I didn't know if she would accept, given my situation with Olivia, but I decided to follow my heart. This right here was big for me because I never even thought about making any woman my wife, but Tami did something to my ass from the first time I saw her ass in the mall that day.

Chapter Eighteen

Tami

Envy's ass was acting strange, but I brushed it off as I stood before the mirror, putting on some eyeliner and lip gloss. He had agreed to go to church with his mother and sister today before having dinner at the house, so I was just putting on the finishing touches. I haven't been to church in a long time, but I looked forward to hearing the word this morning because I've been feeling down about my mother. I saw her the other day, and it hurt me that she was no longer sober. She had let a no-good nigga push her into the arms of the bottle again. I carefully wiped at the tears that fell because I didn't want to mess up the eyeliner that I just finished putting on. When I came out of the bathroom, I felt like I was underdressed, looking at Envy all decked out in a suit and tie.

"Should I change because you're dressed like you about to be preaching this morning?" I joked.

"Ha, I see you got jokes, but no, you don't need to change. You look beautiful as always," he said, grabbing me from behind, kissing me on my neck.

He was about to start something that his ass wasn't ready for because he knew that my neck was my spot, and that I had no problem missing church to get it popping. But he let me go, telling me not to even think about it because he knew I was ready and willing to make it do what it do.

"My mom would kill me if we didn't show up to church as promised," he said, moving my hand from caressing his dick through his pants.

"Well, you the one up in here getting me all hot and bothered," I said, rolling my eyes.

"I was just trying to show you some love with your horny ass," he said, grabbing the keys and telling me he was ready.

When we arrived at the church, it was already packed with people, but Envy's mom had already saved us some seats up front, so I was happy about that. I hugged her and Camille before taking a seat next to Envy. Then the service started, and the preacher spoke about love and forgiveness, and it was hitting home, so I closed my eyes, taking in the testimony he was giving. Then I heard him say, "Welcome Brother Envy. He's going to share his testimony this morning."

My eyes popped open to him releasing my hand and walking up to the podium as I looked on, not knowing what the hell was going on because we damn sure didn't discuss it before coming here this morning. He looked nervous, but then he started to speak, so I did what everyone else did, and that was to listen to see what he had to say.

"Good morning. Some of you may not know that this has been my family church since I was a little boy. Those who do know also know that I haven't been here in a while, but I never strayed away from my religious upbringing. Pastor Troy allowed me to be up here today because I told him about a very special woman in my life who I love. He said to me that if I loved her like I say, I should express it, so I took his words to heart, and that's why I'm here today to do just that. Tami," he called out, with his hand extended toward me.

OMG, I thought as I put my hand to my mouth. I wasn't expecting any of this, and now, Envy being dressed to impress made sense. I didn't understand why he put me on front street with all these people I didn't even know. I knew that I couldn't keep him waiting, so I walked to him, taking his hand as he helped me up the two steps to stand beside him. The only thing that was going through my head was, why didn't he tell me to change if he was going to be putting me on display? I mean, I looked cute, but I could have looked beautiful for whatever he had planned that required me to be in the spotlight this morning. Once I was standing in front of him, he got down on one knee, and that's when the tears fell. I couldn't believe he had me crying in a room full of strangers, besides his mom and sister.

"Tami, I know that you have trust issues, and words really mean nothing to you. When I told you that I love you, I could see the doubt in your eyes because the last person who said they loved you hurt you. That's why I decided to show you just how much my words come from my heart. So, today, in God's house, in front of my mom, sister, and church family, I'm asking you to be my wife."

I stood in utter shock, and I knew he was waiting for an answer, but I was questioning if I wanted to be married again. The ink just dried on my divorce papers, so it would be too soon to jump back into another marriage. And now, he was down on one knee waiting for my answer.

Although I wasn't sure of my answer, I said, "Yes." Everyone started clapping as he stood and put a beautiful ring on my finger, kissing me as if we had already said the "I dos."

Then he walked me back over to my seat, and his mother took my hand in hers and squeezed it gently as we listened to the rest of the service. When it was over, he walked me over to introduce me to the pastor.

"Congratulations, pretty lady. I just want to say that under any other circumstances, I wouldn't have had a proposal done by someone who graces my church whenever they feel like it. But since he's my nephew and begged me to do this for him, I agreed . . . So I'll be the first to tell you that you must be special. I have never seen this side of this 'rough-around-the-edges young man, so, please, don't break his heart, and I hope to see you both next Sunday," he said, looking at Envy after making that last statement.

"We will be here next Sunday, and thanks for giving him the platform to do this," I said before giving Envy the side eye for not agreeing to come back to church.

We went home to change before heading to his mom's house because she was cooking dinner for us. I had no idea that Envy's family owned Precious Lord Baptist Church because his ass was always so secretive when it came to his life. If he wanted me to be his wife, he needed to tell me everything that I needed to know about his ass.

Sami

When I got to Planet Fitness, Tami was waiting for me in the locker room, rocking her sports bra and workout pants, looking cute. All I had on were some sweats and a tee because I didn't know we were coming to the gym to look cute.

"Hey, what's up, girl?" she asked, once she spotted me.

"I'm mad at you and Envy because me and Mason didn't get invited to the engagement announcement," I told her, pouting.

"Well, according to Envy, he did invite both of you, but Mason told him that he wasn't stepping foot into the church. I guess that means you won't be coming to the wedding either," she laughed.

"Trust when I say that I *will* be there, with or without Mason's ass, so you better make sure you give me an invitation," I told her, putting my things in the locker so that we could start our workout.

We worked out for about forty-five minutes before taking our asses to the juice bar because I wanted a smoothie before heading home.

"Oh, I almost forgot to tell you that I'm glad that you decided to be the bigger person in this situation with Olivia and Envy," I said to her, causing her to look at me all crazy.

"What are you talking about?" she asked with her face twisted up.

"Olivia told me that Envy has been paying for her copays and even making a few appointments," I told her, hoping that I didn't just let the cat out of the bag if she didn't know.

"I had no idea that he was doing any of that because he didn't discuss it with me. So how long has he been doing this?" Tami asked, and now, I feel horrible. I honestly thought she knew after telling me about the conversation she had with Envy, and Envy's promise always to involve her.

"I'm sorry. I thought you knew, but he just started doing it last month, and Olivia just had her sonogram appointment last week. He went because they were supposed to find out the baby's sex, but she said that because of the position the baby was in, they weren't able to tell. I feel so bad that you had to find out like this because the shit isn't right that he didn't tell you," I said, now pissed off at his ass for what he did.

I honestly think that Olivia knew that Tami didn't know, and that's probably the reason she made it seem like she did. She knew that I would mention it to her, so that it would cause a problem between the two of them. I swear, her ass could be so grimy at times, and she knows how I feel about her and her games. I'm tired of telling her that she needed to leave Tami alone because Envy was the one who slept with her and got her pregnant, not Tami.

"I'm going to get out of here," she said, hugging me with her voice cracking.

"All right, I'll talk to you later, and again, I'm sorry. I didn't know," I said, returning the hug.

"No problem. It's not your fault. Later," she said, walking to her car.

When I got in my car, I called Olivia up and asked her why she made it seem like Tami knew that Envy was doing those things for her. She had the nerve to laugh on the other end, saying Envy told her that he had informed Tami. I knew that she was lying, so I told her to keep me out of her games. She then had the nerve to get smart, asking me why I was discussing her with that bitch in the first place and to keep her name out of my mouth when hanging with my newfound friend. I just hung up on her ass because I wasn't about to sit and entertain her bullshit. I never knew her to be so damn petty over some dick that she wasn't getting anymore, and I wasn't feeling her new attitude. She was my friend, so I guess I had to take the good with the bad, but it wasn't going to stop me from telling her when she was wrong.

I drove my ass home to shower and try to calm my nerves because I was now in my feelings about how both conversations went down. When I walked into the house, Mason was sitting on the couch rolling up, so I said, "What's up?" and kept it moving upstairs to get out of my stinky clothes. I was a little pissed that I didn't get my smoothie, so after my shower, I was going downstairs to make my own smoothie, and I just might add some liquor to it.

"You good?" Mason asked me.

I didn't even hear him come into the room, and I hope he didn't hear me talking to myself because that has become a bad habit of mine when trying to make sense of something that was bothering me.

"I'm good, just pissed at Olivia," I stressed.

"What did she do now?" he asked.

"She told me that Envy's been paying for her copay at the doctor's office, and that he went with her to her sonogram appointment. When she told me this, she implied that Tami knew this, so I mentioned it to Tami, basically saying how happy I was that she was the bigger person. Come to find out, she didn't even know, and I felt like shit because she was upset that Envy kept it from her."

"So when did this take place?" he asked.

"It happened today when I met her at the gym," I responded.

"No, I'm talking about Envy paying for Olivia's copay and going to the appointment," he said, confusing me.

Who gives a fuck when it happened? I was pissed because I was the reason for an argument that was going to take place between Envy and Tami.

He just came up in here pissing me off to the max, so I didn't even respond to his ass as I grabbed my things and went into the bathroom. I made sure to slam the door for good measure, to let him know just how much he just pissed me off.

Chapter Nineteen

Tami

I was so mad. My hands were shaking as I drove home, and I swear if Envy were in my presence right now, I would be catching a case. I felt like such a fool after hearing that he was doing all these things for that bitch behind my back. I just don't understand fucking men, and I'm tired of trying because the excuse is always the same, so he can miss me with the bullshit. I wasn't even going home tonight, and as much as I didn't want to go to my mom's place, that was where I was going to crash for the night. I wasn't up for an argument with him, so I prayed that I could find something decent in my mom's closet to wear to work tomorrow because I refused to see him tonight.

When I arrived at my mom's place, I used my emergency key to let myself in and found her sitting on the sofa, watching television and smoking a cigarette.

"Hey, Mom," I said, sounding defeated because that's exactly how I was feeling.

"What's wrong with you?" she asked, and to my surprise, she wasn't drunk.

"I'm just so tired of giving my all and getting nothing in return," I sighed, plopping down on the couch beside her.

"Tami, I been telling you for years to stop letting these men walk all over you. I understand how you feel about being loyal, but you already see that all that being loyal only leads you to nothing but a broken heart in the end. I know that I'm in no position to advise because any time one of my men that I call myself loving leaves me, I make love to a fucking bottle. But baby girl, I'm tired too," she said, shocking me.

"So, does that mean you're not going to drink anymore?" I asked her.

"I'm not saying that I will never have a drink again, but what I *will* say is that I'm going to start living for me and start making better decisions when it comes to me. I haven't been someone who you could look up to, and it hurts me to my core that you didn't think enough of me to tell me that you were engaged. Don't worry about how I know. Just know that I do, and it bothers me that your man didn't think enough of me to invite me. I know it's no one's fault but my own, but I'm still your mother, and I promise you that I wouldn't have shown up drunk," she said. I wanted to feel sorry for her, but I just couldn't because I have given her a million chances to do right by me.

"I can see the doubt all in your face, so all I can say to you is that I can show you better than I can tell you," she said, putting out her cigarette and saying good night before she ascended the stairs to her bedroom.

I went upstairs about ten minutes later and went to the room that used to be mine, hoping to find something to sleep in after I showered. My phone was ringing, and I knew it was Envy because of the ringtone that I had set for his ass, but I ignored it and went down the hall to shower. After bathing, I came back to the room with like fifteen missed calls from him. That let me know he knew that something was up, but again, I ignored my phone. I went to my mom's room to look in her closet and see if she had something for me to wear to work tomorrow. We were about the same size, but since she's been drinking, she was a little smaller. I knew she still had clothes that no longer fit her due to her weight loss. She was sleeping, so I went into the closet and picked out a pair of navy blue slacks with a white, button-down shirt. Now the shoes were going to be tricky because she wore a size eight, and I was an eight and a half, depending on the style of the shoe. However, I found a pair of ballerina flats that were an eight medium that fit, so I was good for the morning, and I was thankful I didn't have to go home. I didn't have to worry about Envy coming here because my mom's house would be the last place he would look for me. I laid the clothes on a chair and climbed into bed, putting my phone on the charger, noticing a text message.

Envy: Will you just let me explain?

Envy: Tami, please call me.

Envy: Come on, babe, don't do me like this.

Envy: I'm sorry.

Yes, he is a sorry-ass excuse of a fucking man, I thought as I reached over and turned off the lamp and took my ass to bed. When I got up, my mom was already gone because she had to be to work at eight, but she had to leave at six because she worked in the Bronx. After getting ready, I headed out, praying that I would be able to make it through the day because I was so not in the mood to work. I had a text message from Sami, telling me that Envy came by the house last night, asking them if I was there, but I didn't respond. When I got to work, I had no idea what was going on, but a lot of dudes were posted up outside and inside the hospital. It looked like a war zone, but I kept it moving to clock in and start my day, praying it would go by fast.

"Good morning, Curtis. What's going on?" I asked him.

"Some dude got shot, so all of his homeboys posted up," he told me, causing me to shake my head.

The last time something like this happened, the emergency room was crazy after the friends of the victim were told he didn't make it. I knew that I needed to steer clear of the hallways because I didn't want to get caught up if they started damaging shit, if whoever it was didn't make it. It was going to be hard because I needed to walk that hallway for patients who were going to get registered from the emergency room.

"Good morning, Rose and Shellie," I said to my coworkers.

"Girl, I should have called in today because it's going to be a crazy day. Elle already has you and me working on the adult side," she said. I sucked my teeth because I was not in the mood to be on that side, where it was already a madhouse.

"I should have called my ass out too, and next time, give me a heads-up because it wouldn't have mattered if I was en route because I still would have called out," I told her.

"Hell no, if I have to be here, your ass has to be here too," she laughed.

"Whatever," I told her.

I don't know what the hell was going on, but for some reason it seemed as if the damn day was dragging, and I was so ready to go home. I swear I wanted to go to Elle's office to tell her that I wasn't feeling well and needed to go home. I had plans to go to KFC on my break, but I didn't feel up to it, so I just went to the cafeteria to get something. *The food isn't that great, but it will have to do today,* I thought as I walked over, trying to figure out what looked good enough to eat. I finally decided on a club sandwich and some chips with a Cherry Coke.

"Let me take care of that for you," I heard from behind me, causing me to turn around.

Damn, I thought as I looked up at this fine-ass nigga, standing at like six foot two, with a dark complexion and attractive eyes. He had a bitch drooling, but I wasn't about to let him know that because he was already wearing a cocky-ass smile, knowing he was fine.

"No, thank you," I politely declined, paying for my meal and walking away with a smile on my face.

I sat down at one of the tables, and just as I was about to take a bite out of my sandwich, he asked to join me. As much as I wanted to decline again, I said, "Fuck it," and allowed him to have a seat, but now I sat nervously, knowing that I should have told his ass to keep it pushing. I put my left hand in my lap, trying to hide my ring, and I had no idea why, knowing that I was spoken for, even if I was mad at his ass right now.

Envy

I was pissed off that Tami wasn't answering any of my calls, and I wished like hell I knew where she was staying. I went by Mason's crib, and that's when I found out that Olivia went running her fucking mouth to Sami, and Sami ran hers to Tami. I knew I should have just been honest with her, but I didn't think that she would have understood my reasoning. I didn't want to lose her behind this bullshit because all I was trying to do was help Olivia out, just in case the baby was mine. Olivia had the nerve to be still hitting me up after running her fucking mouth, like I was going to talk to her ass. I hope that she realized that she fucked up whatever it was that I was doing for her because she could bet money that I was done. So I hope she enjoyed running her mouth.

I just pulled up to Tami's job because if she wasn't going to take any of my calls, she was going to talk to me face-to-face, regardless of whether she wanted to. Her coworker, Shellie, told me that she was downstairs in the cafeteria, and when I got down there, I was tight seeing her sitting at the table with some dude. I walked over to the table, and the first thing I noticed was that she was hiding her engagement ring from this nigga, pissing me off even more.

"What's going on here?" I asked her, but looking at that nigga as he stood.

"I'm going to go. Nice meeting you, Tami," his punk ass said, leaving the table.

"So you can't answer any of my calls, but you got time to be down here smiling up in some nigga's face?" I barked at her ass.

"Not at my job, Envy," she said, rolling her eyes as she got up to empty her tray.

I thought she would come back over to the table, but she walked her ass out of the cafeteria with me following behind her.

"Tami, you think I came up here to play with your fucking ass? I get that you're mad, but talk to me and stop acting like a fucking child," I snapped.

"I'm not about to do this at my job," she said. Then she continued walking, so I grabbed her and turned her to face me.

"You wouldn't have to do this at your job if your ass had answered my fucking calls. So, let's not act like you didn't know that I was going to come up here and show my ass. I know you have to get back, so you go on back to your little job, but I promise you, if you don't bring your ass home, there's going to be a problem. And just so you know, let me see your ass smiling up in that nigga's, or any nigga's face, again while wearing my ring, and both of you will have matching body bags," I threatened, walking out of the hospital, meaning every damn word.

I didn't come up here to do that shit. All I wanted to do was talk to her ass and explain why the fuck I didn't tell her about the shit I was doing for Olivia. She got me fucked up if she thought for a second that I was about to play fucking games with her ass not coming home another night. I called up Mason to let him know that I was on my way because we had business to discuss, and I had no intention of making a detour unless her ass kept sending my calls to voicemail.

"Yo, your ass looks stressed the hell out," Mason's ass clowned after opening the door.

"I'm telling you, Tami is going to be the death of me, my nigga. I get to her fucking job, and she sitting in the cafeteria entertaining some nigga, and had the nerve to be hiding her fucking ring," I told him, still pissed.

"That nigga was probably just a coworker, and she probably knew you was going to show up, so maybe she was just trying to get back at you," he tried to convince me.

"Nah, that nigga run those trap houses on the South Side, so I knew exactly who that nigga was, and I'm sure he knew who the fuck I was too. I swear, I felt like snapping her fucking neck, but I kept my cool," I lied. However, he knew me better than anybody, so he knew I *didn't* keep my cool just by the look he was giving me.

"So, let's talk business because I'm not trying to hear that bullshit about keeping your cool. I been thinking about what you said, so if I'm in, what did you have in mind?" he asked.

"I just feel like we been doing this illegal shit for a while and really don't have shit. When I say we don't have shit, just think about it. If we were to get knocked, we have no way to prove how we got the shit. It's time to clean up our money by investing in some legal shit," I explained.

"I feel you. My house and car is in my mama's name, and her ass be threatening me all the damn time about reporting my shit stolen. So, again, what kind of legal business you trying to open?" he asked. I couldn't help but laugh at what he said about his mother because I remember the time his mom was on her bullshit when he was late bringing her some money. She actually reported the car stolen, getting his ass pulled over and taken down to the station.

"That shit not funny, my nigga," he said, but couldn't help but laugh his damn self.

"It was funny the way you ran up out of there when they let you go, acting like she said you had to be home before the streetlights came on," I said, and we laughed together.

"Damn right because her ass was serious about doing that shit again, if I didn't come hit her ass off." We enjoyed the memory.

"Now that I know you're on board, I'm going to think of some shit that we could invest in and get back to you. I got about an hour before heading home to meet up with Tami, so come get your ass kicked in some football," I told him, heading toward the game room.

When I got to the house, it was a little after three, so I knew Tami would be home soon, that's *if* she decided to come home. She walked in the door about an hour later than usual, but I didn't beef about it because I was just happy that she returned.

"I'm here, so speak," she said with an attitude.

"Look, Tami, I know that you're upset, but trust me when I say that I wasn't trying to hurt you. I also know that I gave you my word about including you in any decisions, but honestly, I didn't tell you because I didn't want us arguing about it. I had no idea that Olivia was going to make it more than what it was because all I did was give her a few copays for her doctor appointments. I swear to you that I never went to any of her appointments with her. She just made that shit up because she knew that Sami's ass was going to tell it. Had you answered my calls, we could have nipped this shit. I'm wrong for having any kind of contact with her, but it will not happen again because I helped her out, and she decided to be messy, so now I'm going to fall back."

"Envy, how the fuck am I supposed to marry you when you couldn't be honest with me about something like giving a bitch a few dollars? You must think very little of me to think that I would have been bothered by that shit," she said.

"It's not that. I just figured that the situation that happened at Mason's house between the two of you was enough for me not to mention her asking me to help her out. I was feeling bad about not doing my part if the baby is mine, so when she hit me up for help, I helped her," I stressed, hoping she understood.

"I'm going to explain this one more time, and I hope that you understand it this time because I will not be repeating myself. I have always been a loyal person, even to people who didn't deserve my loyalty. I have been called stupid so many times that I lost count because no one understands how important loyalty is to me. In fact, they take advantage because no matter what the situation, I ride it out. Well, now, I'm tired of riding it out. I want motherfuckers to be loyal to me the same as I am to them. And if you can't respect that and treat me how I treat you, or be honest like I'm honest with you, I want you to take this ring and keep it moving. I don't know how many times I've said that I'm tired, but somehow, I always make the mistake of staying. So, Envy, if you want this relationship like you claim, it's time to show me because I have no more fucks to give, and I will have no problem walking away."

"Tami, I fucked up again, and I know that I probably don't deserve another chance to make this shit right. But if you give me that chance, I will *never* make the mistake of not confiding in you again," I told her, kissing her lips.

"This is your last chance, Envy, and I mean it because I'd rather let you go now if staying means that I will only be hurt in the end. I need you to tell me what you want to do regarding Olivia and her pregnancy. Do you want to be there for her now, or wait until the test proves that the kid is yours? I'm not feeling you going behind my back with the bullshit, so you need to be upfront about what it is that you want to do, so that we can discuss whether I'm okay with it."

I wanted him to be honest with me because if that's what he wanted to do, in terms of being there for her, I needed him to say it. I don't know if I'm ready for whatever his response is going to be, but I needed to hear him say it, so that we will not have any misconceptions about where he stands regarding his involvement.

Chapter Twenty

Tami

I continued waiting for Envy to answer my question, but he seemed hesitant, probably afraid of how I was going to respond. I knew that his mother raised him to be a man who handled his responsibilities, and I get that, but I needed him just to be honest with me. I wanted him to understand that I was being called stupid and many other names because of sticking by Siah, and now, him. So, if I'm willing to be with him with a child on the way, the least he could do is be honest with me. I know that I should care less what is being said about me because I'm sure I'm not the only woman who has been done wrong by a man or stuck with a man when they shouldn't have. Envy is a good man, and I know that he's fighting with himself about what he knows he should do. What kind of woman would I be to tell him that he couldn't do for a woman who may be carrying his child? I'm not upset that he helped her; I'm upset because he gave me his word that he was going to keep me informed.

"Are you going to answer the question sometime today?" I asked him because he still wasn't saying anything.

"I been thinking about it, and the truth is that I would like to be involved now because if it is my baby, I'm going to regret not being there from the beginning," he said, and although I wanted the truth, I didn't like his answer.

He just told me that he's been thinking about being there, and it bothered me because he could have said that shit when we first had the conversation about Olivia. When Olivia first claimed to be pregnant by him, he was kicking some shit about not thinking the kid was his, and how he wanted to wait for a DNA test, so I'm confused. So, he must have just said that he didn't think the baby was his because of me. But if he felt the baby was his, he should have just said that because I would have respected him for it. Now, he's sitting here waiting for me to say something, but I didn't want to say anything at this point because I'm sure it was going to come out wrong. After all, I was pissed. Had he been honest, we wouldn't even be having this conversation right now.

"So you asked for the truth, and when I give you the truth, you don't have anything to say?" he asked me.

"It's not that I don't have anything to say. I'm just a little confused about what changed from the time you found out that Olivia was pregnant, and saying that the baby wasn't yours. I honestly believe that you saying she might have been seeing someone else was a lie, and you just said it because you wanted me to stay. I would have respected you more if you owned up to the baby being yours, since you did have unprotected sex, instead of feeding me bullshit."

"Nothing changed. I may have exaggerated a little bit about her being with someone else, but at the time, that's how I felt because she wasn't in a relationship with me. So, she could have very well been seeing someone else. I just felt like I should be there, so that's why I was trying to help her out, like I said. I haven't gone to any of her appointments, but I would like to go because I feel that I should be there if she's saying it's my baby. I'm not saying any of this to hurt you, but I don't want to keep anything about my feelings regarding the situation from you anymore because all it's going to do is bring us right back to this," he said.

I didn't respond to what he just said and decided to walk away from the conversation because I was now in my feelings and needed a minute. I went upstairs and changed into a tee and some shorts before heading back downstairs to cook dinner for us. Although I wasn't feeling him right now, I was hungry. I didn't get to finish my lunch today because he came and showed his ass, so I was going to make something quick to satisfy my growling belly.

When I got back downstairs, Envy was no longer in the living room, and when I saw that he wasn't in the kitchen either, I went to look out the window and saw his car was gone, pissing me off. I took my ass back upstairs, too upset to cook, let alone eat, so I was going to shower and take my ass to bed at six in the evening to avoid his ass when he got back home. Since he practically threatened me to return home, then to leave, I felt I should have left right behind his ass and returned to my mother's house. But then that was going to require an explanation to her about why I was back. I didn't mind talking to my mother because she gave me some good advice the other night, but I was scared that as soon as I let my guard down, she was going to go back to being her. I wanted my mother back in my life, but this time, I wasn't going to rush it, just to be disappointed again.

I woke up the next morning still pissed off, and seeing him in the bed didn't pacify how I was feeling, so I just showered and left for work. When I got to work, I had a bad attitude and wasn't in the mood for anyone's bullshit today, so I just hoped Elle didn't come at me with any.

"Who pissed you off this morning?" I heard, so I turned around, ready to curse whoever it was the hell out, but was stuck when I saw who it was.

I looked up at him, trying to hold my smile in because he is just that damn sexy, but I wasn't trying to entertain his ass either because I wasn't feeling men right about now.

"I'm not pissed off, just tired," I said, still standing there knowing my ass needed to get to my station.

"What can I do to see that smile from yesterday grace your face again?" he asked, causing me to bite down on my bottom lip, trying to hold that smile in.

"I know you trying to hold back, but release that smile because you're too pretty to be walking around with a frown on your face," he complimented me.

"I have to go," I said, trying to walk away, but he grabbed me by my arm.

"Hold up, shorty. Why don't you meet me in the cafeteria at the same time as yesterday?" he said, and as much as I didn't like that "shorty" shit after I told him my name yesterday, I let it slide and agreed to meet him so that he could let me be on my way.

I was having second thoughts by the time my lunch break came around, but Rose talked me into going, saying that it was only lunch, not a date. She convinced me, but I still felt like I was doing something wrong by agreeing to meet up with him. I sucked it up and decided to take my ass and have lunch, and stop acting like I was cheating on Envy.

When I got there, I didn't see him, so I just proceeded to buy my lunch, slightly disappointed that he wasn't there. I was sitting at my table for about ten minutes before I felt his presence behind me, along with that intoxicating cologne that he was wearing.

"Hey, sorry I'm late. Why didn't you wait for me? I wanted to treat you to lunch," Chase said.

"I couldn't wait for you. My lunch break is only an hour, and I had no idea if you were going to show up," I told him, as he sat across from me.

"So, you're not going to get anything to eat?" I asked him.

"Nah, the food isn't all that great. I just came back because you agreed to meet me here," he said, causing me to smile.

"I know it's not that great, but by the time I get in my car to go get something to eat, it's time for me to go back to work. I'm not trying to be nosy, but why were you here at the hospital so early this morning?"

In fact, I was being nosy because I know the only men who are here that early are men whose significant other just delivered a baby. Not that it would have mattered to me one way or the other because I wasn't trying to be with him, but I did want to know because that would tell me a lot about him.

"My brother, Chance, was shot, so I been up here early every morning, and only leaving his side at night. They tried to tell me no visitors until ten, but I wasn't trying to hear that shit," he said, making me feel like shit for even asking.

"So, your mother named you Chase and him, Chance. Are you twins? Oh, my bad. Is he doing all right?" I asked because I didn't want him to think that I was inconsiderate of his brother being shot.

"You good. We aren't twins, so I have no idea why we were named Chase and Chance. But if you want to know, you could ask my mom when you meet her," he said, smiling.

"So, is your brother going to be all right?" I repeated, ignoring what he just said.

"He's going to be good. He's still not out of the woods, but he's stable for right now," he said, with a stressed look now on his face.

"I apologize," I offered with a smile.

“I’m good. I been meaning to apologize to you if I got you into any trouble with your man yesterday.”

I didn’t want to speak about Envy because all it was going to do was put me in a bad mood, but I knew I couldn’t just ignore his question.

“You didn’t get me into any trouble because I’m grown and can talk to whoever I choose,” I said.

“That shit almost sounded believable,” he laughed, causing me to laugh too.

“It’s the truth,” I told him.

“Prove it,” he smirked.

“I’m here with you, aren’t I? So, I think I proved it to you already,” I sassed, with a roll of my eyes.

“Nah, prove it to me outside of your comfort zone,” he said, causing me to squirm because I think I just wrote a check my ass wasn’t ready to cash.

If Envy even knew that I was sitting here with him again, he would kill me, so just think about what he would do if I were seen with Chase outside of work. I knew I shouldn’t have agreed to meet him here because now, I’ve put my foot in my mouth, so backing out now was going to make him think that he was right.

I nervously played around with the salad on my tray, knowing that I didn’t want any more. I was just stalling because I didn’t know what to say, and Chase was waiting for me to answer him.

Chase

Tami was talking a good game, but I was calling her ass out just to see if she was going to back up that tough talk. I knew that she had a man, and the only reason she was sitting here with me was probably because she was mad at his ass right now.

"So, what did you have in mind?" she asked me nervously.

"How about going to get something to eat when you get off because that shit you eating is going to have you hungry like a few minutes after eating it," I told her because all she had on her tray was some peanut butter with apples and a plain-ass salad.

"I guess I could hang out for about an hour because I'm sure you don't want to be away from the hospital for long," she said.

"I don't have to be back within the hour, but if you have a curfew and need to be home within the hour, that's cool," I said to her because I was good with stepping away for a few hours.

"All right, I get off at three, so meet me in the front. That way, you could tell me where we're going so that I could follow you," she said.

"Cool, I'll see you at three," I told her, giving her a friendly hug before going back upstairs to my brother's room.

I took the elevator up to the floor where his room is. When I got there, his annoying-ass baby mother was sitting in the room. I shook my head because I didn't understand why she kept coming up here every day, knowing that as soon as his girl came up to this bitch, it was going to be a problem. I'm starting to think she gets off on pissing off his girl, because how many times did she have to be told that her ass didn't need to be here?

"So, you just going to walk in here like you don't see me sitting here?" she said, rolling her eyes.

"Hey, Trea," I said dryly, not interested in entertaining her today.

My brother exchanged looks because we both were so confused about why her ass was here right now. He didn't have the strength to argue with her, and she knew that shit, so she swished her ass up here every day, being annoying.

"Trea, why are you here? You know that the two of you are not together anymore, and it's only going to cause problems with Adida," I told her because I needed her to help me understand.

"Chance is the father of my daughter, so I'm here making sure he good, and if his girl has a problem with it, oh well . . . I don't understand why everyone has an issue with me being here when he has yet to tell me not to come up here," she spat, twisting her neck and rolling her eyes, being her typical ratchet self.

"Trea, I told you that I was good and that you didn't need to come back up here, but you just keep coming back," Chance said.

"*Really,* Chance?" she yelled.

"Yo, chill with all that loud bullshit like your ass not in the hospital," I barked at her ass.

"Whatever, and fuck me for giving a fuck," she said, pissed off and walking out of the room, and I prayed she was taking her ass home.

"Yo, son, you have the baby mama from hell," I laughed.

"That's why I stopped fucking with her crazy ass. She be on some psycho shit, just showing up like she supposed to be here. She wasn't even talking to a nigga, just sitting there staring at my ass with this sour look on her face. I kept watching the door, wondering where the hell your ass went," he said, and we both laughed because he wasn't lying. She was missing a few marbles.

"I saw shorty I told you about this morning, so I told her that I was going to meet her in the cafeteria. I hope Adida gets here before three because I'm going to hang out with her for a few hours," I told him.

"Why you acting like I'm going to die or some shit? You been up here every day since this shit happened. I'm good, so do you."

"I know, but I'm just here making sure that you good, bro, but trust, I'm not missing hanging out with short, so you don't have to worry about that," I told his ass.

"Well, didn't you say that she had a man?" he asked me.

"Yeah, but she still agreed to hang out with me, so that's her issue, not mine. I'm just trying to chill."

"Yeah, okay," he said, leaving the conversation alone because he knew that I was feeling shorty already.

I sat with him and kicked it until three, and when I got out front, she was standing there looking sexy as hell waiting on a nigga. I know that she said she was going to follow me, but it didn't make sense for us to take both cars because she could leave hers parked, and I could drop her back at the hospital since I was coming back up here.

"Since I have to come back up to the hospital, why don't you just ride with me?" I said, and she gave me that look. "I know that you don't know me from a can of paint, but trust me, shorty, you good. All I want to do is go out, get something to eat, and drop you back off at your car."

"Okay, but I'm letting you know right now, you better not be crazy or some shit because I don't want to have to put hands on you," she joked, but I could tell that she was serious.

I drove to Junior's and when she said she had never been here, I couldn't believe it because you would have to be living under a rock to have never been to Junior's. And not to hear about their banging cheesecake that they are famous for? She should be ashamed to say she's from New York.

Once we sat down, I decided to see what was up with her and get to know her a little better, that is, if she allowed me to. She still looked like she had something weighing heavily on her mind because she was here, but it was like she wasn't here.

"So, do you want to tell me a little bit about yourself?" I asked her.

"I was married, but he cheated on me with my best friend and had a child with her, who happens to be my goddaughter. He also got another female pregnant, who has his son, so we are no longer married. Then my best friend was killed after I forgave her for sleeping with my ex-husband. Her jealous boyfriend murdered her, and then took his own life after taking hers, but he spared my goddaughter. I'm thankful for that, but now, my ex-husband is playing games when it comes to me seeing the child, so I'm not too happy about that.

"Now, my current fiancé also got someone pregnant, who is carrying the child to term. He originally told me that the baby wasn't his, but now he just told me that he wanted to be there for her, just in case the baby is his. I don't know how I feel about it, and I don't know where we stand as far as my marrying him or even continuing a relationship with him." She said this all in one breath, and that was *not* what I expected to hear. Now, her shoulders slumped, like the weight had increased.

"Damn, shorty, you really have nothing to smile about, and I get it now. I'm sorry that you have so much shit going on with you," I said, feeling her pain because that's a lot for any person to be going through.

"You have nothing to be sorry for. I'm sorry for giving you my whole messed-up life story when you don't know me like that. I honestly have no one to talk to anymore, since my best friend is no longer here. Well, let me rephrase that. I have nobody that I feel like sharing it with without being judged and told how I should and shouldn't handle the situation. Anyway, tell me something about you so that I don't feel so awkward about telling my life story," she smiled, but I saw the sadness in her eyes, making me want to reach across the table and hug her.

"I don't think you're ready for my life story, shorty," I told her.

"Trust me, nothing you can say will be anything close to what I just shared, so believe me when I say that I'm ready."

"OK, so I'm not in a relationship anymore, but I do have a 3-year-old daughter, whose mother is the queen of petty. She only allows me to see my daughter if I'm chilling with her ass, so to keep it real, I haven't seen my daughter in a few weeks. I just got tired of playing this game with her because she wants something that I'm no longer willing to give, so I just figured I'd let the courts handle the situation.

"My job is in these streets, and for the past week, I have been beating myself up about being out here in these streets because my lifestyle is the reason my brother almost lost his life. So, Ms. Tami, my life isn't so much better than yours. I definitely know how you feel."

"Well, I hope your brother gets better, and as far as your baby mother goes, I have no advice because I can't even figure out how to get my ex to let me see my goddaughter. At least you could go to court, but I doubt if I have any rights in court," she said sadly.

Chapter Twenty-one

Tami

I wasn't trying to dampen the mood while chilling with Chase, but I felt comfortable with him, so I just decided to put all my cards on the table. I knew that I wasn't trying to be with him on no relationship-type shit, so I think that's what made me feel so comfortable with him. He had a baby mama, and she sounded like trouble. I didn't need any more drama in my life, especially behind a man who I wasn't even trying to make mine. After getting something to eat, Chase got me some cheesecake to take home before taking me back to my car, hugging me and adding that he hoped he could see me at lunch tomorrow. I didn't make any promises, but I did tell him that I would be there at the same time tomorrow if I weren't too busy. My lunch hour constantly changes if things become busy.

I didn't even realize how late it was until I saw the time on the radio when I started my car, so I just hoped that Envy's ass was out in them streets. When I got home, he wasn't home yet, so I was happy about that because I wasn't ready to have a conversation with him, since he didn't hit me up one time today.

I wasn't thinking about fixing anything for dinner because Chase already fed me and sent me home with dessert, so there was no need to even go into the kitchen.

I smiled at the thought of him and didn't feel no kind of way about it because Envy's ass was tripping any-damn-way. I decided to send Chase a text to thank him for today, and yes, I know what you're thinking. I know I shouldn't have exchanged numbers with him, but like I said, Envy was tripping, and it's an innocent friendship that I wanted to explore. After hitting send, I took my ass into the bathroom to shower and get into bed to watch a few of my shows on DVR that I have yet to see, then read my book.

I was sitting up reading when Envy walked into the bedroom, and since it was only a little after ten, I wasn't going to bitch about it. Instead, I just ignored him, continuing to read. I could feel him burning a damn hole through me, probably trying to figure out why I didn't acknowledge his ass. He's the one who left the house and came home like shit was good last night, not even letting me know that he made it back in, so, nope, I wasn't acknowledging his ass.

"So, you still on that bullshit?" he asked, causing me to look around the room, trying to figure out who the hell he was talking to, pissing him off.

"I'm talking to *you,* Tami," he barked, louder than he needed to because he was standing right in front of me.

"I'm not on no bullshit, but it's crazy how you left the house yesterday getting back who knows what time, and now, accusing *me* of being on some bullshit." I rolled my eyes, giving my attention back to my book.

"I left because you asked me a question, and when I gave you an honest answer, it was too much for you, so you bounced, and so did I," he said.

"I left because I was confused about how you went from telling me one thing and then flipping it to be something else. I wouldn't have had a problem had you kept the shit real from the door, but you didn't. Don't tell me you don't think the baby is yours because a bitch is claiming to be pregnant by you, but then switch it up, claiming you want to be there for her," I said, not in the mood to discuss Olivia and her fucking pregnancy again.

If he wants to claim the kid, then by all means do that, but leave me the fuck out of it because I no longer want any part of him and Olivia's unborn child. All I wanted to do was read a little more before calling it a night because I had work in the morning.

"So, you're going to turn your back on me and continue reading?" he asked with an attitude.

"Envy, I don't know what you want from me. You already said what you wanted to do, so do it and leave me out of it. I wasn't there when you made that baby, so I don't need to be there or involved while you and Olivia figure out the shit," I told him, reaching over and turning off the lamp, after giving up on trying to finish reading my book.

I heard him leave the room, slamming the door behind him, and I was tripping because the door didn't do a damn thing to him. It was open when he walked his ass up in here, so he didn't have to slam it. He was just trying to get a reaction out of me, but he wasn't going to get one because, after all, this was his place, so he could do whatever the fuck he wanted to do in his shit. I fluffed my pillow to my liking, closed my eyes, and let my mind take me to a place of peace as I drifted off to sleep.

"Oh shit . . . ohhhh!" I screamed out, thinking that I was dreaming . . . until I opened my eyes to Envy in between my legs.

I was mad at his ass, but I wasn't about to turn down no head, so I grabbed his head and rode his face until I came in his mouth. I started to leave his ass hanging, but I wanted to feel him inside of me, so I assumed the position as he entered me from behind. I figured he was upset with me still because he pounded in and out of me with so much force, the shit turned me on as I came again on his dick. I don't usually like it rough, and I'm not going to lie, when he was pounding in and out of me, my mind drifted to Chase being the one fucking me. I know I was wrong for thinking about another man, but I honestly have no idea why I was consumed with the thought of him.

I screamed out Envy's name, feeling his dick pulsating inside of me as he grabbed my hips, hitting me with deep strokes. He was on the verge of coming, so I backed my ass up, helping him release every drop inside of me before collapsing on the bed, drifting back into a peaceful sleep.

When I woke up the next morning, I didn't even want to get out of bed because I was tired as hell, and I had Envy to thank for waking me up out of my sleep. He was sleeping peacefully, causing me to roll my eyes as I dragged myself out of bed and into the bathroom. Chase invaded my thoughts again, which caused a pep in my step as I showered, then quickly got dressed so that I could be on my way.

As I pulled up to the hospital employee parking lot, my text message alert went off. I figured it was Envy, probably asking me why I didn't wake him up, but it was Chase. A smile graced my face as I read the text message with him saying good morning, and telling me that he wasn't at the hospital yet, but he hoped to see me later. I texted him back before going inside, letting him know that if I had the same lunch break as yesterday, I would see him later. I have no idea why I was entertaining the thought of him when I knew that it wasn't going to happen. I may be a lot of things, but I wasn't going to see him in *that* way, since I was with Envy and still wearing his ring. I think it had more to do with the attention that I was receiving from him, something that I was missing.

I have yet to feel like I was the only one when it came to my relationships because it was always Tara when I was with Siah, and now, it's Olivia since I've been with Envy. Having Chase's attention all to myself felt good.

Chase

Tami and I have been chilling for the past two weeks, and although I was starting to feel something for her, I knew that I shouldn't. I feel like she put me in the friend zone. Honestly, feeling something for her was going to do nothing but fuck with my feelings. I didn't want to be in the friend zone, but if it meant spending time with her, I would just have to rock with it for now. My daughter's mother let me get her this weekend, after promising that we would do something together with the baby next week, but I was lying. I just wanted my daughter because Tami had her goddaughter, and we were meeting up to take them to the park. The park was out of my comfort zone, since I'm in these streets, and I never know who the hell is gunning for my ass, but I agreed just to see her again. When I pulled up to the park, I saw her with the prettiest little girl near the swings, so I pulled into the spot next to her car. After getting Gaby out of her car seat, we walked over to them.

"Hey, who is this pretty little girl?" she asked, admiring Gaby.

"This is my daughter, Gaby, and who is this you got with you?" I said, indicating the shy goddaughter who was hiding behind her leg.

"This is Phoenix. She's a bit shy, so it's going to take her a few minutes to warm up to you and Gaby," she said, picking her up and putting her in the swing as I did the same with Gaby.

We hung out in the park for about thirty minutes before taking the kids to get some ice cream, then going our separate ways, but not before I got her to agree to let me take her out tonight. She was taking Phoenix back to her grandmother, and I was taking Gaby home, so she agreed to go out to get something to eat. She didn't want me to pick her up at her crib, which was understandable, so she gave me her mom's address. I was going to pick her up over there.

The tapping on my window had me ready to reach for my .380 . . . until I saw it was Tami, and the crazy shit about it was I didn't even see her coming out of the house. I was reaching for my phone to call her and let her know I was out front, but that's still no excuse. My ass was slipping, and I needed to get my head back in the game, especially after my brother got caught slipping.

"Hey, I didn't even see you leave the house," I said to her as soon as she got in the car.

"Really? Well, I saw when you pulled up, so I saved you the trouble of getting out of the car or calling me to tell me that you were here," she smiled.

"Thank you. Now, where would you like to go?" I asked her.

"So you invite me out, but you have nothing planned?" she said, giving me the side eye.

"I invited you to dinner, but let's keep in mind that the little time that I've gotten to know you, I know that you're picky as hell. So, again, where would *you* like to go?" I laughed at the face she was making, like what I said wasn't true.

"There's a spot near the Williamsburg Bridge where we could get something to eat and drink. It's more of a lounge, but I love the food and drinks there, if you don't mind trying it out," she said, and I knew exactly the place she was speaking of.

"Cool, we could do that. I know the place you're talking about," I said, pulling out en route to Lenny's Bar and Grill.

We were chilling, enjoying the food, drinks, and conversation until I saw my baby mama and her sidekick walk in, causing me to take a deep breath.

"What's wrong?" Tami asked me, and before I could even answer her, they walked over and were now standing at our table.

"So, is *this* bitch the reason why you couldn't keep your daughter for the whole weekend?" she asked me, while looking at Tami with a disgusted look on her face.

"Meeka, move around with that bullshit," I barked. I was pissed the hell off that she would even come over here with that bullshit, knowing that I didn't play that disrespectful shit. I respected the fact that Tami sat back and let me handle that shit like the lady that she was, but I could tell that she was pissed too.

"No, nigga, I asked you a fucking question, so no, I won't be moving around until you answer my question," she said, getting in my face like I wouldn't knock off her fucking head.

"Trea, you need to get your fucking sister the fuck up out of my face," I said to her.

I swear my brother and I had to be on crack, fucking with these two fucking sisters and having kids with their asses.

"Nah, I'm waiting to hear why the fuck you're here with this bitch when you always blanking when she doesn't let you see Gaby. She finally let you see her, and you dropped her back a whole day early to spend time with a bitch," she barked with her hand on her hip.

"I'm not about to be too many more bitches, so I'm going to need both of you to focus on Chase because I didn't have a baby with either of you," Tami spoke, unable to ignore them any longer.

I knew that they were trying to get a rise out of her, and I think she knew it too, and that's the reason she wasn't trying to give them the satisfaction. By her being quiet, they must have thought she was a punk, but I knew better. I could see it in her eyes, but clearly, they missed it.

"It doesn't matter if you had a baby with us or not because you're the bit—" Trea attempted, but Tami punched her in the mouth before she could finish her sentence.

Trea tried to grab Tami, but she didn't have a chance because Tami caught her in the face, punching like she was at the gym, hitting a punching bag. Meeka jumped across the table to assist her sister, but Tami was handling them both, and as much as I wanted it to continue, I knew she didn't sign up for this shit, so I grabbed Meeka. She was calling me all kinds of bitches, then grabbed the drink off the table and threw it at Tami, catching her with it on the side of her face. Finally, two dudes came over to help me because it was out of control by this time. The glass didn't faze Tami, as she was still fucking up Trea. I put Tami in a bear hug and carried her outside, kicking and screaming. Once out of the lounge, I let her go, and she started pacing back and forth, trying to calm herself down.

"I need you to go back inside to get my phone and my bag," she said calmly, but still heaving heavily.

I didn't want her to go back inside because I already knew that it would start all over again, so I told her to get in the car. After that, I walked back inside and didn't see Trea or Meeka, so I assumed that they were in the bathroom. I grabbed Tami's phone and bag and stepped outside. When I got there, I saw a black car pulling up with tires screeching before coming to a stop with Meeka's cousin, Zha, jumping out with three other bitches with her. *So, they called backup because they couldn't handle one female with their wack asses?* I thought, smirking.

"Zha, go on because it's not even about to go down," I told her ass. I didn't have a problem hitting a bitch. If they thought they were going to jump Tami because she handled them bitches, they had me fucked up.

Meeka's family was known for that jumping shit, and I wasn't about to let them because it was a fair fight on Tami's part. So, what Zha needed to do was go inside, get her cousins, and take them the fuck home. I didn't feel sorry for any of them. They always talking shit but can never back that shit up unless they jump someone, and besides, Meeka shouldn't have had her ass out here anyway. Sweating me about dropping my daughter off at home, but she had her ass in the streets like she didn't have a fucking daughter, who was just dropped off at home.

Chapter Twenty-two

Tami

I sat in the car, pissed that those bitches tried to jump me when I heard tires screeching as this car came to a stop with four girls jumping out. I watched as Chase talked to one of them, but she wasn't trying to hear him as his baby mother and her sister emerged from the lounge. They were trying to come for me, but he was holding them back. So much yelling was going on, and just as I thought about getting out of the car, I saw Chase reach into his waist, pulling out his gun, and causing all of them to fall back. His baby mother screamed at him about pulling a gun on her, telling him that he was never going to see his daughter again. He walked to the car, got in, pulled off, and I'm not going to lie. I was a little shaken by the whole ordeal. I didn't know hanging out with him was going to cause all this drama. I thought back to when I mentioned the lounge, and he seemed hesitant, so maybe he knew she would be there.

He didn't say anything, and I could tell that he was trying to calm himself as he handed me my phone and bag, but he kept driving, offering no words, so I spoke.

"You didn't tell me you had a ghetto-ass baby mama," I said, looking at him.

"And you didn't tell me that you had hands, and I hope you got those bitches registered," he joked.

"No, my hands aren't registered. I didn't knock no one out. I just beat the brakes off those bitches. I can't believe they called for backup on little ole me," I said.

"That's just how they do, always starting shit and can never back up all the shit they talk. Instead of taking that ass whooping like they deserved, they called their cousins to handle it. A typical bird move, but I had your back."

I didn't get a chance to respond because my cell started ringing, and I decided to let it go to voicemail because it was Envy.

"Why you send dude to voicemail?" he asked, looking at me.

"I'm in the car with you, so it would be rude to take his call," I said, turning my head toward the window, sighing.

Envy and I haven't been on good terms because I wasn't honest with him when I told him to do what he needed to do regarding Olivia and the baby she was carrying.

The truth of the matter is, it hurt me every time he went to one of Olivia's medical appointments, because that child should have been mine. I feel like a champion who always wins the fight, but never takes home the prize because of these trifling-ass tricks that these niggas keep falling victim to. I know it wasn't fair to blame them, but that's just how the fuck I felt, and although I love Envy, I don't think that I'm going to be able to do this with him. I felt like I needed to walk away from the relationship and return his ring because I wasn't about to be stuck in another marriage where I was the chosen one, but not the one to carry my husband's firstborn child.

"Are you all right?" Chase asked, as I wiped at the tears that fell at the thought of no longer being with Envy.

"I'm good," was all I said to him.

He pulled into a long driveway, causing me to look at him for an explanation as he parked the car and turned off the engine.

"This is my crib. We're just going to chill for a while, and then I'll take you back to your car," he said, telling me and not asking if that was okay with me.

His home was beautiful, and I was impressed because it looked like some lavish home that you only get to admire in a magazine. It was one of those homes that belonged to celebrities, so I was taking it all in before he took me by the hand, leading me to the living room. Envy and Mason's places were impressive too, but this nigga here had their places looking like an apartment that could fit inside of his home.

"I love your home," I said, sitting.

"Thanks, and if you're good, maybe I'll give you a tour," he winked.

Something about him had me mesmerized as I just sat stealing glances at him as he stood to put on some music.

"So, what do you want to eat? I don't know about you, but a nigga starving," he said, rubbing his stomach.

"What did you have in mind because I can eat since I worked up an appetite fighting off your baby mama and her sister," I laughed.

"So, I better whip up something good because that was a hell of a workout you had," he joked before telling me that he would be right back.

He came back downstairs wearing sweats and a beater, showing his tatted muscles, and his sexy ass couldn't be denied. I understood why his baby mama would be tripping. She had to be mad that she fucked that up and was no longer getting dicked down by his fine ass. I would have been feeling the same way too, if I weren't waking up to his ass anymore.

I sat back on the sofa singing K. Michelle's new song that just came on the radio, bopping my head and snapping my fingers, not even noticing him watching me until I looked up.

"Don't stop, you have a nice voice," he complimented.

"Thank you," I offered shyly.

He walked me into the kitchen and whipped up some burgers and onion rings, and my ass enjoyed every damn bite. As promised, he drove me back to my car, hugging me good night, telling me to give him a call to let him know that I made it home safely after I told him that I wasn't going to stay at my mom's house. When I got home, Envy was sitting in the living room with a pissed look on his face, and trust, if that look could kill, I would be dead right now.

"What's going on with you?" he asked me.

I thought about whether I should be honest with him or say nothing like I've been doing, but did I really want to continue having animosity between us, or should I get on my grown-woman shit and just say what's bothering me?

"Talk to me, Tami," he said, with a stressed look on his face.

"What do you want me to say, Envy?"

"I want you to tell me what the hell is going on with us because I feel like you're pushing me away," he expressed.

"How do you figure I'm doing that, Envy?"

"For starters, you've been going out every weekend, not giving me the time of day anymore, and when I call you while you're out, you always send me to voicemail. You never did that shit unless you were mad at me, so again . . . What's up? You not fucking with Sami like that anymore, so who has your attention these days?" he said, and I could tell that he was getting angry.

Tears fell from my eyes before I even said what it was I needed to say because I wasn't ready. I knew that I was going to have a conversation with him, but I didn't think that it would be tonight. I went to join him on the sofa, and that's when he frowned at me, and his jaw tightened, leaving me confused.

"What nigga was you with tonight?" he asked, his fist balled up, scaring the shit out of me. "Is it the same nigga I saw you with, and don't lie because I smell that nigga on you," he barked.

I was fucked because he wasn't lying. I smelled it on me too as soon as I got into my car. It was from the hug that Chase gave me before saying good night to me. I didn't know if I wanted to be honest about the situation or lie my way out of it and deal with it another day. I've been through so much shit lately, and I must admit that since I started kicking it with Chase, I have had something to smile about, and that's the same feeling I had when I met Envy. I know that it was my fault that he entertained Olivia, but I just felt that he should have been more patient with me if he was feeling me like he claimed. Had he just waited, he would not have fucked the first bitch who threw the pussy at him, and that bothered me. It bothered me so much because if he was going to take the pussy, why didn't he think enough of me to wear a condom? I told him that I needed time, and since he didn't take heed to that, I feel like he's going to hurt me again. I know it sounds like I'm making excuses or looking for a reason to be with Chase, but I wasn't.

Envy

I called Tami after I finished handling some business, but she sent me to voicemail, pissing me off because I called her three times with the same result. I don't know what was going on with her, but I didn't like it because I felt she was pushing me away. So I waited for her to get home to let me know what the hell was going on. She walked in around eleven o'clock, and I was pissed because she came up in here smelling like another nigga . . . a nigga that wasn't me. I asked her who the nigga was, and she was just sitting there playing with her damn fingers, like she was nervous or some shit.

"Who the fuck is he, Tami?" I barked, ready to fuck up some shit.

"I don't want to talk about that, but I will talk about what the problem is," she said, waiting for me to respond, but I didn't. I just let her continue.

"When I told you that you could do whatever it was that you needed to do concerning Olivia, I wasn't completely honest with you. I hate the fact that you're going to doctor appointments and being in her presence, period. I just got out of a marriage dealing with the same shit, and I don't feel I can handle what comes with dealing with another woman and a child who isn't mine," she said.

"Okay, Tami, so what are you *not* saying because we had this conversation, and you're saying the same shit you said before. So, I'm confused right now," I told her.

"Envy, I'm saying that I'm not going to marry you, and I don't want to be in the relationship anymore," she said, letting her tears fall, but I didn't give a fuck about her tears.

"So, you spent every fucking day with that cheating-ass ex-husband of yours, who kept doing you dirty, but you stayed. And now, you telling me you want to leave a nigga for some shit that I did when we weren't kicking it like that because you took your ass back to him again? I'm a good man, and I've done nothing since we made our relationship official besides try to do the right thing about the mistake I made, and *this* is how you do me? Would you rather I just say fuck her and the baby? Is *that* what you're saying?" I asked her ass.

"That's not what I'm saying, Envy. I'm saying I can't do it, but by all means, do what you need to do, like you been doing," she said, removing the ring from her finger.

I wasn't about to sit here and beg her not to go once she removed her ring. Her decision hurt me because I love her, but she just crushed my heart, which is why I never gave it to anyone before. She sat there crying when I should have been the one crying, since she was the one leaving me. I felt like whatever nigga she was seeing helped her with her decision because a month ago, she was good with the relationship, and that's why she accepted my ring.

I got up and went upstairs to the bedroom because there was nothing left for me to say, so I left her with her thoughts. When I got up the next morning, she was gone. I looked in the closet, and most of her things were gone too, causing my chest to tighten. I frantically checked all her drawers, and they were all empty. I went downstairs, praying that she hadn't left yet, but she was gone. She left me a damn Dear John letter on the table, so I picked it up to read.

Envy, if you're reading this letter, you know that I left and took all of my things with me, but I just wanted to tell you that I love you and will always love you. I have to love myself this time around because, in the end, I know that I will be the one left with a broken heart. I wish you nothing but the best, and I'm sorry that things had to end this way. Tami.

I crushed the letter and threw it across the room as angry tears surfaced because I was pissed at myself for falling in love. Just like that paper I just threw across the room, I was crushed. I picked up the phone because I needed to talk to her to tell her that this isn't what I want, and that we could make it work. I just needed her to understand that I was willing to do whatever for her just to come back home, even if that meant leaving Olivia alone altogether, because Tami was more important to me. She let the phone go to voicemail, but I was on some stalker shit as I dialed her phone repeatedly until the voicemail informed me that her inbox was full. I threw down my phone, feeling defeated, and thinking about where she could have gone so that I could tell her how much I loved her and didn't want to lose her. I needed to convince her that I could make this right if she just gave me the chance to prove it to her, but I had no idea where she ended up going. I called my nigga, Mason, and asked him to ask Sami if Tami gave her a call, but she said that she hasn't spoken to her. Feeling defeated once again, I let it go.

It had been two months since the breakup between Tami and me, so I was knee-deep into the new business venture that Mason and I had opened. Tonight was the grand opening. We were stuck on what kind of business we wanted to open because niggas in the hood were always opening a club or a strip joint, so we wanted to do something different. After peeping what the Bronx *didn't* have, we decided to open a lounge with two floors. On the top floor was a game room with a bar. On the lower level, music, food, and drinks with flat-screen televisions throughout the lounge. I loved the game room because it was also a lounge area where you could play pool, shoot darts, and enjoy a variety of arcade games. We named the lounge Flex Zone. We were proud to be business owners, but it was a bittersweet moment for me. I wished that I had Tami here with me so we could share this day together. I swear, not a day went by that I didn't think about her, looking for excuses to call her.

I wanted Sami to invite her to the grand opening, but she informed me that Tami was seeing someone. It hurt me that she moved on so fast after breaking my heart.

I was en route to pick up Olivia because she had an appointment this afternoon, so I tried to focus on that and the fact that I needed to meet Mason at the lounge to get things situated for the opening. We were going to be open on Fridays and Saturdays every weekend, so that the opening will include both days this weekend, with door prizes and the winner of the raffle. I knew it was going to be lit because we had an ad run on HOT 97 for the entire month. Based on that ad alone, we should have a large turnout. The appointment went well. Olivia found out that she was having a little boy, and I felt bad that I didn't share her excitement because I was blaming her for the reason I no longer had Tami in my life.

Chapter Twenty-three

Tami

I was feeling a little uncomfortable as I sat in the living room waiting for Chase to finish getting ready because we were going to Flex Zone. I have no idea if he knew that Envy owned that lounge because all he had been talking about was going to the grand opening for weeks, and I still hadn't built up the nerve to tell him. It shouldn't matter because Envy and I were no longer together, but he might feel a way about it. I already gave Sami a heads-up that we would be there, and she said it should be all right because, after all, it's a business open to the public. She felt that as long as Chase and his boys were coming to have a good time, it shouldn't be a problem, and I agreed with her.

When we walked into the lounge, "Do You Mind" was playing by DJ Khaled, and I was feeling the vibe and very proud of Mason and Envy. The guys headed up to the game room, leaving Adida and me downstairs, which I was fine with because I didn't see Envy on the lower level. I thought he had to be on the second level. I sent Sami a text message asking her if she was here yet because I was sitting across from the bar on the lower level and didn't see her ass either. The lounge was crowded, and everyone seemed to be enjoying themselves, which was a good sign. I noticed that Envy and Mason had heavy security, so I wasn't worried about anything jumping off.

"Hey, girl," Sami sang in my ear, hugging me around my neck. I could tell that she already had a few drinks and was enjoying herself, and I was ready to join her and have a good time as well.

"Sami, this is Adida. Adida, this is a good friend of mine," I introduced them.

"Nice to meet you," Adida said to her.

"Nice to meet you too," Sami said before getting all up in my personal space with her drunk ass. "So, where is the new boo?" she asked, looking around.

"He went upstairs to check out the game room," I told her, and in return, I wanted to ask about Envy, but I didn't. I kept trying to tell myself that I made the right decision, but my heart still yearned daily for him. I led everyone to believe that I was in a relationship with Chase, but it wasn't like that. We were just two friends who hung out. He knew that I wasn't ready to be in another relationship, so we were just chilling. He suggested I stay with him, but I told him that I wasn't doing that again, so I stayed with my mother for about a month after leaving Envy. Now, I have my own place in Queens that Chase helped me with by paying my first month's rent, security, and furnishing it because he refused to take no for an answer, so I let him do it.

"So, you're not going to go upstairs and check out the game room, girl? Envy and Mason did the damn thing. Come on, you mad wack if you trying to just sit in the cut," she said, pulling me up out of my seat and telling Adida to come as well.

Adida was cool people, and although I was kind of skeptical about meeting new friends, she seemed nice enough. I met her a couple of weeks back when Chance was finally released from the hospital. She said she's been waiting to meet me, which made me realize that Chase was speaking very highly of me. We got to talking, and she was cool as hell and praised me for beating the brakes off Meeka and Trea's asses because she said they be fucking with her every chance that they got. She said she never had to put hands on them because Chance always saved the ho, and not because he still had feelings for Trea, but because he didn't want Adida fighting. I tried to sit back and let Chase handle his business that day, but the bitch got out of pocket with me, so they both got served, and I have no problem serving them again.

When we got upstairs to the game room, I was once again impressed, and Sami wasn't lying. They did the damn thing, and I was feeling the disco lights that bounced off the walls. Adida and I walked over to the bar because Chase and Chance were playing on one of the pool tables, so we decided to get a drink. I ordered Bacardí Limón on ice, and Adida ordered Hennessy and Coke. I looked at her like she was crazy because I wasn't trying to get fucked up off no dark liquor. I knew that my limit was two drinks and two drinks only on light liquor, but fucking with dark liquor, my limit was not to fuck with it at all because it always had me done. I couldn't help but wonder where the hell Envy was since this was his grand opening. I figured that he would be around, but nope, I didn't see him or Mason.

"Sami, where is Mason?" I asked her, trying to whisper.

"Bitch, don't even try it because if you wanted to know where Envy's ass was, all you had to do was ask. You know good and well your ass couldn't care less where my nigga at," she said, pulling my card, being extra loud, and causing me to shake my head at her ass.

"Whatever. Nobody's thinking about Envy's ass," I mumbled . . . as he suddenly appeared out of nowhere, with me hoping that he didn't hear me.

"How are you, ladies?" he asked, looking at me, causing my heart to skip a few beats.

Adida was staring at Envy with lust-filled eyes, and I swear I saw some drool on her bottom lip from how hard her ass was staring. I know that we are no longer together, but her ass better put her eyes back in her head and go find her man before I beat the brakes off her ass too. I gave her a look, and she caught that shit quickly as she sat back and sipped on her drink, leaving Sami laughing and shaking her head at me. Envy's ass even had a smirk on his face, and now, I was embarrassed at how I just acted, so I took a sip from my drink and tried to refocus for a second.

"I didn't think you would be here tonight," he said to me.

"I didn't think that I would be here tonight either, but I got invited by a few of my friends. I also want to say how proud I am of you, and I love the place," I told him.

"Thank you. I really appreciate that, coming from you. How have you been?" he asked me.

"I've been good, just working, and I finally have my own place, so I feel good about that," I said, causing him to stare at me intensely.

"What?" I smiled up at him, but he didn't get a chance to respond because Chase and Chance walked over.

Envy winked at me and walked off, and I was cursing under my breath that Chase walked his ass over here at the wrong damn time. I wanted to go after Envy, but I knew that it wouldn't have been smart since I came here with Chase, so I wasn't trying to be disrespectful.

"Drinks on Chance because I busted his ass in pool, so drink up," Chase said, sitting beside me as I sat and watched Envy, who was watching me before a waitress said something to him, and he walked away.

"Did you know that this was my ex's place of business before you invited me here?" I asked him.

"Nah, shorty, I didn't know, and I still didn't know until you just said something. What's up? Is there a problem with us being here?" He turned, looking in my face for my reaction.

"No problem. I was just wondering if you knew," I said.

"You knew when I invited you, so why didn't you say anything?"

"I didn't think it was a big deal, and I was only asking you now because I was curious if you knew, that's all," I said, now thinking that I just should have left well enough alone because it was sounding as if I still cared for Envy.

"Girl, let's have some fun because I know you didn't come here just to sit down all night," Sami's intoxicated ass whined.

I looked at Chase to see if he was going to have a problem with it since I came with him, but he told me to go ahead, so I grabbed Adida by the hand and the three of us bounced to the arcade. I sat in one of the racing car game chairs and just watched Envy do his thing. I couldn't help but admire how good he looked in his slacks and button-up, causing some moisture between my legs. Seeing him tonight made me regret my decision to leave him because I still loved him, and I know it was written all over my face. I instantly caught an attitude as I watched some female all up in his face and whispering in his ear, causing him to smile. Our eyes met briefly, and even in the dimly lit room, I could see him wink at me again before walking off, with the female trailing behind him, and I swear, I felt like crying.

I sucked my teeth as I saw Meeka and her flunkies enter the game room, and I just prayed that they didn't start no shit because I didn't want to be the blame or cause of Envy and Mason's opening night being ruined. Since I spotted them before they spotted us, I told Adida and Sami to follow me and see what was popping on the lower level. We made it as far as the entrance of the game room . . . before loudmouthed Trea started calling Adida out of her name.

I convinced Adida to keep walking and ignore Trea, but Trea hit a nerve when she said that she was with Chance last night.

"Bitch, my nigga wouldn't dare touch your ho ass again," Adida spat.

"That's what his mouth says. Ask him what his tongue says," she said, and they all laughed.

"Adida, let's just go because it's not even worth sitting here arguing with her, when you know that your man is at home with you every night," I tried to reason with her.

"Bitch, please, it may not be worth it, but you can ask Chase what that tongue do too because it was all up in my sister last night," Trea said, trying to get a rise out of me, but I wasn't going there with her.

I already beat both of those bitches' asses, so I wasn't about to do that shit again because I was above the bullshit she was kicking. Whatever Chase did with his tongue was no concern or issue of mine because we were just friends, so she could keep it pushing with that bullshit. I know from experience that if they were still getting the dick, they would have no reason to be upset or be trying to fight the females who are holding that man's attention.

I took Adida by her hand and used my other hand to pull Sami's drunk ass with us, so that we could separate from the hood squad. I didn't want anything going down. Suddenly, I felt someone pull my hair, causing my neck to jerk back, and when I turned around, it was that dyke-looking bitch, Zha. I should have known it wasn't Trea or Meeka because they didn't want it again. I let go of Adida and Sami and punched her in her fucking mouth, and then it was on and popping from there. I didn't give a fuck that she was a big bitch and that I weighed half of what she weighed, but I was giving it as good as she was throwing them. It turned out to be an all-out brawl because Adida and Sami were both throwing hands, but I couldn't concentrate on that because this bitch just flipped my ass on the floor and tried to go ham on my face. I took my fingers and tried to dig out her fucking eyeballs because I'll be damned if she was going to fuck up my face.

Security came to intervene, and I was thanking God that they pulled her big fucking ass up off me, but I was pissed the fuck off because this is *not* what I wanted to be doing. I fucking left Envy alone because I didn't want to deal with baby mama drama, but here I was dealing with a baby mama—when I wasn't even fucking the baby daddy.

When Envy walked over, I couldn't even look him in the face, so I just let Sami explain what went down as I left. Chase and Chance's asses still didn't know what happened because they were missing in action right now, so I called an Uber and took my ass home, promising myself that I was so done.

Chase was blowing up my phone, but I didn't want to speak to his ass because, like I said, I was too pissed, and I wasn't going to stop being pissed tonight, so he could stop calling my phone. I hit Sami and Adida up to make sure that they were good because I didn't stick around once security got involved. Adida said that they were still outside the lounge, and things were still popping off, with Chase slapping the fire out of Zha. Trust me when I say I don't promote no man putting his hands on no female, but that manly bitch probably needed that shit. I told her that I was just checking to make sure that she was good before ending the call, not even asking about Chase's ass.

I'd just finished my shower and was in my bed because my neck was killing me from that bitch banging my head on the floor. I suddenly heard someone knocking on my door, and I got pissed, already knowing who the hell it was. No one knew where I stayed but Chase, so I knew it was his ass and since he showed up unannounced, he was about to get this verbal ass kicking that I was saving for another day. However, when I opened the door, I was shocked to see Envy standing there, and I wondered how he knew where I lived because I hadn't told anyone but my mother. Now, where would he have seen her even to ask her?

"Are you going to let me in or continue being rude by just staring at me?" he asked, with a smirk on his face at the confused look on mine.

"How did you know where I live?" I asked him.

He walked in and looked around my place like I had invited him over for a tour, ignoring my question as he finally made himself comfortable on my couch. He didn't know it, but he was minutes from getting cursed out because I could see he wanted to play games.

"Envy, if you're not going to tell me how you knew where I lived, can you tell me why you're here?" I questioned, getting agitated. I missed him like crazy, but I wasn't about to let him know that, but I think he knew already. That's why he was ignoring me, acting like I wasn't happy to see him. I watched as he pulled a bottle from his back pocket, and when I saw that it was a bottle of Hennessy XO Cognac, all I could do was shake my head at his ass.

"So, you robbed your bar?" I asked, still shaking my damn head.

"You can't rob something that belongs to you. Come have a drink with me and talk about what went down tonight," he said, now with a serious look on his face.

I didn't want to talk about what happened at his grand opening because I already knew what he was going to say, and I wasn't ready to hear the truth. I decided to buy myself some time by getting two glasses. I went into the kitchen, but instead of getting the glasses right away, I leaned up against the counter, taking a deep breath and asking the good Lord to give me the strength to deal with Envy's ass.

"Bring that ass, Tami," I heard him say from the living room, causing me to suck my teeth as I grabbed two shot glasses.

When I returned, he was cracking open the bottle, so I set the glasses down on the table and took a seat across from him. He looked at me because, yes, I was treating him like he had the cooties, but I didn't care. I didn't want to be too close to his ass because the way my hormones were set up . . . distance was good.

"So, the reason I showed up on your doorstep unannounced is because you left, so I didn't know if you were good or not. Also, I wanted to know what the hell happened tonight with you and those girls," he said, handing me my shot that I chugged before answering his question.

"Well, thank you for caring enough to find me to make sure that I'm good, and I'll be the first to apologize for what went down tonight. Chase's baby mother and her sister decided that they wanted to fuck with us, and we did attempt to walk away, but the girl that I was fighting pulled me by my hair, so I had no choice but to defend myself," I told him, keeping it short. I took the bottle and poured my next shot, knowing that it needed to be my last.

I swear, if I didn't see him open the bottle, I would have sworn he put something in my drink because I was feeling something I couldn't explain. I was imagining myself sitting on his lap with him entering me as I held on to his ears, riding him for dear life.

"Tami," he called out, causing me to look at him strangely because this liquor had me bugging, and the smirk on his face told me that he knew that it would. "I'm going to need you to focus because I need you to explain to me how you go from saying you weren't willing to deal with a baby mother, which we don't know if I even have one yet, to fighting a baby mother."

"I already explained to you that she started the shit, so I was only trying to defend myself, and trust me when I say that I will not be dealing with his baby mother anymore," I told him, feeling light-headed as I put my head back against the couch.

"And why is that?" he questioned, with a look on his face like he didn't believe me.

"Because he's not my man, and I'm not going to keep dealing with her because she thinks that he is. After the first encounter with her, I told him to handle it, and obviously, he didn't, so I don't even know if I want to continue being friends with him," I stressed.

"So, now that you see the grass isn't greener on the other side, you need to bring your ass back home and stop playing with a nigga," he said, but I didn't think the grass was greener. I was just tired of bullshit.

"Why would I do that when the reason I left hasn't changed?" I lifted my head to look at him.

"You acting like I was sleeping with her again. All a nigga was trying to do was the right thing because if she were my sister or my mother, I would want a nigga to step up and handle his business like a man. I explained that to you, and instead of you being proud that you had a man who wasn't willing to be a deadbeat, you left me. That shit doesn't make any sense to me, and then you get caught up in this situation that's causing you to fight every time you run into this chick. And trust, that's a situation that isn't going to change." He looked at me, daring me to challenge what he just said.

I knew what he was saying had some truth to it, but I honestly didn't want to hear it because I didn't think he should be comparing the two. I didn't feel like talking anymore because the liquor had me wanting to fuck, so I was going to need him to shut up and come give me some dick because I haven't had any since his ass.

Chapter Twenty-four

Chase

I swear, I tried to break Meeka's fucking neck when I found out what the fuck she did last night, and I was mad that I wasn't there. Chance and I stepped out to smoke in his truck, and when we got back inside, Adida told us what had popped off. After hearing that, I went looking for Tami, but she was gone, and I was pissed.

Meeka's dumb fucking ass had the nerve to try to flex on a nigga, so I dragged that bitch outside, kicking and screaming, as she yelled for her ratchet-ass family to help her. I told all those dumb bitches if one of them jumped, I was going to lay every one of them the fuck out, and I meant the shit. My brother was trying to get me to chill when he saw that her eyes were rolling to the back of her head, but I didn't care. I told that bitch to stop lying on my fucking dick. She knows I hadn't touched her stank-ass pussy in months. Yeah, I let the bitch suck my dick, but that was the extent of it, and she knows why. I swear, if Chance didn't pull me off that bitch, I would have killed her, and at that moment, I didn't have two fucks to give.

I got into my ride and called Tami repeatedly, but she just kept sending my calls to voicemail. It was kind of pissing me off because I felt she shouldn't blame me for that stupid bitch's actions. I decided to just go by her crib and try to talk to her, but I saw that fuck nigga's car parked out front, so I just bounced, even more pissed off.

I've been in the crib all day chilling and smoking, trying to get my head straight before heading out to handle some business. Afterward, I was going to go back to Tami's crib to see what was up. I heard the knock at my door and knew it was my brother because I was waiting on his ass to come pick me up so we could ride out together. I let him in, and he still looked pissed about what happened last night, so I just said what's up to my cuz, Rich, and left Chance's ass sulking like a little bitch. Rich and my cousin, Jamar, have been here for about a month. They came from out of town to help us with some fuck niggas who needed to be dealt with, but don't get shit twisted. I had hittas for these niggas, but I enlisted niggas who I trust for this business.

"Why you still sitting over there acting like a bitch, Chance?" I said, sick of the silent treatment he was giving me when we needed to discuss this business.

"Why the fuck I got to be a bitch because I'm pissed about your ass being reckless. You pissed off about a bitch, who didn't even let you smell the panties, then bounced on your dumb ass. You could have killed Meeka last night in front of a million fucking witnesses because of some pussy. So, that shit makes you more of a bitch than me, so miss me with that shit, my nigga," he spat.

"First off, I said *acting* like a bitch, and trust me, nigga, I wasn't mad at that bitch for being the reason shorty left. I was mad at that bitch for lying on my fucking dick to every fucking female that I meet, so, yeah, I was going to dead that bitch and deal with the consequences," I said, not giving a fuck, causing him to shake his head.

"You sound mad fucking stupid right now, my nigga, because you supposed to have your head in the game, handling these niggas who shot me. But instead, you beefing with bitches. That's why those niggas felt that they could come for my ass because they know you out here being a bitch in these streets," he barked.

"What the fuck you say, my nigga? Say that shit again to my face, and I promise you, your ass will be back in the fucking hospital. Then you could tell me how much of a bitch I am," I said, as I had his ass yoked up.

"You niggas bugging the fuck out, and I didn't come up here guns blazing to watch both of you acting like fucking bitches," Rich said, laughing. Rich wasn't new to this because Chance and I were always going at each other, and he knew that I wasn't going to hurt my brother, but I *would* fuck up his ass.

"Keep talking that slick shit," I told Chance, letting him go.

"Fuck you, and if you done playing my daddy, let's go so we can handle these niggas," he said, fixing his tee that I pulled out of shape.

We all hopped into the car and drove across town. Usually, we wouldn't handle business in the daytime because of witnesses, but I wanted those bitches to know I didn't give a fuck about nothing when it comes to fucking with my family. I know that I was about to fuck up Chance, but I could do that because he's my brother. However, I'll be damned if I let a nigga try to take him out and live to tell about it.

We got word that this nigga was chilling at some bitch's house, so we parked directly behind the bitch's crib and hopped the fence, causing a dog no bigger than a cat to start barking like he was a protect dog or some shit. Rich kicked his little ass so hard that it sent him running off, crying, causing us to bust out laughing at his crazy ass.

Rich knocked the hinges off the door, busting that shit open, and we walked in, guns pointed, ready to shoot first and ask questions later. We walked into the living room and caught a glimpse of the female trying to run, but she didn't get too far because her protruding belly wouldn't allow her to move any faster. I put my finger to my mouth, telling the bitch to be quiet as I signaled for Chance and Rich to check upstairs. We ran up in there through the kitchen, and no one was there. She was the only one downstairs, so if his punk ass was here, he had to be hiding upstairs.

I heard gunshots ring out, causing me to tell that bitch not to move as I took two steps at a time, trying to get up the stairs. When I reached the top of the stairs, I saw that nigga, Messiah, laid out, leaking from being shot in the chest. I sent Rich downstairs to make sure that bitch didn't try to run as I popped his ass twice in the head, making sure that his ass was dead this time because Chance fucked up the first hit on this nigga's life. I wanted to empty the fucking clip in his ass, but I just made sure that his punk ass was dead, then went downstairs to handle the bitch so that we could get the fuck up out of there.

I walked into the living room where she was now crying uncontrollably, and although I felt sorry for her and her unborn child, I wasn't about to leave any witnesses. I popped her ass in the head twice, and then we got out of Dodge with the quickness. I couldn't help but laugh at the dog shying away from us this time when he saw us come out of the house.

"Rich traumatized that fucking dog," Chance said, causing us all to laugh.

"Fuck his li'l ass, barking like he was about that life," he cracked up.

They dropped me at my crib as I left them to tie up the loose ends, and as soon as I got inside, I pulled out my phone, calling Tami. She again let my call go to voicemail, and I was starting to think that what my brother said about me losing it over her ass was the truth. I never chased no pussy, and if a bitch were mad at me, I would just move on to the next, but there was something about her ass that wouldn't allow me to move the fuck on. I just hoped that she wasn't considering going back to that nigga because I was feeling her ass, and I wanted her to be my girl, but playing the friendship card might have backfired on my ass. I decided to leave her a voicemail, telling her to get at me when she got my message. That's when I knew she had me gone, because I *never* talked on anyone's voicemail.

I disposed of the clothes that I was wearing and hopped my ass in the shower, washing away all my sins that I participated in for the day, praying that that bitch didn't have that one nosy neighbor watching. I knew nobody reported shit in the hood because they knew what happened to snitches. I needed to know that all was good, so I called Chance, and when he picked up the phone, he already knew what I was calling about. All he said was it was handled before ending the call, causing me to relax a little. Then I went to my minibar and fixed myself a glass of Hennessy and finished the blunt that I rolled earlier, thinking about Tami.

Tami

I woke up with a hangover and a sore pussy because Envy tore up my shit last night, making me realize how much I missed the dick. He was in beast mode, and I wasn't complaining because that liquor had my ass doing shit that I would normally frown upon. He was still sleeping as I limped to the bathroom to shower, trying not to wake him up because I knew he was going to be ready to hit it again, not caring that he had already beat up the pussy. He'd have my pussy out of commission for at least a damn week if I let him.

After my shower, I sat on the bed with just the towel wrapped around me, putting lotion on my legs when my cell phone rang. I thought that it was Chase calling again since he had been blowing up my phone, so I started to let it go to voicemail, but then I looked at the screen and noticed that it was my mother calling. I panicked because she never—and I mean *never*—called me this early unless something was wrong, so I quickly answered. She didn't even say hello; she just yelled for me to turn to NY1. I ended the call, grabbed the remote off the nightstand, and put on the news. My heart dropped upon seeing Tara's house, so I knew that it wasn't good news. The news report was ending, but with NY1, they consistently reported the story again after the commercial, so I waited, wishing that my mom would have just told me what she saw. That's why I knew that it had to be bad because it's hard for her to deliver bad news, and although I didn't like the bitch, Tara, I didn't want nothing bad to happen to her. I thought about calling Siah, but dismissed that thought as quickly as it came because we weren't on the greatest of terms because of his ill feelings for me.

Once the news came back on and reported that a pregnant woman and an unknown male were found dead in the home, my heart started racing, and my fingers couldn't move fast enough, trying to dial Siah's number. I received no answer and panicked. I started cursing the television because it didn't have any other information. They kept talking about not releasing the names of the victims until they notified their relatives. I nervously called Siah's mother's phone, and when she answered, I already knew who the "unidentified" male in the home was because she answered the phone, trying to talk, but couldn't. His father got on the phone and said that the police had no information on who killed them both in broad daylight, with no sympathy for the unborn life. He was thanking God that MJ was at the house with him and his wife, and once he started crying, I told him that I would be by the house later.

When I ended the call, my heart hurt, and the tears fell because no matter what Siah and I had going on, that didn't mean I didn't care if he lived or died. My cell phone rang again, and it was my mother, asking me if I was all right, and if I needed her to come over. I told her that I was all right and that Envy was here. There was a long pause on her end before she told me that if I needed her, I should give her a call. I promised I would. She was maintaining sobriety, and I was proud of her, but I still had my doubts about how long it would last this time since we'd been here before.

I tried to get myself together before Envy got up because he had seen me cry time and time again over my ex-husband, and although my reason for crying this time is valid, I just wanted to be strong. However, when he got up, he knew that something was going on with me, and I took a deep breath, praying that I didn't cry when I told him that Siah was murdered.

"You good?" he asked, probably thinking something concerned me about Chase because of the look on his face when he asked me.

"Siah was killed yesterday," I responded, as the tears fell and my throat became dry, making it hard to say anything else.

He came over to me and hugged me, telling me that he was sorry for my loss because it was indeed a loss to me. Like I said, I still cared about him. I cried in his arms, wondering who would do this to them, but I had to remind myself that he was in the life. The streets had finally succeeded in killing him.

Envy helped me dress because I was still sitting on the bed wearing only my towel, but to be honest, all I wanted to do was lie back down. I felt bad because all the guilt of my not being there the first time that Siah was shot started to get to me. I was so busy beefing with him that I never got the chance to be a grown-up about the situation, so he died not knowing that I didn't hate him, and that I just disliked the way he was treating me.

"They killed Tara too, not even caring that she was pregnant," I cried.

"Damn," was all he said as he held me tightly, trying to calm me.

I wanted to go to Siah's mother's house, but I didn't want to go alone because I knew she still felt some type of way when I didn't come to the hospital when he got shot. I thought about asking Envy to go with me, but felt that would have been disrespectful, so I was going to call my mother and ask her if she would go with me. I told Envy of my plans to visit his parents' home, and that I was going to take my mother with me, and he said that he understood. I finished dressing after speaking to my mother, and she agreed to go with me, so I was on my way to pick her up.

Envy left to return home. I told him that I would call later to let him know how it went because he was worried, not knowing if someone would be gunning for his parents next. I assured him that I would be fine, but at the same time, I was praying that I would be fine because whoever did this was heartless.

My mom and I were invited into the home where Siah grew up, but I could tell that we weren't welcome. I just felt fucked up by the vibe that I was getting from his family. They were treating me like I hadn't been in this home a million times before, but that's just like family. They don't care that I left a relationship that wasn't working for me because they believed whatever he told them about me. I went over to Phoenix and picked her up because she had no idea what was going on, but she looked so sad, it made me think that maybe she did.

As soon as I sat down with her on the couch, Siah's cousin, Shalonda, came and snatched her from me. My mom was ready to go off, but I told her to let it slide. Now was not the time or place to be up in here arguing when his family is here grieving, and I also had to remind her that they were in their feelings. I know most of them were probably wondering what I was doing here when I wasn't with him anymore, or the fact that I didn't care to see him in the hospital. By now, my mom was fed up with the way the family was acting, so she told me that if I didn't want her to show her ass, it was time for us to go, and I agreed. I knew that she wasn't going to take much more before she ran through that house like a tornado, so I said my goodbyes to his father because he was the only one who showed us that he appreciated us coming.

After I dropped off my mom, I headed home because I had a headache and was stressed. Phoenix had cried to leave with me, but, of course, they wouldn't allow me to take her. His mother said that she needed to be with family right now, like I wasn't family to her, when she's been in my life since the day I saw her born. I swear, I wish that Rema were still here because I probably will never get to see my goddaughter again, and that hurts me to my core.

I called Envy on my drive back to my house, telling him how I was treated at Siah's parents' house. He didn't like their treatment of me, but told me that they all were grieving right now and in their feelings, and to give them time to come around.

I wanted to tell him that they probably weren't going to allow me to attend the funeral and, if that happened, it was going to hurt like hell. I was getting upset just thinking about it, so I told him that I would call him later because I just wanted to get home and be alone.

When I pulled up to my place, I sighed heavily upon seeing that Chase was parked in front of my house because I didn't want to see him right now.

I got out of the car and proceeded to my front door, not even attempting to ask him why he was here, but I didn't have to because he was now standing directly behind me.

Chapter Twenty-five

Chase

I sat in my car waiting for almost an hour for Tami to get home, and as soon as she pulled up, she walked to her door without even acknowledging me. I got out of my ride and was now standing behind her, but she still didn't say shit to me. I grabbed her arm to ask her why she was treating me this way, and that's when I noticed the look on her face. She looked like she'd been crying all night, and I hoped that it didn't have anything to do with Meeka because I handled that shit, and I was going to let her know that.

"What is it, Chase?" she asked just above a whisper, but aggravated at the same time.

She was making me feel like I was bothering her, and I started to say fuck it because I wasn't about to kiss her ass. I couldn't walk away, though, because something told me that it had to be deeper than what happened with Meeka.

"What's going on with you? Why are you crying?" I asked, but she pulled away from me, going inside. However, she didn't close the door, so I took that as a sign that I was invited inside. I closed the door behind me and followed her to the living room to see if I could get her to tell me what was happening.

"Tami, what's wrong?" I attempted again.

"My ex-husband, Siah, and his pregnant girlfriend were murdered yesterday," she said, as the tears fell from her eyes.

I had no idea that Messiah was her ex-husband, and although she called him "Siah," I knew that she was talking about him. *What are the odds that I was the one who murdered her ex?* I knew it had to be the same killing. I felt bad for her, but not bad enough that I would have spared his life had I known he was her ex-husband because his death certificate was signed the day he shot my brother. I tried to comfort her the best that I could, but it was hard because of how I felt about his ass. I had no idea why she was crying over this nigga. She told me how the nigga treated her and why she left him, but she never told me who he was or who he cheated on her with. I feel that his ass didn't deserve her tears, but I knew that I needed to be here for her if she allowed me to.

"Is there anything that I can get you? Are you hungry?" I asked, not knowing what else to say because I couldn't offer any kind words. Truthfully, I hoped his ass was burning in hell right about now.

"I'm going to be fine, and if you don't mind, I would like to be left alone," she said, pissing me off.

Just as I was going to insist that she let me stay with her, someone knocked on her door, and I knew it could be only one other person. My suspicion was confirmed when she opened the door, and he was standing there looking at me, like *I* was the unwanted guest. I wanted to tell his ass that if anyone should have been uninvited, it should have been him because I was the one who was here for her when she got this place, so he could lose the mean mug he was rocking.

When I heard her say to him, "He was just leaving," I knew that it was time for me to go since she played me in front of his ass. She just told me that she wanted to be alone, so why was it that *I* was leaving, and she wasn't asking *him* to do the same?

"Nigga, you got a problem with your fucking eyes?" I asked him.

"Bro, I'm not the fucking nigga you want to be fucking with right now," he barked.

"I know the two of you are not about to do this right now. Chase, please leave, and I'll give you a call later," she pleaded with me, causing him to walk inside like he was *that* nigga.

I was going to give him that, and since she asked me to leave for the second time, I was going to do just that, but I was pissed at her ass right now. I didn't say shit to her as I walked out the door, and I heard her let out a deep sigh, but I didn't give a fuck because she was on some sucker shit right now. If we got to speak again, it would be *her* ass reaching out to *me,* and I meant that shit. I didn't care that I was feeling her because I wasn't about to keep letting her play me like I wasn't that nigga with her rude ass.

I was even more pissed that I sat in my car for that damn long, waiting on her ass, just for her to put me out like it was nothing to her. I know that she and that nigga have history, but I've been there for her ass, and for her to treat me like a bitch nigga had me not wanting to fuck with her. She was probably still upset with me about what happened with Meeka, but I have no control over what that girl says outta her mouth. I would never play her in front of Meeka, like she just did me in front of that nigga. That nigga didn't want to square up, so I wasn't even going to take that tough talk seriously because those weak-ass words didn't mean shit to me.

I pulled up to my mom's crib because I hadn't seen her in a minute, and I was shocked to see Gaby there with her since Meeka's ass told me that I wasn't going to see her again.

"Hey, Mom, when did Gaby get here?" I asked her.

"No, what you should be telling me is why you do that girl like that because I didn't raise you to put your hands on any female," she spat.

"You act like I just walked up to her and put my hands on her for nothing," I defended myself.

"I don't give a fuck what she did to you. You had no business putting your hands on her, and she should have had your ass locked under the fucking prison," she said angrily.

I knew she was even more upset with me, since my father had a problem with his hands when it came to her. I remember how I felt watching him come home from work and putting his hands on her for no reason at all. I understand how my mom felt, but Meeka forced my hand, so *that's* why I put hands on her ass. I can't believe she would come here and tell my mom that I put hands on her and not tell her why. Just the thought makes me want to put hands on her ass again.

"I'm sorry, Mom. I just let my temper get the best of me," I apologized.

"Sorry doesn't make it better because it doesn't take away the pain she's feeling, and I'm not the one you need to be apologizing to," she said, pointing to the guest room.

"Meeka's here?" I questioned.

"She is," was all she said.

I had no idea why she was here, and my mom had started with the short answers, so I knew she wasn't going to tell me why. I love her, but she be doing the most because had I not come by, she wouldn't have even called me to tell me that my daughter was here. Meeka must have told her a hell of a story for my mom to allow her to stay here and not get me on the phone to tell me what was going on with her.

I took a deep breath before walking into the room to ask her what the fuck was going on, and as soon as I saw the marks on her neck, I felt bad. I wasn't a woman beater, but there was something about her that pushed at my buttons and made me want to kill her ass.

"Why you here?" I asked her.

"Somebody shot out all the windows at my place, and I had nowhere else to go because my mom's house is already overcrowded, so I called your mom," she said.

"So, why the fuck didn't you call me?" I barked, causing her to jump. "You couldn't stay with any of those motherfucking cousins of yours?" I asked her, confused about why she didn't run to one of those bitches.

"They all have live-in boyfriends, so I didn't want to stay there with Gaby," she said, and I wanted to believe her, but something just didn't sound right.

I didn't believe her when she said someone shot up her place, but if it was shot up, it was because of the neighborhood that she refused to move out of. Her ass stayed in Fort Greene, right around the corner from the projects. I kept telling her ass that she needed to move, but that's where most of her family stayed. Since she wanted to be hardheaded, I should make her figure out the shit because when I kept asking her to move for the safety of my daughter, she refused, but look at the first place she ran to. I knew if I told her to leave, my mother wouldn't have it because of Gaby, but I wasn't trying to put Gaby out. Her ho-ass mother, on the other hand, could kick rocks for all I cared.

Her family always came with the quickness when it was time to fight, but her ass couldn't stay with any of them when she needed them. That's why I be telling her to get off that bird shit when it came to her family. All they cared about was drama and not her stupid ass, but you couldn't tell her that shit.

"So, what now because you can't stay here?" I told her.

"I have nowhere else to go, and I can't take Gaby back there," she whined.

"Gaby should have never been there in the first fucking place. She can stay with me, but you have to go," I told her ass.

"So, you hate me that much that you would see me on the street?" she cried.

"You can't be serious right now because I recall a nigga trying to get you to a safe neighborhood with my daughter. It was *your* ass that let *your* family deter you from receiving my help, and you didn't have any problem listening to them. So, if you have nowhere to go, that should tell you something about your fucking family, so miss me with the 'I hate you' talk. If I hated you, trust that we wouldn't even be having this conversation right now," I said, keeping it real with her ass.

"So, can you please help me with another place?" she begged.

"I'm not making no promises," I told her, walking out of the room.

As much as I didn't want to do shit for her ass, she was still my daughter's mother, and I knew that I couldn't just leave her assed out. I swear, I don't know how I even got caught up with her ass because she has always been a hood rat, so what possessed me and my brother to go slumming that night, I have no idea. We both were gone off that Henny, but we knew to stay out of the hood zone, so they must have been looking good as shit that night because, not only did we hit, but we also ran up in both their asses raw. I didn't hate her ass, but I didn't like her ass, either. She has put me through some unnecessary bullshit. And if she didn't have my daughter, I would have killed her ass.

"Mom, I'm heading out. I'll be back to pick them up because it's not your responsibility to give them a place to stay," I told her. She said she didn't mind, but I still told her that I would be back.

I picked up Gaby and held her for a few minutes to quiet her down because she wanted to leave with me, but I couldn't take her with me. After taking her to the back with her mother, I hugged my mom, just thanking her for being here, before heading out.

Tami

I knew that Siah's family was upset with me, and I thought that they might not allow me to attend the funeral, but I was allowed to. I didn't want to attend by myself, and it would have been disrespectful to invite Envy to go with me, so Sami attended the funeral with me. When we got to the funeral, too much was going on because there were so many females claiming to have been his girlfriend. There was a pregnant girl in attendance, who claimed to have been with him for a year, and she was carrying his baby. It got so bad that they started escorting females out because they were trying to fight, not showing any respect to his family. I knew that Siah was a dog, but this was a bit much. I had no idea who that man was whom I had been crazy in love with, and I wondered if he was ever capable of loving anyone.

We didn't sit with the family, and as much as I wished Phoenix were in attendance so that I could see her, I knew that Siah's mother wasn't going to allow children to attend. One of his aunts told me that she had the children say goodbye privately, and I honestly wished that I had gotten that option because I would have loved to tell him that I didn't hate him. Sami and I decided not to go to the repast, so I thanked her for being there with me today and dropped her off at home, telling her that I would call her later.

I didn't go home. I decided to go by Chase's place to see what was up with him because I hadn't heard from him. I was guessing he was upset that I asked him to leave. I parked the car and was now standing on his porch waiting for him to answer the door, but instead, his ratchet-ass baby mother answered the door.

"Yes?" she said with an attitude.

"Is Chase here?" I asked, not in the mood to go back and forth with her ass.

I had no idea why she was here because I heard how he almost killed her dumb ass, but here she was, so she must have liked that ass whooping. Gaby came and ran into my arms, probably remembering me from the day that we hung out at the park, and her mother didn't like that shit at all.

"Chase, I know you didn't have my baby around this bitch," she yelled, grabbing Gaby from my arms.

I stood there just smirking at her stupid ass because she was about a dumb bitch, almost snapping her daughter's fucking arm from snatching her up so roughly. I swear I wanted to beat her ass again for doing that stupid shit instead of her just asking me to put her down.

"Bitch, don't you ever snatch my fucking daughter up like that again. Take your ass somewhere and don't answer my fucking door like you live here," Chase said, dismissing her.

I swear, if he thought I was impressed by that, he was wrong because any man who didn't respect the woman who birthed his child wasn't the man for me. He could have checked her without being disrespectful about it, and trust, I know how hard it is to be nice to her, but that shit wasn't cool. He just said that shit so that I didn't think she lived there, and to be honest, I didn't care because he wasn't my man, and we were just friends.

"What's up?" he said.

"I haven't heard from you, so I came to see if you were good," I told him.

"I'm good. I just fell back because you weren't trying to let a nigga be there for you, so I figured when you were ready, you would reach out," he said, sounding salty.

"I was just trying to keep the peace, that's all. And since I had already said that I wanted to be alone, I didn't think you would mind my asking you to leave. If it makes you feel any better, I asked him to leave too," I lied.

"It's all good. I'm not sweating that nigga. You trying to come in?" he asked me, like enemy number one wasn't inside.

"Nah, I'm good. Just hit me up when you're not on rat patrol," I told him, laughing as I backed up off his porch.

"I see you got jokes, but I'll hit you up later," he promised.

I wasn't about to ask him why she was even there because, like I said, I didn't care. I just came to make sure he was good, so I was now taking my ass home to a glass of wine and a hot bubble bath to get my mind right. Envy called to ask how I was feeling and if he could come through later, and, although I wasn't up for company, I told him that it was fine.

After bathing, I just put on a pair of leggings and a tank, waiting for him to get to the house, and I couldn't wait because he said he was going to bring something to eat. I didn't even realize that I hadn't eaten anything today because I opted out of going to the repast, so it was fair to say that I was starving. I told him to bring me some Chinese food because I wanted some honey barbecue wings with fried rice mixed with onions and hot sauce.

He arrived about forty-five minutes later, so we sat in the living room, eating and watching *Honeytrap* on Netflix. It was a pretty good movie, but I was pissed off at the end. I couldn't believe that the star set Shaun up to die, when all he tried to do was be there for her. I swear I wanted to punch her in the face because she could have screamed or even tried to help him, but her ass just stood there.

Envy was laughing because he couldn't believe how tight the movie had me, and I'm not going to lie. I felt like crying at how they did him. Suddenly, Envy's phone rang, and just by what he was saying, I knew that it was Olivia. When he got off the phone, he said that it was her and that she needed him to meet her at the hospital. She claimed to be having contractions, and I wanted to believe that she was, but for some reason, I didn't. He looked at me, waiting for me to tell him what he should do, but I wasn't deciding on whether he should go. I asked him what he was going to do because I couldn't make the decision for him. He said that he was going to go and asked me if I would go with him, so we both were on our way to the hospital.

I was thanking God that she wasn't going to the hospital where I work because I would have told him I wasn't going. When we arrived there, we got on the elevator to labor and delivery after we were told that's where she was. New York Hospital didn't have many restrictions because they allowed both of us to go to her room, and when she saw that he had me with him, the look on her face was priceless.

"So, what's going on?" he asked her.

"Why would you bring her here?" She ignored his question.

"Olivia, I didn't come up here to play twenty questions with your ass. Why she's here isn't important, so tell me what the fuck is going on with the baby," he snapped.

"I'm being monitored, so the doctor will come in and tell me what's going on," she said, but I think the bitch was lying about being in pain.

If she was having contractions like she said she was, as soon as they hooked her ass up, they could have told her if they were contractions or not. I think she just wanted to see Envy, so she made up this bullshit lie, but the shit backfired because she didn't expect me to accompany him. I know Sami told her that we weren't together anymore.

"Well, I need you to press that button for the nurse so that we can see what the hell is going on with you," he told her.

"If you're in a rush, you shouldn't have even come to the hospital," she stated, rolling her eyes.

"It's not about me being in a rush, but I did come to see what's going on with you, not come chill in the room with you without knowing anything," he said, trying to stay calm because I could tell she was pissing him off.

"I just hate how you flip the script when you get around her because you don't be giving me this attitude when it's just you and me. So, if her being here is going to deter you from acting like you give a fuck, then you can leave," she said, causing me to shake my head.

I swear this girl is always trying to get a rise out of me, but she could have that because I wasn't feeding into that bullshit. I could tell she still didn't learn not to fuck with me because if she keeps up with the slick talk, I don't have any problem snatching her bald-headed ass up out of the hospital bed, pregnant or not. The fact that she didn't press that button, but instead kept going at him about me, told me she knew wasn't shit wrong with her ass, and I hope he saw right through her drama-queen ass.

When the nurse finally came into the room, she checked the monitors and told her that she wasn't in labor, but that the doctor would be in soon to give her a vaginal exam to make sure everything was all right.

"Can I ask you a question?" I asked the nurse.

"Sure, what can I help you with?" she said.

"I just wanted to know if there was a procedure to determine paternity before the birth of the baby," I said.

"Why the fuck you asking questions about *my* fucking baby? That doesn't concern you," Olivia spat, causing the nurse to look around like, *What the hell did I walk into?*

"Did you hear me mention you or your baby, or did you hear me just ask an innocent question?" I spoke rudely, then looked at the nurse, waiting for her to answer my question.

"Yes, there is a test, but it carries a slight risk of miscarriage, so that is something that you would have to discuss with the doctor. He could explain it to you in more detail, along with all the risks," she offered before leaving the room.

"I don't care if there were a million tests that determine the paternity before my baby is born, because I will *not* be doing any testing until I push my baby out. So, thank you, but no, thank you, bitch," she said smartly.

"And that's your right. I was just asking because I wanted to know, so you can miss me with all the tough talk," I spat back at her ass. "Envy, I'm going to wait in the waiting area because I see that Olivia's 'pretending-to-be-having-contractions' ass is going to come up missing if she keeps talking shit," I told him, leaving the room.

I was falling asleep because it seemed like we were there forever before they decided to release her crazy ass. As we were leaving the hospital, Olivia looked like she was about to shit on herself as a few guys passed by us. She moved closer to Envy, making me wonder what the fuck *that* was about. Ole dude didn't say shit, but it didn't stop me from wondering why he had her so shook. Envy was oblivious to what just happened, but I sure wasn't, and since she likes to be petty, I was going to be petty too.

"So, who was that?" I asked her.

"How should I know who he was?" she answered, letting me know that she knew the dude.

If she didn't know him, she would have asked me who I was talking about, since there were a couple of them. She was full of shit, and I have no idea why Envy doesn't see the shit, but he will learn soon enough.

"So, the dude that just walked by with the fitted tee on . . . You saying that you don't know who he is?" I asked again, just to make sure.

"Didn't I just say that?" she said, rolling her eyes.

I knew she knew exactly who he was, but I was going to leave it alone since she wanted to play stupid. Her ass was so nervous, she almost tripped and fell off the sidewalk, and had she not been pregnant, I would have been rolling. But I knew if I laughed at the bitch, Envy was going to think that I was childish, so I didn't laugh out loud. But I couldn't wait to get home because I was tired after sitting in the hospital for all those unnecessary hours with her lying ass. I swear before God, if her ass called him again about "not feeling well" while we were together, I was going to pass on the ride-along.

Envy was quiet, and I had no idea why, but I hoped that his ass wasn't mad at me because again, he didn't have to involve me in his situation. If he thought that because she was pregnant, I was going to let her keep coming out of her mouth being disrespectful, he was wrong. I was going to give it to her as good as she put out the shit, and if he didn't understand that, then, oh well . . .

Sami

"Are you sure it was him, Olivia?" I asked her.

"Sami, it *was* him, and I have no idea what he's doing here," she stressed.

Olivia's ex-boyfriend, Rich, was crazy as hell, and she wanted nothing to do with him, so she broke it off with him before moving back here. He just didn't understand that no meant no and tried to force her to stay with him, so she left, not telling him where she was going. She thought that she saw him, but I was trying to convince her that if it were him, given his aggressive nature, he would say something to her. "Well, like I said, I don't think it was him because, trust, he would have said something to you," I told her.

"It *was* him, and he probably didn't say anything because I was with Envy and Tami, or maybe he didn't think it was me because of my pregnant belly. I don't know his reason for not speaking, but he has me shook, not wanting even to leave the house. Girl, driving over here, I kept looking out my rearview mirror, making sure that I wasn't being followed—*that's* how shook his ass has me," she admitted.

"Olivia, I wouldn't even worry about it because even if you do run into him again, it's not like he's going to kill you or some shit," I told her.

"I don't know what he's going to do because, before I left, he threatened me, saying that if I ever left him, he would make sure that no one else would have me. I don't want to have a run-in with him, and he hurts me or my baby, Sami," she said, on the verge of tears.

"So, maybe you should let Envy know what's going on because, if someone is out there who may hurt his baby, he needs to know. I mean, I don't think that he wouldn't get involved if you told him the truth," I told her.

"To be honest, I'm not too sure about Envy and his thought process lately since he's been hanging back with Tami. I called him two days ago, and he still hasn't returned my call, so I have no idea if he's going to this appointment with me tomorrow. Now that Rich is staying somewhere in New York, I really don't want to ever go to another appointment alone. I'm thankful that I already took maternity leave," she said.

"Well, I just hope you take my advice and tell him because I don't want to see nothing bad happen to you. These niggas out here crazy with that, 'If I can't have you, no one else will' bullshit, like they own you or some shit."

"I just hope his crazy ass keep it pushing because I left his ass for a reason, and I don't want no parts of him. I'm going to try to call Envy, but I already told you now that he's back with Tami, his ass acting brand new. You should have seen him at the hospital the other night, acting like he didn't want to be there, and then he lets her ask the nurse about a paternity test before the baby is born. He didn't say anything to her, and I just felt that it wasn't her place because, at the end of the day, I didn't lie down with her ass," she said, pissed, but I already knew because Tami told me.

I felt bad for her because I could tell that she was scared. See, that's why I told her she should have never fucked with his ass and left him with the bitch he was with. I tried to tell her fucking around with other females' men was going to catch up with her ass, but she never listened. I bet her ass will listen now. Then again, I can't even say that because she knew that Envy had a situation when she met him. I know because I told her he did, and it attracted her to him even more.

She called Envy to see if he could come over so that she could talk to him, but he sent her straight to voicemail. She tried a few more times, but he still didn't answer, so I came up with an idea that probably would work.

"Mason," I called out to him.

"What's up?" he asked, coming out of his man cave.

"Can you call Envy and ask if he could come over here? Olivia has something important to talk to him about, but he's not answering her calls."

He pulled out his phone and, *bingo!* Envy answered, letting us know that he was ignoring her calls, and I felt sorry for her because her face showed she was hurt. I hate that she put herself in this situation because it hurt me to see my friend hurting, and I could tell that she was trying to hold back her tears. Mason said he'd be in the game room and that Envy was on his way, but to let him know when he got there. He said that he told him that Olivia was the one requesting his presence because he didn't want him walking in here like he set him up, which I understood.

Olivia went upstairs to use the bathroom, so I went into the kitchen to get myself something to drink, praying that all went well, and he didn't tell her that he didn't give a shit about her situation with Rich. Envy's ass showed up with Tami, and I never had a problem with Tami coming here, but all it was going to do was complicate the situation.

"Hey, Tami, I didn't know that you were coming," I said to her.

"Well, Envy and I were out when Mason called, so he wasn't going to drop me off when I live in the opposite direction," she said, getting defensive when I was just stating the obvious.

"No problem. I was only asking, so stop trying to act like you about to square up," I joked.

"Girl, please," she said, walking in.

I was praying nothing jumped off as we were all now sitting in the living room, with me giving Olivia the signal to talk to Envy. I know she felt uncomfortable doing it in front of Tami, but I needed her to say what she needed to say and get it over with. Tami already seemed frustrated being in Olivia's presence, so I just wanted her to speak. I wished that I'd told her to talk to Envy about it when he was over here, chilling on his own with Mason. That way, Tami wouldn't have been with him.

Olivia looked scared to talk to him in front of Tami, and I understood because he was probably going to put on a front. After all, she's here. However, this might be her only chance to talk to him because, once he leaves, he's not going to answer her calls. I could tell that he was getting impatient waiting for her to speak, so I gave her another look, letting her know that it was going to be all right. I think that she was intimidated by Tami, but she'd said it herself; she lay down with Envy, not Tami, so she needed to talk to that man.

Chapter Twenty-six

Tami

I sat in disbelief as I listened to this bitch, Olivia, tell Envy about some ex-boyfriend who threatened to cause her harm if he ever saw her again. I knew that bitch was lying the other night at the hospital when she said she didn't know who dude was, but now, she's sitting here admitting to it because she's scared.

I wanted to say something so badly, but I decided to let Envy handle it. But then I heard him asking her if it was the guy she was talking about when they first met, and it pissed me off. He'd led me to believe that it was just a one-night stand to him, but it sounds like he was getting to know the bitch before hooking up. I know it may sound crazy, and one might wonder why it even matters, but fuck that shit. Anytime a nigga sits listening to a bitch talk, it tells me that he was feeling that bitch if he engaged her in conversation. I promised myself that I wasn't going to say anything, but I'm going to stop this conversation right now, and I could give two fucks about him and me not being back together because I still have a claim on his ass.

"So, let me get this straight. You have a crazy-ass ex who threatened to kill your ass for whatever reason, on sight. Right? So, please, enlighten me as to why Envy should get involved when he knows nothing about why this man threatened you. You could be telling us anything right now. Shit, knowing you, your ass probably did something to that man and ran your ass here to New York, thinking you was safe. I'm not going to sit here and have him be a part of this shit because you sound stupid right now, asking for someone to protect you when they have no idea the reason you need protection. Envy fucked you, so now he should be obligated to protect you? I think not, sweetie, and if you're so fucking scared, I suggest you get a dog," I said, shutting her ass down.

"Why you always coming for me when I didn't address you? What you need to do is stop being so fucking insecure, acting like this man isn't about to have a child with me. That alone obligates him to protect me until I deliver his baby safe and sound, so do me a favor and stay out of what doesn't concern you," she said.

"Bitch, you sound stupider than you look, and trust me when I say that it *does* concern me because I bet money that he will not be fighting your fucking fight for you. And you haven't seen insecure, but I'm about to show you, so from here on out, don't call my man about nothing that concerns you or that baby until you push out that bitch. Let's go, Envy. And, Sami, I think you and Mason are cool, but please don't send no messages for this bitch again unless you're calling to say that this bitch had the baby and is ready to do the DNA test," I said, getting up and waiting for Envy to follow.

I wasn't trying to make him feel like he wasn't a man and couldn't handle his own business, but that bitch just pissed me off. Now, she was sitting there looking stupid because I guess she expected him to go against what I just said, but he didn't. He just gave Mason a head nod, and we bounced. I knew that Mason was going to clown his ass, but I didn't care. I was sick of that bitch with her fucking demands—like somebody owed her something.

She fucked that man, and whatever his reason is for wanting to fuck her up is between the two of them and has nothing to do with Envy. Sami is her best friend, so what she should have been doing was having Sami recruit Mason's ass because, trust me when I say, Envy better not get involved in that bullshit.

"So, I'm your man now?" he asked me, once we got in the car.

"No, nigga, you're not my man because my man wouldn't have been in there entertaining that bitch," I told his ass, causing him to sigh deeply.

I didn't care if I was pissing him off because his fucking ass had no business sitting up there reminiscing with that bitch about whatever she told him about her fucking ex in front of me. Call me petty or whatever. I didn't care because that's the reason I left the relationship. He needed to consider *my* feelings when it came to her, and I don't think that was asking for much. When he got the call from Mason telling him exactly why he was being requested to his house, he should have shut that shit down, but since he didn't, that was the reason I rode shotgun and wasn't taking no for an answer.

"What the fuck do you want from me?" he barked with attitude, pulling over.

"That's just it. I don't want always to have to jump in when I feel you not handling shit, so that's what I want. I want you to handle your shit when it comes to her. Why didn't you shut that bitch down instead of entertaining the idea of protecting her, not knowing the real reason that nigga gunning for her? Why should *I* have to risk losing *you* for protecting someone you have no obligation to? That's all I'm saying," I told him, letting the tears fall at the thought of losing him to a beef that has nothing to do with him.

I honestly think that Olivia exaggerated the situation because, if that dude felt that way, he would have fucking said something to her ass. A real nigga wouldn't have cared who the fuck she was with. He would have snatched her ass. So, that tells me that she did some shit to him, and *that's* why she was scared when she saw his ass. She was trying to get Envy's ass caught up, and I bet money, there's more to what she's telling, and Envy needs to stop acting so damn gullible.

"Listen, you didn't give me a chance to say anything. All I asked her was if it was the ex that she had told me about. You jumped in and said all that you felt you needed to say and shut the shit down, so you can't sit here and say anything to me about what I should have said when you didn't give me a chance to say it."

"If you were going to shut the shit down, you wouldn't have cared who she was referring to. You would have just told her, hell no," I insisted.

"Tami, you and I are two different people, so the way you chose to handle it was not the way I would have handled it. Yes, I was going to tell her that I wasn't getting involved, but you should have trusted that and let me handle the shit myself. Once again, you let your feelings for her get in the way of you letting me handle the shit. And then, you claiming me when it's beneficial to you, and that shit ain't cool," he said, ending the conversation and pulling off.

Envy

Tami was on some bullshit, and it was starting to piss me the fuck off. I let that shit back at Mason's house rock because I would never disrespect her in front of others like she did me. Regardless of whether she knew it, she had me looking weak as fuck, and had it been anybody else, I would have gone the fuck off. So, now, we were in the car headed back to her place, and she was still with the bullshit, so I had to put her in her damn place. I'm a fucking man, and how I handle my shit is how I handle my shit. She apologized, but I didn't say if I accepted that shit or not because I was just that mad, so I just dropped her off at her place and kept it moving, en route to my mom's house.

My mom wanted to see her, but she would have to set that up on Tami's time because she wasn't rolling with me. I used my key to let myself in, and she was in the kitchen making tea when I walked in.

"Hey, son, where's Tami?" she asked.

"So, is that why you asked me to come by, because you only wanted to see Tami?" I asked her.

"What's going on because it's written all over your face? And I know something had to happen because I spoke to Tami, and she said that she was with you and that she would be coming here with you," she said, waiting for me to explain.

"Mom, that girl bugging, and it's starting to piss me off because she tells me that she didn't want to be with me and started seeing someone else. But the crazy part is that she's dealing with the same thing with him that she said she couldn't deal with in our relationship. I'm just starting to feel like my trying to get her back just isn't worth all of the stress that I've been feeling lately," I said, being honest with her.

"Son, you have to be real with yourself and understand that Tami hasn't been in the best relationship with her ex. You also need to understand what it feels like to finally meet someone who makes you realize what you been missing, just for that person to put you in the exact same situation. When she returned your ring and left, I understood completely because she's scared that she's about to go through the same thing she just got out of. She knows that the girl wasn't going to make things easy, especially if that is, in fact, your child. Did you hear me ask about that girl or ask about meeting her? No, I didn't, and you know why?" she paused, waiting for me to answer.

"No, I don't know why," I answered.

"I refuse to get attached, just to be disappointed in the end. I've always taught you to do right and own up to your responsibilities, but a 'possibility' isn't your responsibility, so I understand why Tami left," she said, and to be honest, it gave me something to think about.

I needed to have a conversation with Olivia and then handle my business with Tami. I called Olivia and was now en route to her house, and although I didn't want to go there, I had no choice because she was acting like her ass was on house arrest. She said she didn't want to leave the house because she was worried about running into dude. So now I was sitting outside her home, wondering whether to go in. My phone rang. It was Olivia asking me if I was coming inside or if I was going to stay in the car. I ended the call, saying nothing. *Instead of being in the window checking for me, she should be checking for that nigga she running from,* I thought as I got out of the car. I walked in and sat down, trying to figure out how to say what I needed to say without having to argue with her because that was not what I came to do.

"First, I just want to apologize for the other day because I should have said something. We both know I was trying to do right by you, but let's state facts: we both know that there is a possibility that I'm *not* the father of your baby. I was trying to do the right thing because that's how I was raised. So, the right thing for me is doing right by Tami and not continuing to do the things I've been doing until we have a paternity test done," I said, feeling good that I finally said it.

"So, you came all the way over here to deliver bullshit, once again, because of Tami. If she cared for your ass, she wouldn't be trying to control you. This baby is yours, and you need to accept it and be here for me, helping me with the arrival of your child," she yelled.

"Olivia, I didn't come over here to argue with you. I came to reason with you. I have a situation that I need to respect if I want to keep it, so I'm begging you to fall back. Once you give me proof that the baby is mine, you will not have to worry about anything because I'll take care of mine," I told her.

"I find it hard to believe that once you find out the baby is yours, anything will change because you're too worried about what Tami wants. Any real bitch wouldn't dare ask you to fall back from what we both know is *your* baby," she said, knowing that there was no guarantee, but if that's what she wanted to believe, then so be it, but I wasn't changing my mind.

I look at her skeptically because she needed to keep it real with herself, and if she chose not to, she should at least respect that I was willing to step up if the child were mine.

"I know that this isn't easy for you, but it's not easy for me either because we didn't just make a baby," Olivia said. "I was feeling you. I knew that you were honest with me about everything, but that didn't stop either of us from hooking up, so I feel that I shouldn't be the one to blame and have to deal with this alone. It's not like we're sleeping together or conversing outside of my doctor's appointments, so I don't see what her problem is. Yes, what I requested was a bit much yesterday, but I was scared and didn't know what else to do, so since I'm carrying your baby, I thought about you," she said, tearing up.

I understand some of what she was saying, but she should put her feet in Tami's shoes because then, she would feel the same way. It's not like I said I didn't want any part of the child, regardless of whether it was mine, so why couldn't she accept this? She doesn't have that many months to go, so the shit is almost over with. Then we can get the test done and go from there. I was getting nowhere with her, and I've been here longer than I expected to be, so I was going to have to wrap regardless of whether she agreed.

"I'm about to get up out of here because we're not getting anywhere," I said, standing up.

"Envy, this is so not fair, and I don't understand why you're treating me this way. I promise I won't say anything else to Sami or anyone, but don't make me do this on my own," she said, letting the tears fall, and I felt bad.

"Listen, Olivia, I'm sorry, and I'm not trying to hurt you or blame you because, like you said, we both crossed that line. My hands are tied right now, and had you not opened your mouth to Sami, we wouldn't even be having this conversation," I told her.

"I know. I was trying to make Tami jealous, and I know that I was wrong, but if you just give me another chance, I promise you I will not say a word," she pleaded.

"Olivia, I don't want you to feel that you have to beg me to do what's right because, if the baby is mine, that's a given. Just give me a call tomorrow when you get off work, and I will come by," I said, not knowing what else to say.

I felt like I was losing my damn mind being pulled in so many directions, and although I knew what I wanted to do, I didn't know if I should. If I wanted to be with Tami, I knew that I needed to respect her feelings, but it made me feel bad having to leave Olivia to do it on her own. When I got to my house, Camille was sitting in the living room, eating a bag of chips, watching *Basketball Wives*.

"What I tell you about just popping up without calling me first?" I said, plopping down on the couch next to her.

"Well, the key that I have in my possession says I can visit whenever I want," she replied, dangling her keys in my face.

"What brings you to my neck of the woods, and I hope it's not money?" I laughed.

"No, I still have money from all the monetary gifts that I got for graduating. I just came here because I was talking to Mom, and she told me about your struggle. So, instead of going home, I came here, expecting you to be home, but you weren't, so I used my key," she said, causing me to take a deep breath because she didn't know the half of what I was dealing with.

"So, from what Mom told you, what advice does your young, never-had-a-man ass have to offer?" I joked, causing her to punch me in my arm.

"I don't need to be in a relationship to know right from wrong. I love Tami to death because she was there for me when I needed her the most, but I disagree with her when it comes to her telling you not to be there for Olivia. After all, you decided to lie down with that girl unprotected, so if she says that it's your child, I feel that you should be there for her because she shouldn't have to do it alone. Now, if it's proven that you're *not* the father, then you take that as a learning experience, never to make that same mistake again, so you don't have to waste time and money on a kid that isn't yours.

"To be honest, I'm disappointed in you for having unprotected sex when you told me how important it was always to protect myself," she said.

"Tami already left me because she couldn't handle me supporting Olivia as far as doctor appointments and money for what she needed for the pregnancy. Now that she's willing to give me a second chance, she's just going to leave again if I continue to help Olivia," I said, defeated.

"Envy, as a woman, Tami shouldn't want you to turn your back on your responsibility as a man. I know Mom agrees with Tami, but I must disagree with them both. It hurts me to say this, but maybe Tami *isn't* the woman for you. She seems bitter about the situation because her ex-husband put her in a similar situation, so she would never see clearly when it comes to standing by you. And to keep it real with you, you were single when you slept with Olivia, regardless of whether you want to believe it. She went back to her husband at the time and left you hanging, so I feel that she shouldn't hold what happened against you."

"I really don't know what to do, to be honest with you, but I do feel that I was doing the right thing," I admitted.

"I feel you were doing the right thing too. You also have to keep in mind that Tami is broken, and she comes with a distrusting heart because of what she went through. I feel that you should move on because Tami isn't going to be able to love you until she loves herself first. I say that because any woman who put up with all that she did couldn't possibly love herself or even know her worth. You're going to get the backlash of all her hurt and pain, and I would hate to see you lose yourself trying to please her. I'm not trying to tell you what to do because that decision is yours, so I'm done. And just know that any more advice I give you is going to cost you," she said seriously.

She said that she had to go, and I hugged her, thanking her before she left because she gave me some good advice, and I had a lot to think about. As soon as I made sure she was in her car safely, I went to pour myself a drink and light up because I needed to be in a different space, even if it was only for the night. I already made up my mind about what I needed to do, so before I called it a night, I hit Tami up, telling her that I was going to come by her crib when she got off work tomorrow to talk to her. *My life has become a damn soap opera, and now, I know why I never wanted to fall in love, let alone wife anyone,* I thought, as I took my ass to bed.

Chapter Twenty-seven

Tami

I couldn't stop the tears from falling from my eyes because I was hurting, but I knew that it was my fault because I pushed him away. When Envy said that he was coming to talk to me after I got off work, I thought that he was coming to say that he saw things my way, but I was wrong. He felt that the baggage I was carrying was holding me back from loving him, and he thought that I was changing him, and he was allowing it because of how he felt about me. He said that I needed to concentrate on healing before being in another committed relationship. My heart was hurting because I didn't want us to end like this, and I feel that I should have let him be a man instead of trying to control him. I had no one to talk to, so all I did was go to work, come back home, and drink until I'm numb to this thing called life.

I can't tell you the last time I saw Phoenix, and that was starting to take a toll on me because she and Envy were the only two that I gave a fuck about. After getting off work, I stopped at the liquor store because this has become my routine, and when I pulled up in front of my place, I couldn't help but roll my eyes and curse under my breath. Chase was sitting parked in front of my house, and I didn't understand why he always felt the need to pop up instead of calling. I wasn't in the mood to entertain him because I just wanted to drink until I numbed my pain and took my ass to sleep.

"Hey, you," he said, once he got out of the car.

"Hey," I said dryly.

"Damn, you haven't seen me in like forever, and that's how you greet a nigga?" he smiled that sexy smile of his.

"I apologize. I'm just tired," I told him.

I walked to the door, fishing my keys from my purse as I opened it, allowing him in before locking the door behind me.

"Can I get a hug?" he asked, so I obliged, getting lost in his arms and feeling a sense of warmth wash over me.

I didn't realize how much I missed him until I was in his arms, but I knew it had more to do with missing the attention I hadn't been receiving. He released me, and I told him that I would be back as I climbed the stairs to change because I was still going to get into my comfort zone and have a few drinks.

When I went back downstairs, I went to the kitchen to pour myself a drink, offering him one. Soon, we were sitting on the couch, drinking and smoking. I was feeling nice, knowing my ass had to be to work in the morning, but I didn't care. I lay my head against his chest after passing him the blunt. I wanted him to make me feel good, even though we had never been intimate before, but I needed him right now, so I started to massage his dick through his pants. He looked at me to make sure that this was what I wanted to do since I'd told him many times that I wasn't ready. I gave him a nod that I was.

He gently pushed me off him as he removed his boots and pulled his hoodie over his head.

"Not here," I said, pulling him toward the stairs to my bedroom.

I swear, his tongue wasn't in the pussy for no more than five minutes before we both heard glass shatter. He jumped up, only wearing his boxers as he ran down the stairs, and I grabbed a pair of shorts and a T-shirt before going downstairs behind him. I stood in my doorway, watching this bitch Meeka destroy Chase's Lexus with a tire iron, and I was pissed that she was at *my* house with this drama. My ass was high and feeling good, so since that bitch didn't touch my ride, I wasn't going to say a damn word. I just watched.

"Why the fuck you here?" she asked, with her hand coming down, shattering the back window.

"Meeka, I'm going to fucking kill you, bitch," he yelled, jumping off the porch, but she just ran around the other side of the car.

"You're a lying bastard. You told me that you weren't fucking with this bitch anymore. So, again, Chase, why the fuck you here?" she yelled, and I'm sure the whole neighborhood heard her ass.

"Chase, I'm going to need you to come inside and put your clothes on, so that you and this crazy bitch can leave my house," I said, and he turned back to look at me for a second.

I thought he would say something disrespectful to me, but he wanted her to believe that he was distracted, and it worked. He ran up to her and grabbed her by her neck. She was scratching at his hands as she struggled to breathe. I was getting nervous now because I thought he was going to kill her ass, so I ran down the stairs to try to reason with him to release her. She was crying as I pleaded with him to let her go, but he had this crazed look in his eyes and wasn't trying to hear me. I even told him that I was sure someone had already called the police, but that didn't work either. He didn't stop until we heard the cries coming from her car. I couldn't believe that she brought her daughter out here with her to do this bullshit.

"I know you didn't bring my daughter out here while you on some bullshit," he barked, releasing her, but slapping the shit out of her as he walked over to her car.

Meeka was on the ground, gasping for air, and I honestly didn't know if I should help her or go into my house and lock my door. When I saw Chase take Gaby from the car and go inside my home, I was confused because I just needed him to get dressed and get the hell out. I attempted to help Meeka up off the ground, but she pushed my hand away, so I left her ass where she was.

I walked into the house, and he was on the phone telling someone to come and get him, and that was music to my ears because I needed him to leave. I have no idea why I even allowed him inside my house when I told myself that I wasn't fucking with him and his baby mama drama, and now that he brought that shit to *my* front door, I was done. I watched him get dressed, afraid to say anything to him because his ass looked like he was ready to snap at the slightest thing.

I picked up a crying Gaby, trying to calm her because she was screaming at the top of her lungs, and it only seemed to infuriate him more.

His phone rang shortly after, so he took Gaby from me, telling me that he was going to have a tow truck come and pick up his car tomorrow. He didn't offer an apology, and no thanks for the little taste of pussy that I did give him. He said nothing as he walked his ass out my door, and my being pissed would be an understatement. I slammed my door so hard, I knocked my fucking clock off the wall with glass breaking everywhere, pissing me off even more. I didn't even bother to clean it up. I needed to shower and take my ass to bed because I had to be at work in the morning.

When I woke up the next morning, my head was banging, and I didn't want to go to work, but I knew that

I couldn't afford to take any more days off. I made sure to clean up the glass from my broken clock before heading out the door. Chase's car was no longer parked in front of my house, so I guess he sent someone out while I was sleeping. I couldn't believe the night I had. Just the thought of going through all of that with his ass and didn't even get the dick pissed me off. I felt like my life was spiraling out of control with this "I-don't-give-a-fuck" attitude I was rocking since Envy broke off things. I knew that I shouldn't have allowed Chase to even enter my house after the way he'd treated his baby's mother, only to see him do the shit again. If he didn't have any respect for her, I don't know what made me think that he would have any for me.

After clocking in at work, I went to the emergency department to see if Trina was working because I needed some Motrin before starting my shift. My head was still banging. The day dragged, but I was relieved that it was time for me to go to lunch because it wasn't that busy today. I went to the cafeteria and sat in deep thought, wondering if I should give Envy a call because I was missing him like crazy. I fucked around and pushed his ass out of my life because something in me wouldn't allow me to believe that he was going to do right by me.

"Girl, you all right?" my coworker Shellie asked me, taking a seat and joining me.

"I'd be lying if I said that I was all right because I'm fucked up right now," I admitted.

Shellie and Rose knew just about everything that was going on with what I was going through with Envy, so there was no reason for me to lie.

"What's going on now?" she asked.

"Well, you already know that I broke things off with Envy, but he and I kind of reconnected until Olivia pulled another one of her stunts, and I lost it. He felt like I wasn't allowing him to be a man when it came to taking care of his responsibility," I told her.

"Well, you already know how I feel about it, so you know that I agree with him and don't understand why you don't. You know that if you had sex with a man and got pregnant, regardless of who he was with, you would want that man to do what he needed to do concerning your child." Shellie paused, then continued. "Yes, even if it was just a possibility," she added, knowing what I was going to say next.

"I just don't understand why no one sees where *I'm* coming from," I said, letting a few tears of frustration fall from my eyes.

"Tami, don't cry, and trust, it's not that I don't understand where you're coming from because I do, but you're wrong. I hate that Envy's and your relationship had to come to an end behind this, but it's for the best. If you couldn't handle the possibility of this being his baby, then you wouldn't have handled the baby being his. He asked you to be his wife, so that says a lot about that man, and he deserves a woman who is going to stand by him through the good and the bad. He stood by you when you went back to Siah, and we both know that his straying was nobody's fault but your own. I'm not saying any of this to hurt you, but if I didn't say it, I wouldn't be a friend," she said, only causing my tears to fall harder.

I knew everything that she said was true, but hearing it come from someone else made me feel like shit.

"Tami, I wasn't trying to make you cry. All I'm doing is keeping it real with you. If you love Envy as you claim, you need to make it right by accepting that he isn't Siah. If you're not ready to be shown what real love is, I'm going to need you not even to attempt a relationship with him."

"Thank you," I said, wiping my tears.

Her break was only half an hour, so after she went back, I continued sitting and thinking about all she had said. I was ready to be loved, but I didn't know how to receive it, or how to tell if it was real, because Siah claimed to love me, and looked at how he treated me. I was going to leave well enough alone for now as far as Envy was concerned, because I wasn't going to engage back into a relationship with him until I was ready to accept all of him. I knew that I was taking a chance that when I was ready, it might be too late, but it's a chance I'm going to have to take.

After work, I went home and decided to do something that I haven't done in a long time, and that was cater to myself. I was going to make myself something to eat, and after eating, I was going to soak in a nice hot bath, sipping on some wine, and eating some strawberries. After my bath, I would sit in bed and cuddle with a good book until I fell asleep, dreaming about my book bae.

However, reading a book didn't go quite as I planned because it only made me realize how much I missed having Envy in my life. I tried hard not to let the tears fall, but I failed miserably. I was tired of crying, but I couldn't help it because the more I thought about him, the more it hurt me. I closed my eyes, trying to stop the tears from falling, but the more I thought of him, the more the tears fell. I wanted to call him and tell him that I was sorry, but I wasn't ready, so instead, I just forced myself to sleep.

Envy

As I stood in the hospital room, holding Olivia's hand as the doctor was coaching her to push, all I could think about was coaching myself not to faint. Sami was on her other side, being strong and shit, telling her to push like it didn't faze her. A nigga was feeling queasy from the time the doctor asked me if I was going to cut the umbilical cord. My eyes went toward the door nervously because I had been on edge since we arrived at the hospital last night, since we were at the hospital where Tami worked. I thought Olivia was being petty when she requested that I bring her here, but she assured me that her plan was always to have the baby at the hospital where her aunt worked. I haven't seen Tami in months, and I was hoping that I wouldn't run into her while I was here.

"Come on, I just need one more big push," the doctor said, causing me to focus back on the matter at hand.

Olivia squeezed my hand as she grunted really hard and pushed, but I guess that push wasn't big enough because he still wasn't out. She screamed. I think she was getting frustrated that the baby wasn't out, so I told her to try to calm down and that it would be over soon. Olivia and I have become closer since I've been spending time with her, getting things ready for the arrival of the baby, but it was on a friendship level. I wasn't ready to be with anyone on an intimate level, but I have been enjoying her company, which is why I happened to be at her crib when she went into labor. After two more pushes, she pushed out a baby boy, and he was screaming at the top of his lungs. I looked over at Olivia, and she looked exhausted, but she wasn't too exhausted because she was asking to hold him.

While cutting the cord, I was trying to get a good look at him, but was unable to because the nurse snatched him up so fast. She briefly placed him on Olivia's chest but didn't keep him there long, so I waited patiently as she cleaned him up.

Olivia was sleeping by now, so Sami waited for the nurse to finish up with the baby. It took her about ten minutes to finish with him, and when she asked me if I wanted to hold him, I quickly told her yes. I took him in my arms and stared at him. I didn't see any resemblance to me, but he did look like his mother. I knew that I couldn't base it on whether I was his father solely on his looks, so I had to rely on the paternity test. We already planned for the test that cost me $700 because I requested express testing, which takes anywhere from twelve to seventy-two hours, as opposed to the five working days.

During one of her doctor's appointments, we were informed that the hospital didn't do DNA testing unless there was a medical reason for it, so an outside lab was doing it. I just needed to call them to let them know that she had the baby and we were ready to have the test done, and let them know what hospital we were at.

I called my mom to let her know that Olivia had the baby and that the test was going to be done, hopefully tomorrow, once I got in touch with them. She asked me if I thought he looked like me, but I told her that he didn't, and that he looked like his mother, just a lighter version of her.

After I ended the call, I waited until Olivia was put into a room before leaving the hospital. I let her know that I would be back after I received the call with the lab's arrival time. I think she expected me to stay with her at the hospital, but we weren't a couple, so I decided not to stay even though I could see the disappointment on her face. I didn't want her to make our friendship more than what it was, so staying the night wasn't something I wanted to do. I probably would have stayed a little longer, but we've been at the hospital since last night, and she just had the baby at 8:00 p.m., so a nigga was tired.

Sami looked like she wanted to object to my leaving the hospital too. But I did my part by not missing the birth and holding Olivia's hand throughout the entire delivery, so they needed to consider that.

When I got home, I took a shower and was now lying across my bed on my back, with my eyes closed in deep thought about how I was going to feel if the baby weren't mine. I couldn't get his little face out of my mind, or how it felt when I held him in my arms. I didn't want to put him down. I didn't even realize that I fell asleep until my alarm woke me up. I'd forgotten that I set it to go off at 8:00 a.m. because I wanted to get up early to make sure that the lab would be sending someone this morning.

By the time I finished showering and getting dressed, the lab called back to let me know that someone would be there by 10:00 a.m.

After taking the test at the hospital, I left the hospital without visiting with Olivia or the baby, and I knew she was pissed because she expressed it via a text message. I wasn't trying to get attached to li'l man if he weren't my child, so I felt that not seeing him for two days wouldn't do any harm, even if he were, in fact, mine. Olivia said that she wanted me there so that we could pick out a name for him, but I didn't feel that I should be a part of that if he weren't my son.

I'm not going to lie and say I wasn't feeling some way when I got home about not going to see him because he was all that I was thinking about. I called my mom and told her how I was feeling, and she said it was normal, which is why she didn't want to meet him until she knew if he was mine.

Olivia

I was upset that Envy didn't come see me after he took the test. However, after he explained what he was feeling, I understood. However, I still felt that he shouldn't have stayed away this long. I thought that we were still friends since we've been hanging out, but I guess not.

I had to use the bathroom, but I couldn't because the baby was in the room, and I didn't want to leave him unattended. I buzzed that damn button so many times, and the nurse still didn't come, so I thought about calling downstairs for my aunt because I needed to go. But after I buzzed the nurse a few more times, and she still didn't come, I decided to use the bathroom anyway. I was going to make it quick, so I figured the baby would be okay for a few minutes because I couldn't wait any longer before I had an accident in bed.

I got out of bed slowly because I was still in so much pain, but I made sure to check on my son before going into the bathroom, and saw he was still sleeping. However, when I came out of the bathroom, my heart stopped. Rich was standing there, holding my son, and I had no idea how he knew I was here.

"Rich, what are you doing here?" I asked him, shaken by his presence.

"Nice-looking kid, but it's a shame he has a ho-ass mother," he said.

"Rich, please, put my son down," I pleaded, knowing what he was capable of.

"Bitch, you need not worry about your son. Instead, you need to worry about what I'm going to do to *your* ass," he barked, placing my son back into the bassinet.

"Rich, I'm sorry," I apologized.

"I don't give a fuck about your 'sorry' right about now. You told my wife about us, causing her to leave me, and I haven't seen my daughter since. Bitch, you're not sorry. You did that shit to hurt me, and then to add insult to injury, you fucking *robbed* me?" he said, grabbing me by my neck.

I couldn't breathe, and he was killing me slowly, so I dug my nails into his arms, causing him to release me finally.

"Bitch, are you fucking crazy?" he yelled, slapping the shit out of me, like I was his whore, and he was my pimp.

I was silently praying that the fat-ass nurse I paged a million times walked her ass up in here before this nigga killed me. I backed away from him because I wasn't going to let him get his hands back around my neck again, and when I heard my room door open, I thanked God upon seeing Envy and Mason walk in. I didn't know that he was coming to the hospital, but I wasn't complaining as I ran into his arms.

"What's going on?" he asked, pushing me behind him, so I take it his question was directed toward Rich.

"Why the fuck you asking me? I don't answer to no nigga, so you better ask that bitch what the fuck is going on," he spazzed on Envy, scaring the shit out of me. I saw Mason move closer to Rich, and Rich pulled a gun on him, preventing him from getting closer.

I thought that Mason would have backed down, but the gun didn't seem to faze him or Envy. But it sure had me frozen where I stood. I didn't want any shooting going on with my son in the room, so I just prayed that they remembered he was present.

"My nigga, you *do* realize that you're in the hospital, and my son is in his bassinet, sleeping, right? Now, I don't give two fucks about you holding because it wasn't necessary to pull out when I ain't said shit to make you feel threatened. That gesture alone tells me you a scared nigga, and a scared nigga becomes a reckless nigga, so I'm going to let you live to see another day on the strength of my son," Envy told him, moving to the side, allowing him to exit the hospital room.

I let go of the breath that I was holding, once again thankful that nothing popped off. I went and sat back on the bed because my stomach was killing me.

"Why the fuck was that nigga here?" Envy asked me, like I invited a nigga to come and take my life.

"Envy, I have no idea why he was here or how he knew that I was here," I told him.

I wasn't ready to tell him the truth about why Rich was threatening my life because he wouldn't understand the position that I was in back then. I needed to have a serious talk with Envy, but Mason being here was making me feel uncomfortable, and I hoped that he wasn't going to be here long. I knew why Mason showed up because he had been texting me, and I had been telling him that my son wasn't his, but I guess he wanted to see for himself. I know what you're thinking, but just know that I didn't pursue him. He had been in Sami's ear about a threesome, but she didn't want to do it with any random chick, so she asked me. At first, I told her hell no, but she pressured me into giving in, so I agreed. But when it was over, she was acting like she had an attitude with me. I didn't understand where her attitude was coming from because it wasn't like I slept with him behind her back or something. It took her a week to get over the fact that she was upset with herself and not me, so when she apologized, we went back to being friends as if nothing had happened.

I tried hard to stop thinking about all the things Mason did to my body that night, but every time I was in his presence, I would get hot and bothered. So, one night and too much to drink, I fucked him. We have been fucking around since that night on and off, but when I got pregnant with my son, I hadn't had any sexual encounters with him that would make him a possibility.

There was only one other person who could be the father of my son, other than Envy, and I was praying that he wasn't the father. I guess after seeing my son and not seeing any resemblance to him, he left the hospital, so it was just me and Envy now, and I could tell that he was already attached to the baby. He sat holding him and making silly faces as he talked to him, making me smile because "big bad" Envy said he wasn't going to claim my son until the DNA test, but he's already in love with him. He called him his son three times when he was talking to Rich, so I prayed this was his son because he is going to be heartbroken if he isn't.

"I have to name him, but if you want me to wait to see if we get the results tomorrow, we can wait," I said to him.

"No, you don't have to wait. I think that we should name him," he said, surprising the hell out of me as we brainstormed on what name we were going to choose.

Chapter Twenty-eight

Tami

"Curtis, let me go. I need to get to him. Please just let me go," I cried in Curtis's arms as he held me, not letting me go to Envy.

I was on my lunch break when I saw Envy exit the hospital, and since I hadn't seen or spoken to him, I couldn't resist as I tried to catch up with him to say hello. But I didn't get the chance to say anything to him because, as soon as he stepped through the double doors, gunshots rang out. I took off running upon seeing Envy go down, but Curtis grabbed me, stopping me from going outside because people were still shooting.

After the shooting stopped, I just wanted Curtis to let me go to him. I needed to make sure he was all right, but he still wouldn't let me go. When he finally decided to release me, I wasn't allowed near Envy because hospital personnel were on the scene, and nobody was allowed out of the building. I couldn't stop crying, but I knew that I needed to call his mother to let her know that Envy had been shot. However, my hands wouldn't stop shaking.

Elle was now instructing everyone to get back to work, but I wasn't trying to hear her, and just as I was about to lose my job for telling her to leave me the fuck alone, Shellie let her have it. I know that we both were going to have to deal with a write-up, but neither of us cared.

Shellie took my phone and called Envy's mother. I asked her if she would call Sami too, so she could let Mason know.

Envy was rushed to the back, and no one told me anything. So, Shellie told me to calm down as she left me to see if she could get any information on his status. I was sitting in the emergency waiting room with my leg shaking a mile a minute as tears poured from my eyes, not caring how I looked to my coworkers right now. I was hurting and thinking the worst because he had been hit multiple times before going down, and I just knew that he wasn't good.

"What happened to my brother?" Camille walked up to me in panic mode, crying, and her mother, who was behind her, was also crying.

"I don't know much. All I know is that I saw him leave the hospital. Since I haven't seen or spoken to him in months, I was going to say hello to him, but I never got the chance because, as soon as he left the hospital, shots started, and I saw him go down. They wouldn't even let me go to him, so I don't even know if he's okay," I cried.

"Please, let my baby be okay." His mom rocked back and forth in the chair, holding the crucifix that hung from her neck.

I felt so bad, and I was getting impatient because Shellie hadn't returned to tell me anything. All they kept telling Camille was that someone would be out soon to speak to them. Camille told me that Olivia had the baby, which is why he was here at the hospital. She left me wondering if this had anything to do with Olivia and the dude that she was so afraid of. This was why I didn't want Envy to get involved, and I wished he had understood that at the time.

An hour passed, and a doctor I was unfamiliar with told the family that Envy was still in surgery. He would be out to update them once his surgery was finished. Hearing him say he would return later, post-surgery, gave me hope because, to me, that meant he was going to make it.

Mason and Sami were now in the emergency room with us, and Mason was telling us about the incident that Envy had with the dude who was in Olivia's room today. He was blaming himself for leaving Envy behind after telling us that the guy pulled out a gun on them in Olivia's room. Just as I was about to say something, this bitch Olivia came running toward us, wearing a fucking hospital gown and nothing on her feet but a pair of socks, looking stupid as hell.

"Sami, is he going to be all right?" she asked while crying, making me wonder if she and Envy were a couple now.

"Olivia, I told you that I was going to let you know something as soon as I knew something. You shouldn't be down here. Just go back upstairs, and I promise you, as soon as I hear something, I'll let you know," Sami told her, trying to comfort her, walking her out of the waiting area.

I swear that bitch was always doing the most, and she better be lucky that I was just as concerned as she was about Envy because I owed her an ass whooping. We sat in the emergency room waiting area for another hour before the surgeon finally came out and spoke to the family. Envy suffered gunshot wounds to his chest and torso. He said that it was touch and go because he lost a lot of blood, but they removed the bullets, and he was now stable and resting.

"Can I please see my baby?" his mother pleaded with him, so he allowed her to see him, but he said, "Only for a few minutes."

I wasn't worried about not being allowed to see him because I knew that I would be able to get back there to see him later, even if that meant having one of the security guards walk me back. When everyone left the hospital, I waited around until they put him in a room, and that's when I called up to the floor they had him on to see who was on duty. Nurse Stephanie was on duty, so she allowed me to sit with him in his room without any problems, and if anyone asked who I wasn't cool with, I would tell them that he was my husband.

He was sleeping, so I just sat in the chair, making sure not to wake him because I knew he needed his rest after being shot and operated on. I knew that he wasn't going to wake up tonight, so I lay my head back against the chair I was sitting in and closed my eyes to get some rest as well.

I had no idea what Elle was going to say about my absence from work tomorrow because I was calling out and using one of my sick days. I refused to leave his side until he told me from his own mouth that he was all right. Only then would I be content that he was good. I knew that I had no right to be here, and I hoped that when he opened his eyes, he wouldn't turn me away since we're not together anymore.

The night turned into morning, and he still hadn't opened his eyes, but I wasn't budging until he did. I was happy that the nurse on duty never questioned me about my relation to him, but she did tell me that he was heavily sedated, and that was the reason he still hadn't opened his eyes. I was now sitting near the bed and holding his hand when his mother and sister walked in. I got up to hug them both. His mother walked over to him and kissed him on his forehead, and he stirred a little, but he didn't wake up. I told her that the nurse said he was heavily sedated, so she just talked to him as if he were awake.

"Envy, I need you to open your eyes because your son needs you. Yes, he's your son, baby. They sent the results to the hospital, and Olivia received them, so I need you to open your eyes and name your son," she said, as tears cascaded down her face.

I wanted to let a few tears fall from my eyes too because, although it may be a happy moment for them, it was a dreadful moment to me. Camille looked at me and asked me if I was all right, and I told her that I was. I wasn't going to voice how I felt about it because what I felt didn't matter.

Sami walked into the room and went over to Envy's mom and asked her if it would be okay if Olivia came to see Envy. I held my breath, waiting for her response because, like I said before, it didn't matter how I felt because he wasn't my man, and I wasn't his family. When she told Sami she didn't think that it was a good idea to visit him because I was here visiting him, I had to hold my smile in. I don't know if Envy told her we were broken up, but this was one of the reasons why I loved his mother. She didn't have to consider my feelings, but she did. Sami didn't like her answer, but she didn't disrespect her. She just said that she would let Olivia know as she left.

"Thank you," I said, wiping at my tears because that gesture touched me.

"No thanks needed, baby. I just need you and my son to get it together. He loves you, and I know that you love him too," she said.

"I do love him because, if I didn't, I wouldn't be here right now," I told her.

Envy

I managed to open my eyes, and although they still felt heavy, I fought to keep them open. I was in pain and tried not to move my body. Instead, I slowly moved my head, looking around the room, and spotted Tami. She saw me, so she jumped up and walked over to the bed with tears in her eyes.

"Hey, you, how are you feeling?" she asked me.

"I'm in a lot of pain," I struggled because my throat was dry as hell.

"I'm going to get the nurse so that they can give you something," she said, but I stopped her.

"Nah, no more pain medication if the shit is just going to have me feeling like I'm high and still in pain. Can you get me some water, please?" I asked her.

I watched her as she grabbed the pitcher of water and poured some into a cup, but she didn't hand it to me. She raised the bed before helping me drink some water, and that shit felt good going down my throat.

"Your mom and Camille are here. They stepped away for a few minutes to get something from the cafeteria," she said, and I nodded.

I heard my mom talking to me earlier, and I tried hard to open my eyes, but they had me doped the fuck up. That's why I didn't want any more of whatever they were giving me. I heard her say that the results came back and the baby was mine, but I didn't need the test. I felt a connection with him, so, in my heart, there was never any doubt.

"My baby," my mom screamed, walking into the room, hurrying over to the bed, and kissing me all over my face.

"Hey, bighead. I'm glad that you're all right because we thought we were going to . . ." Camille started, but she couldn't finish before the tears fell.

"I'm good, baby girl. Your brother is made of steel." I smiled, wishing that shit was true because I wouldn't be in so much pain right now if it were.

"Do you know who did this to you?" she asked me.

"I just know that I had words with Olivia's ex, and when I left the hospital, a black Explorer pulled up, and they just started shooting. I didn't have a chance to go for cover, so my ass got lit up, but if it was his punk ass . . . Don't worry, I'm going to handle it," I told her, getting pissed just thinking about that fuck nigga.

"You let the authorities handle that. All I need for you to do is get better," my mom said with a worried look on her face because she knew that I wasn't going to leave it alone.

My mom and sister stayed at the hospital for another hour before leaving, and I knew that my mom was still upset that I wasn't going to leave the shit alone. I wasn't about to let that nigga live to tell about what he did to my ass over some shit that had nothing to do with me. He started the shit, now I'm going to finish it, and I put that on everything I love.

The doctor made his evening rounds and said that I would probably be in the hospital for about a week, so I knew that I wasn't going to be able to see my son. I needed to get in touch with Olivia so she could have Sami bring me the paternity papers so that I could fill them out. I didn't want her to make him a junior, but I did want a say in naming him, so I was going to let her know that as well when I texted her later. We were about to name the baby before I got shot, but Olivia wanted something to eat, so I told her I was going to go up the street to Burger King, but I never made it back.

"So, what's been going on with you?" I asked Tami because I haven't seen or spoken to her in a while.

"Working and paying these bills have been the highlight of my life these days," she said.

"So, are you still fucking with dude?" I asked her.

"No, I'm single."

"Since?" I inquired.

"Since you broke it off with me," she said, rolling her eyes.

"Why you rolling your eyes? I'm just asking," I smiled, letting her know the shit wasn't that serious for her to get upset.

"I'm good. What about you? Are you seeing someone?"

"Nah, I'm not seeing anyone. I haven't even fucked anyone since I stopped fucking with you," I said seriously.

"Well, I can't tell, the way Olivia's ass came running into the emergency room, when she found out that you were shot," she said, with jealousy written all over her face.

"I have no control over Olivia having love for the kid," I said, just to get her upset.

"Whatever."

"So, did you hear that the baby is mine? I heard my mom say that shit, but to be honest, I already knew because I felt it the first time I held him in my arms," I told her, watching for her reaction.

"Yeah, I heard, so I guess congratulations are in order," she said smartly, causing me to crack the fuck up.

"Why you tripping? You know I still got love for your ass."

"So much that you told me that you couldn't be with me, right?"

"I couldn't be with any woman who's not willing to accept a child that belongs to me, no matter how he was conceived. You broke things off with me for trying to do the right thing, so I just couldn't continue with you controlling the situation. You weren't even trying to meet me halfway. Instead, you wanted to call the shots and expected me to be your 'yes-man.' I couldn't do it, shorty."

"Trust me when I say that I get it now, and I fully understand your position. I hate that I had to lose you to get it finally," she said, looking in my eyes.

I wanted to believe her, but I wasn't sure if I could. I did not doubt that she loved me, but I did doubt that she could handle me being a father to Olivia's son.

"I know what you're thinking, and trust me when I say I have been beating myself up about how I handled the situation."

"So, why didn't you call a nigga and express that shit?" I asked her.

"I didn't want to reach out until I knew that I was ready to accept that you were possibly about to be a father to Olivia's child. I never missed any man the way that I'm missing you, and I know to be in a relationship with you, I have to accept your son, and I'm willing to do that," she said.

"That's all I wanted from you, but you were acting like my having a son with her meant that I was going to ask her to marry me. So, are you trying to fuck with a nigga?"

"Well, if that's your way of asking me if I want to be a part of your life again, then yes."

He smiled. "*That's* what's up. Now, I need you to tell that nigga that he had you on loan until you got some act right. Now that I got you back, his ass needs to bounce, and I don't want to hear no shit about that nigga being your 'friend.' *I'm* your friend, and I'm the *only* friend you need," I told her seriously.

"Chase is no longer a part of my life. I haven't seen him since the night his baby's mother showed up at my house, destroying his ride," she said, and I believed her just by the look on her face when she said it.

We spent about another hour together before Tami left the hospital, telling me that she would be back to see me on her break tomorrow. I sent Olivia a text and was waiting for her to respond, but I didn't get a response, so I was going to lie down because my chest was hurting. I paged the nurse to see if they could give me something that wasn't going to have my ass zoned out. I like getting high, but that shit had a nigga too high.

Soon, my room door opened. I thought it was the nurse, but it was Olivia, causing me to sigh deeply because I wasn't in the mood to argue with her. I knew she came down here with ill intent because I could see it on her face, but I needed her to respect the fact that I was laid up because of defending her ass from her bitch-ass ex. The nurse walked in right behind her, so I was thankful for that because I needed something for this pain.

"So, I understand that you don't want the OxyContin, but you do want something for pain?" she asked.

"Yes, I just want something that isn't going to have me zoned out," I told her.

"OK, I could give you something that isn't as strong, but I don't know if it will help with your level of pain," she said, but I assured her that I'd be good.

Olivia

I was hurt when Sami came back to my room and said that Envy's mom didn't think it was a good idea for me to visit him. Last I checked, he and Tami were no longer together, so why was it an issue for me to come and make sure my son's father was good? I know he and I aren't together, but we developed a friendship these last few months, and I cared to know if he was going to be all right. When I got the text from him, asking Sami to bring the papers for him to fill out, I knew that it wasn't just his mother who didn't want me there. If he could text me, that told me that he could make decisions on his own, so why was he asking for Sami to bring the papers and not me? I had questions, and I wasn't about to play the texting game with him. I got permission from the doctor to go to his room to visit him, and that's exactly what I was going to do.

I walked into the room, and yeah, I was pissed by this time, but I didn't get to express anything that I was feeling because the nurse walked in. I waited patiently until she finished with him so that I could talk to him. I knew that now wasn't the time, but I needed and wanted answers. After he took the medication that she gave him, she left the room, so I walked closer to the bed, trying not to let my feelings for him deter me from checking his ass.

"Hey, how are you feeling? I tried to see you, but I wasn't allowed to," I told him.

"I'm in pain, but other than that, I just want to get up out of here so that I can see my son," he said, not even addressing why I couldn't see him.

"Your son was circumcised today, but he's doing fine. We are being discharged from the hospital tomorrow, so I need these papers filled out. I just don't understand why you would text me, requesting that Sami bring you the papers, when this is *our* child. So, you wanted to name our son via text message? Because I'm not understanding why you didn't just request that I bring the papers," I said, getting angry.

"I didn't know if you were going to be able to bring the papers since you just birthed my son," he said, but he was spitting bullshit because he knew that I could come down. If I couldn't, I wouldn't have had Sami ask if I could visit.

"So, did you have a name in mind because I was thinking about making him a junior?" I told him, and he was staring at me crazily. "What?" I asked him.

"I don't want to make him a junior. I'd prefer he has his own identity," he said, spitting bullshit again.

"Well, what would you like to name him, because I was thinking about naming him Enzion, if that's okay with you?" I asked him.

"What the hell is an Enzion, because it damn sure isn't a name for a baby," he snapped.

"You of all people shouldn't be snapping on nobody's name because I could say the same thing about 'Envy.' Enzion is my deceased father's name, and the first two letters in his name will be the same as yours. I like it, but if you have something different, speak now," I told him.

He looked like he was thinking, and I knew he didn't even have a name picked out already, so I hoped that we could name him after my father.

"All right, we can name him Enzion, but I will be calling him Zy. So, let's get this paperwork done so you can take it back upstairs," he said, but when we finished up, I still wanted to talk about a few other things.

We ended up naming him Enzion Zi'are Jacobs, and I was pleased with the middle name he picked since he agreed to name him after my father. I wanted to make him a junior, but it was all good. I wasn't going to stress about it. He probably was saving his name, hoping Tami would give his ass a fucking son.

"Now that we got that out of the way, I would like to know why it was a problem for me to see you today," I asked him.

"I didn't have a problem with you coming down, so stop trying to make something out of nothing. I'm in this hospital bed because I was defending your ass for reasons I know nothing about, so be thankful and stop being petty."

"I'm not being petty. I just want to understand why your mother would tell Sami that I couldn't visit you, like I was a nobody."

"She probably said that because Tami was here, and everyone knows that the two of you don't get along, so why would she invite you to visit? You have no consideration that I'm laid up in this hospital bed in pain because, if you did, you would have waited until I was released to discuss this shit," he said, getting pissed.

"You're right, and I apologize. I'll talk to you about it another time. I'm going to go back upstairs to be with our son and take care of these papers. Feel better," I said, walking out of his room even more pissed than when I arrived.

I was pissed, and since he called me petty, I was going to show him petty. As soon as I got back to my room, I went on Facebook and posted photos of my little man, making sure to tag Sami. I noticed that she and Tami were friends, so I knew that she would see the pictures. I put up a pic of Envy holding Enzion, with the caption that said, Handsome, just like his daddy. Not even minutes later, my phone rang.

"You know that your ass is wrong for that, right?" Sami asked as soon as I answered the call.

"I'm not wrong for shit. All I did was post a picture of my baby and his father," I said to her with attitude, ending the call because she was acting like she was bothered by what I did.

Chapter Twenty-nine

Envy

Walking into my house, I was surprised to see Camille in the living room and my mom in the kitchen because, when I spoke to her this morning, she said nothing about coming over. Tami came to pick me up from the hospital today, taking another day off and not caring that I told her not to and that I would be fine getting home. I limped over to the couch, sitting beside my sister, breathing hard, feeling like I had walked a few miles. The doctor had already let me know that I would have shortness of breath and to take it easy. I was just ready to get back to being 100 percent so that I could hit that nigga up with his punk ass.

"Hey, bighead," Camille said.

"Hey, I take it you're here to help me out, so go get me a bottle of water," I said, pushing her.

Today was my first day home from the hospital, and I wanted to see my son and have my mom and sister meet him too. I've been calling Olivia since this morning, but she has yet to answer my calls, and I know it's because I told her to take my picture down off her page. Had she posted my pic without ill intentions, I wouldn't have had a problem with it, but I knew she was doing it just to be petty. If she didn't answer the phone in the next hour, I didn't care about being in pain; I was going to be pulling up to her crib. I didn't want to have to do that, but she wasn't giving me a choice. I haven't seen my son in a little over a week, so I was missing him, and she wanted to play games.

"Mom, she's still not answering the phone, but I'm going to give her another hour, and if she doesn't answer, I'm going to go over there," I told her, after she asked if Olivia was still bringing him.

"No, you just got home, so you don't need to be going out here acting a fool because that's what she wants you to do. I'm going to tell you now, if she continues to give you a hard time about spending time with your baby, you know what you're going to have to do," she said, and I knew she was talking about taking her ass to court for visitation rights.

I just wanted to see my son without all the extra bullshit, and trust, I wasn't going to court for someone to tell me when and if I could see my son. If I wanted to see my son every day, that's what I was going to do. Olivia was going to see a side of me that she has yet to see, fucking with my having a relationship with my son. My mom decided to fix plates because she saw that I was getting upset, knowing that I was about to fly off the handle at any second.

"You good?" I asked Tami because she's been quiet.

"I'm good," she said, getting up to help my mom.

An hour later, Olivia still hadn't reached out to me, and my mom and Camille had already left, so I told Tami to take me to Olivia's crib. She was telling me to give her another hour, saying that her phone might be dead and making excuses for her, but I wasn't trying to hear her. If she wasn't going to take me, I was going to drive my damn self over there, not giving a shit about the pain I was in. She finally gave in, so we were en route to Olivia's house, with her telling me to keep in mind that my son was there and to try to stay calm. I appreciated her concern, but if Olivia got out of pocket with her mouth, I was going to punch her in that shit, real talk.

When Tami pulled up to Olivia's block, I swear it felt like déjà vu, seeing two police cars and an ambulance in front of her place. My heart dropped to my stomach, giving me a bad feeling as I slowly got out of the car, grimacing because I was in pain again.

Tami was by my side as we walked up to the house, trying to find out what was going on from the officer who was telling everyone to step back. Another officer was putting up the police tape, and I started to panic. Just as I was about to go off, Olivia was being brought out of the house on a stretcher. I'm not going to lie. I went into panic mode, needing to know where the fuck my son was. I told the officer that my newborn son lived at this residence, and I needed to know if he was all right, and that fuck nigga told me that someone would be out to talk to me soon. Tami tried to calm me because I was about to lose it. After all, nobody was telling me shit.

Tami called Olivia's aunt, who was her supervisor at the hospital, to let her know that she needed to get here. We were still waiting for someone to come out and tell me where the fuck my son was when some white bitch came out, asking me a million fucking questions. She had the nerve to tell me that she needed proof that I was the father of Olivia's son, and I wanted to slap that bitch. She was trying to play me because why would I be here claiming to be the father of a baby who didn't fucking belong to me? I was about to go off on that bitch, but Tami intervened and told her that Olivia's family member was on her way, and she could confirm that I was, in fact, the father of the baby.

A detective came out, asking about our relationship with Olivia, and if we knew of any enemies or anyone who may have wanted to cause her harm. I didn't want to lie, and these motherfuckers didn't give me my son, so I just told them that some guy had threatened her at the hospital, and when I left the hospital after having words with the dude, I was shot. So there was a possibility that it was the same guy. I gave the same bogus description that I gave the officers at the hospital who came to talk to me because, on my son, that nigga was going to get dealt with. I didn't need him locked up because his ass was going to be still breathing and living life, and I wasn't trying to hear that shit.

Olivia's aunt, Elle, finally got to the house, but they'd already taken Olivia to the hospital. She let the officer know that I was the father of her niece's baby, and they allowed me to take my son. Elle and her husband left for the hospital, stating that they would keep me updated on Olivia's condition. I was honestly ready just to go home and pop a few pills because that's how much pain I was in right now. It hurt like hell, sitting in the back of the car and holding my son, but I had to suck up that shit until I got home to my meds.

"Do you think you should go to the hospital?" Tami asked me.

"I'm just going to wait to hear something from her aunt because I'm in a lot of pain," I told her.

"When we get to the house, I'll call her to see if she's heard anything about Olivia's condition," she said.

We had to stop to get a few things for my son because we weren't allowed in Olivia's house. All the police did was hand him over to me. I have no idea what Olivia did to this fuck nigga, but I'm pissed that my son was put in danger. But at the same time, I prayed that she would be all right because, even though she was petty as fuck, she didn't deserve this shit.

I called my mom and asked her if she and Camille could come back over to the house after explaining what happened, and she said that they were on their way. After thinking about it, I realized that Olivia was still the mother of my child, so I needed to be there, and Tami agreed, so once my mom and sister got to the house, we left to go to the hospital.

About an hour later, we arrived at the hospital, and the only update that the family had was that she was still in surgery. She had so many family members there, it was unbelievable. The hospital staff offered them a private room because they took up the entire waiting room. Elle was a mess. Some of the hospital staff were there offering kind words of support. Tami and I stepped out of the room because the scene was overwhelming for her. I asked her if she was ready to leave the hospital, and she said she just wanted to wait to hear that Olivia had made it through surgery. She was shot twice in the chest, so I was silently praying for her to be all right because we had a son to raise, and he was going to need his mother.

Sami was just getting to the hospital, and she was a mess, so we went back inside with her to see if they had any updates. As soon as we walked into the waiting area, I knew it wasn't good news because now, everyone was crying. Tami walked over to Elle's husband, and he confirmed that Olivia died. Tami began crying. Sami fell to her knees, crying out that she didn't get a chance to tell her that she wasn't mad at her anymore. I helped her up, pulling her into my arms and trying to console her, but she was inconsolable. After telling Olivia's uncle that we were sorry for their loss, we left the hospital.

We drove Sami back to her house because she was in no condition to drive home. Mason was there, waiting for us. I was feeling fucked up right now because my son had just lost his mother, and that shit hurt like hell. Tami asked me if I was okay, and I told her that I was, but I wasn't.

"I just want to say how sorry I am about Olivia. I know we were always going at each other, but I would have never wished this on her," she offered.

"I know you wouldn't, and I just want to say thank you for being there with me," I told her.

We got out of the car and went inside, and I went straight to my son because I needed to hold him tight, knowing that I could have very well lost him tonight too. I have no idea why that punk ass spared my son's life, but I'm not going to be so generous because I'm touching anything that means something to that nigga.

Tami

On my way home from work, I stopped at the liquor store to pick up a bottle since it was Friday. Envy and

I were having date night in my living room because we haven't been spending much time together. As a single father, the baby has taken up most of our time, so we decided that we needed a night alone while Zy was with Olivia's mom. Getting out of my car, I started walking toward the liquor store, and it was just my luck running into Chase's ass. He was with his brother and two other guys, and as I got closer, I realized that one of the guys was the man who had shaken Olivia. Envy was hell-bent on this dude being the one who shot him and killed Olivia, so I pulled out my phone to send him a text. I just knew the dude was going to recognize me from the night he saw me leaving the hospital with Olivia, but he didn't. They were drunk, so I figured that was the reason he didn't remember me, but whatever the reason, I was thankful.

Chase was walking toward me, so I quickly read Envy's text message before putting my phone back into my bag.

"What's up?" he said to me.

"Hey," I responded, not interested in engaging in conversation with him.

Envy told me to get the hell out of Dodge, but if I left abruptly, dude might have gotten suspicious and remembered that I was with Olivia that night. I made small talk with Chase, telling him that I needed to get into the store and get home because I had no idea what the hell Envy was going to do. I just knew I needed to go.

"So, you just cut off a nigga, no call-no show?" he said, causing all of them to laugh.

They were fucked up, and I wasn't getting good vibes from their asses, so I just wanted to go without all the extra bullshit.

"Look, Chase, you already know what it was, so don't go there," I told his ass.

"So, it's like that, huh?" he said.

"It's like that," I said, walking into the store with them coming in behind me.

I didn't even get what I came to buy. Just picking up the first thing I saw, I went to the front to pay so that I could get the hell out of there. I was happy that his drunk ass left me the hell alone, letting me leave the store without following me out. My phone rang in my bag, so I answered it quickly as I walked to my car. It was Envy screaming at me about my leaving the store now when he'd told me to go five minutes ago. I told him that I was leaving, and he said that he saw me, and he needed me to get the hell out. He didn't have to say anymore as I got into my car and pulled out.

I wasn't even off the block before I heard gunfire, and I knew that whoever was with Envy was getting revenge on dude. Although I wasn't fucking with Chase like that, I hoped he didn't get caught in the crossfire.

My heart was beating rapidly by the time I arrived at my house because I was worried. Now, I was also praying that Envy was all right. An hour passed, and I hadn't heard anything from him. He wasn't answering his phone, so I didn't know if he was okay. I started pacing the floor, not knowing what to do, and then it hit me to call Sami to see if Mason was home, but she said that he wasn't and she hadn't heard from him, either. I told her what was going on, and now I had her worried, but she needed to know, so I told her to hang up the phone and try calling Mason. If he answered, I told her to ask if they were all right and to call me back.

I swear I was losing my mind because a few hours had passed, and neither of us heard from them. I knew that I needed to calm down because I was making myself crazy right about now. I thought about calling Chase, but I knew that I couldn't do that.

I was desperate. I was even thinking about getting in my car and going to the liquor store to see what had happened. Instead, I decided to lie down on the couch with my phone next to me, waiting for a call from Envy, and ended up falling asleep.

I don't know how long I was sleeping, but I was awakened by someone aggressively pounding on the door, and I just knew that it was someone coming to tell me that Envy was hurt. I rushed to the door, and when I opened it, he was standing there, and the tears fell as I ran into his arms, crying uncontrollably.

"I'm good," he said, and I lost it.

"Why didn't you pick up your phone to let me know that you were all right? I was in here going crazy, and all you can say is that you're good? I thought I lost you," I cried out.

"I'm sorry, but I had to handle some shit, and you know if I were able to call you, I would have. I'm sorry I had you worried, but it was out of my control," he said, pulling me into his arms.

After I finally calmed down, I asked him what happened, but he told me that it was best if he didn't share the details. I wanted to know if Chase was all right, but I didn't dare ask him. I would find out on my own, but something in my gut was saying that he wasn't.

The next day, Envy left to go home, so I searched social media to see if there was anything on Chase's page, but there wasn't, so I turned on the television. My heart sank, confirming what I already knew, as I was listening to the news as they reported a shooting at the liquor store, stating that all four victims were pronounced dead at the scene. Tears fell from my eyes as guilt tried to seep in. After all, I was the one who called Envy and told him that I saw the dude, but it was either them or my man. *I'd rather Envy caught them slipping, than them catching him slipping, so I did what I had to do,* I thought, as I convinced myself that I had no reason to feel guilty. I don't know what the future held for Envy and me, but I was so in love with him. I was going to ride with him until the wheels fell off.